"There's alre~~ady been eno~~ugh ~~deat~~h. So just put the sword down..."

But Awena wasn't prepared to give up on her vengeance. She wanted Annja to pay, and lunged at her, slashing wildly. She had no skill with the weapon, but pure rage still made her more than dangerous.

Annja parried blow after blow, fending off the attacks, knowing that like any fire, Awena would burn herself out. She didn't have the stamina to match Annja, even if the blade somehow imbued her with unholy strength.

Again Awena swung, coming at her, but the intensity of the attacks lessened as she tired. Annja felt the strain, too. The muscles in her sword arm burned where it had been touched by the blue flame.

Annja blocked each parry, swords ringing out as they clashed.

Tears streamed down Awena's face. She seemed to shrink in on herself, drawing a shallow breath before launching the next blow.

Annja knew that this was the moment to strike.

One chance. One opening. That was all she needed.

She had to end this now....

Titles in this series:

ROGUE Angel

Alex Archer

CELTIC FIRE

A GOLD EAGLE BOOK FROM

WORLDWIDE®

TORONTO • NEW YORK • LONDON
AMSTERDAM • PARIS • SYDNEY • HAMBURG
STOCKHOLM • ATHENS • TOKYO • MILAN
MADRID • WARSAW • BUDAPEST • AUCKLAND

Recycling programs
for this product may
not exist in your area.

First edition September 2014

ISBN-13: 978-0-373-62170-5

CELTIC FIRE

Special thanks and acknowledgment to
Steven Savile for his contribution to this work.

Printed in U.S.A.

The
LEGEND

...THE ENGLISH COMMANDER TOOK
JOAN'S SWORD AND RAISED IT HIGH.
The broadsword, plain and unadorned,
gleamed in the firelight. He put the tip against
the ground and his foot at the center of the blade.
The broadsword shattered, fragments falling
into the mud. The crowd surged forward,
peasant and soldier, and snatched the shards
from the trampled mud. The commander tossed
the hilt deep into the crowd.
Smoke almost obscured Joan, but she continued
praying till the end, until finally the flames climbed
her body and she sagged against the restraints.

Joan of Arc died that fateful day in France,
but her legend and sword are reborn....

1

Clouds covered the moon. The garden was in near-perfect darkness but for the ambient orange glow of the streetlights pushing at the edges of the shrubbery. Deep among the medicinal herbs there was nothing but shadow. A short distance away two cats fought, hissing and squealing as they duked it out over territorial rights for a scrap of land not worth the urine it took to mark it. And among those deep shadows in the darkest part of the garden, the woman in black let out an almost-silent breath she'd held a second longer than was comfortable.

Awena had walked the narrow paths between the flower beds every day that week, admiring them, passing comment to the gardeners and tourists as she went, making sure that she knew every inch of them. There was no way she was going to stumble into a replica urn or turn her ankle on a shallow border or do anything else to cause undue commotion. A certain amount of noise would get put down to badgers and foxes and other nocturnal scavengers, but a woman crying out—no matter how strangled her cry—only ever sounded like a woman crying out. It was the kind of sound hardwired deep into the human psyche to draw the attention of heroes, especially after the sun went down.

The last thing she needed was any heroes.

The garden was only a brisk five-minute walk from the police station, though through a geographical and town planning quirk it was longer if a car was sent thanks to the twisting one-way streets.

She was playing the law of averages. First responders would instinctively check the front of the building before making sure the perimeter was secure, then eventually make their way over the wall she had climbed and into the garden at the rear. Each action bought her a few precious extra seconds to do what she'd broken into the garden to do.

Lights still burned at the front of the museum, small halogen spotlights meant to entice casual passersby visiting the town in the evening, their glow saying *Stop, look around, marvel at the glass display of the frontage and the great pillars of the portico, imagine what it's like inside.* A notice promised free entry, with opening times from ten in the morning until five in the afternoon, Monday to Saturday, and from two on Sunday afternoons. It was an imposing building, even in the dark. More so in the dark. It was a mixture of classical Roman and modern architecture. At the rear of the main building stood the Roman garden and a smaller entrance that was invisible to casual prying eyes.

She moved silently, feet ghosting across the ground with the lightest of steps, her black trainers, black jeans and sweatshirt making her almost invisible in the darkness. A navy blue woolen hat kept her hair tucked out of sight and gloves ensured that there would be no fingerprints to give her away. It was all in the planning. Be methodical. Take no unnecessary risks. Idiots took risks. Idiots thought it was cool to make stuff up on the fly and improvise. Awena was not an idiot. The lock wasn't going to be a challenge. As far as the world was concerned there was nothing in there worth stealing. She knew different.

It was a calculated risk: trying to avoid setting off the alarm would only slow her. It would also make the job exponentially more difficult. She knew exactly how long she had from the moment she deliberately tripped the alarm to the second she disappeared into the night, knew exactly what she was looking for, where it would be and how to get out of there before the first responders were even in their cars.

She broke it down into segments.

Ninety seconds to break the lock—it was fractionally longer than it had taken for her to crack an identical one at home, but then that hadn't been in the dark. Pressure situations added a few seconds. The risk came as those seconds added up.

One hundred and twenty seconds from opening the door to be in and out before anyone came running. Another sixty seconds to get her treasure to the car—which was parked on the other side of the wall—and a final seventy-five seconds to move the car to a carefully chosen parking bay where no one would notice it.

Two hundred and fifty-five seconds.

There were few houses close by. None overlooked the garden. It was unlikely that even the nosiest of parkers would be out of their beds and twitching their curtains because of the commotion, but even if they did all they'd see would be a car driving away. In the middle of the night a car was a car was a car, almost impossible to differentiate a Volvo from a Ford from a Volkswagen. That was what she was banking on.

Awena took a deep breath and opened the door, starting the stopwatch on her wrist, and stepped inside.

Immediately inside she heard the high-pitched whine indicating the alarm had been triggered.

These systems were set up with a sixty-second grace period for people to enter the code into the alarm box. That meant she only risked one hundred and ninety-five seconds with the escalating shriek of the alarm. One hundred and ninety-five seconds was a lifetime in the silence of a little town in the middle of the night but there was nothing she could do about that. She didn't have the code. Once the tone changed that signified an alert had been sent to a private alarm company, the alarm company would try to ascertain if it was a genuine alarm call or a mistake, which would eat up a few more precious seconds before they contacted the police. There could be delays at any link along the chain, but she couldn't rely on that. One hundred and ninety-five seconds, in and out. That was all she had.

Awena moved quickly, making her way into the main exhibits room. The faint glow of the streetlight outside leached through the window, bathing everything inside in its curiously otherworldly orange glow. She pulled the jeweler's hammer from where she'd carried it tucked into her jeans. As the tone of the alarm changed to an escalating shriek, she delivered a single swing of the hammer, shattering the display case's glass top into a million orange-filled fragments.

She ignored the cache of denarii in the broken pot and reached inside for her prize.

It was the only thing in the whole museum that held any value as far as Awena was concerned.

She lifted it out of the case.

It was heavier than she'd expected, needing two hands to carry.

When the two-minute timer she'd set on her stop-watch beeped before she was halfway across the floor she realized she wouldn't be able to get out in time and felt a rising panic as each step seemed to take a little longer than the last. She'd planned this meticulously, down to the second, but the reality of the break-in de-fied all of her best-laid plans. She was going to need whichever god or devil looked down on thieves to do her a favor if she was going to get out before the police showed up. And even then she had to move quickly. But like it or not, the weight slowed her down. She hadn't bargained on that. But then, how could she have known how heavy it would actually be?

She pushed the back door open again, leaning into it, and hitched her burden a little higher, trying to run across the gravel until the fire in her legs became too much to bear. The alarm grew progressively louder. Every dog in the neighborhood tried to compete with it. She couldn't hear anyone shouting to silence them. She couldn't hear any footsteps or wailing sirens of police cars.

Perhaps someone was looking out for her, after all.

Awena staggered the last few strides to the wall, and as much as she wanted to drop her burden, at least for a moment to catch her breath, she knew if she did there was no way she'd get it up and over the wall. Momen-tum was vital. All she could do was grit her teeth against the rising tide of agony and push on until she'd strained every single muscle in her body to lever the treasure up and onto the top of it.

She braced herself against the wall, balancing the

treasure while she struggled to catch her breath, then hauled herself up and rolled off the wall onto the roof of her Land Rover. She'd parked it right up against the rear wall. It meant leaving tire tracks, but she'd switched the wheels out that evening, using a set of radials meant for a much smaller vehicle. She'd switch them back tomorrow. Awena lay on her back looking up at the moon as clouds drifted across it, then pulled the weight after her, putting it onto the roof beside her, then slid down the side of the car. She'd lost track of time. She couldn't waste so much as a single second checking her watch.

She managed to get her prize into the Land Rover—hiding it on the floor behind the driver's seat—just as she heard the sound of a siren in the distance.

Even with the weird night acoustics of the town, she could tell the patrol car was still making its way through the one-way streets. *Close but no cigar,* she thought, grinning for the first time that night.

She fired the engine up and threw the car into first, pulling away from the grass verge without turning on her lights.

The police siren was closing in, but instead of turning right and following the road out of town, she drove straight across into Broadway, a narrow lane that led only to the Roman amphitheater and the rugby field. There, without so much as a streetlight to guide the way, she had no choice but to turn on the lights so she could navigate what amounted to a dirt track.

It was a calculated chance. She knew how the police thought. They'd expect her to run. Hiding in plain sight wasn't in their playbook. Hiding out in the parking lot outside the old Roman amphitheater was not logical, so it was her best shot at getting away with the robbery. She'd watched the parking lot over the past week, making sure that it wasn't unusual for cars to be left overnight. Every night there'd been a handful of motors in there, left by people who'd spent the evening in the rugby club and decided to return to collect their car in the morning.

She pulled into a space beyond the last vehicle and turned off the engine.

She sank back into the soft leather bucket seat and closed her eyes, tension flooding from her body.

She'd done it.

She gave herself a minute to savor the fact, then climbed onto the backseat and settled herself beneath a picnic blanket to wait for morning.

2

Daybreak began somewhere over the horizon.

The faint glow in the sky signaled the start of the day.

For the curate, there was more than enough time before the 8:00 a.m. service to unlock the doors of the cathedral and make the preparations for Communion.

He hurried along the path in the slowly brightening gloom, enjoying this time of the morning as he always did, when God's glory was there for all to wonder at. He was a simple man who enjoyed simple pleasures. Anyone who had ever heard him in the pulpit knew that. The curate crossed the old wooden footbridge spanning the brackish water of the narrow River Alyn before it moved out to the sea. The man in the shadows knew that it wouldn't be long before he arrived—the curate was a creature of habit—and like it or not he was going to have to give up his search for now if he wanted to slip away unnoticed.

He had already spent a couple of days checking the grounds, examining individual gravestones, crossing them off on the rough map he had sketched out to be sure he didn't return to overlapping areas of the bone garden.

But he still hadn't found what he was looking for.

More than once he had been approached by staff and clergy of the cathedral asking if he was all right, or if he needed any help looking for a particular grave. Each time he smiled politely, said thanks but no, and they left him to wander the huge grounds. It was more attention than he wanted to draw to himself, but it was of the natural sort, in keeping with what the staff saw every day. That was the trick, to remain inside the ordinary, not to do something outside of it that would be remembered. There were tourists doing wax rubbings of some of the older gravestones, school groups being given a guided tour of the noteworthy dead and told the stories of the old town in hushed voices.

The curate's shuffling figure drew closer, the man looking like something out of a cartoon as he held up a hand, conducting the nature around him in time with the music he was humming, and the man knew he'd have to stay where he was now until the holy man had gone inside. He was a genuinely happy man. There were so few of those in the world. He almost skipped as he came through the lych-gate, his footing sure on the cracked and broken cobblestones that lead up to the main cathedral doors. A huge weeping willow overhung the path. Its long thin dagger-leaves rustled in the breeze. To hide from the curate, the man had taken to the deep shadows the willow cast rather helpfully.

He was silent, still, allowing the shadows to shroud him. That meant he was as good as invisible to the curate.

As the curate neared he took a single slow step back, allowing the tree trunk to come between them.

When his heel came down it was on something

harder than grass, but as he placed his weight on it a sound cried out.

A strange noise...

A voice calling?

The curate stopped in his tracks, his head cocked on one side as he looked directly at the man even though he couldn't see him for the protection of the shadows.

"Hello?" The curate waited for a response, his eyes scanning the shadows for any sign of movement, which proved he couldn't see the man hiding there. The man didn't answer. "Who's there?"

The man held his breath, readying himself in case the clergyman moved closer.

He would hate to have to kill him.

Mercifully he stood still, too.

He had no idea what had caused the "voice"—the sound of stone grinding against stone. Some sort of echo effect caused by being so close to the great cathedral?

"If you need food or shelter you are welcome," the curate called. "I can get you a hot drink as soon as I have done my duties inside. Would you like that? Tea? Coffee?"

The man tried hard not to laugh.

There was something about do-gooders that brought out the worst in him. Put them in the robes of the church—which they stupidly believed gave them a cloak of invulnerability—and they were insufferable. He decided to have some fun. "I could murder a cup of tea," he replied in a voice more gruff and deeper than his usual tone. It masked his accent. "Thank you."

The cleric waved in his direction, the smile on his face broader than the simple act of boiling water warranted, and made for the main door of the cathedral with his keys jangling in his hand. The curate was clearly a trusting soul. But then why would he imagine the man would need anything more than that? Why would he conjure imaginary thieves intent on mugging him? Why indeed.

No doubt there were processes and procedures in place to protect the relics—triggers that would dispatch a silent alarm to the police if anyone tried to force their way inside. That didn't concern him. He had no interest in what was *inside*. None of the ritualistic paraphernalia held any fascination for him. It wasn't about value. While there was a chance that what he was searching for lay inside the building, it was a slim one because by rights it would have been discovered long ago if that was the case. No. The only thing that interested him about this particular patch of hallowed ground was a long-lost burial plot he knew must lie somewhere within the property.

And what was buried there along with the old bones was worth more to him than anything the church in Wales held precious: it was the final resting place of Giraldus Cambrensis, Gerald of Wales.

Once he was sure that the curate was inside he waited another moment, then heard other voices carrying in the air as the holy man was greeted by his brethren. The man then ran as quickly and as lightly as he could to reach the car he had parked in a pay-and-display lot tucked at the bottom of an overgrown country lane a couple of hundred yards beyond the towering spires of the cathedral.

He was intrigued by the "voice" and the curious stone that seemed to have triggered it, but it wasn't worth the risk of returning in daylight. At least not today. A few days, maybe, to allow the curate to forget about the poor soul who was too timid to come in to claim his cup of tea.

He started the car and drove carefully through the narrow lanes and one-way system until he found himself on the road to Haverfordwest. Once he reached Solva he pulled off the road to take advantage of the unob- structed—and spectacular—view over the bay, then settled back to catch a couple of hours' sleep.

3

Another day, another flight, another country.

World traveler or not, Annja had flown enough long-haul flights to know she'd want nothing more than sleep when she reached her final destination, but more likely than not the room wouldn't be made up. That was the problem with an evening departure from New York. It was great in theory, if you could sleep on the plane, but she couldn't so she'd effectively been up all night without the joys of dancing and pounding nightclub bass to keep her going. That'd slow the whole body clock adjustment thing along with her screwed-up circadian rhythms. One thing she'd noticed was the older she got, the more difficult the adjustment was. A few years ago jet lag barely touched her.

Through the window to her left she saw nothing but cloud below her, thick, white and impenetrable.

She checked her watch. There was still about an hour until landing, which meant somewhere below her lay the endless deeps of the Atlantic Ocean. Soon enough they'd hit the change of air as they traversed Ireland. That was always an invitation to turbulence, like Greenland. It was something about the warm air and cold air colliding.

Annja had been looking forward to this trip for a while.

She'd already earmarked a bunch of places she wanted to visit to research possible segment ideas for *Chasing History's Monsters,* not that she'd shared them with Doug Morrell, her producer on the show. As much as she loved Doug, there was a limit to how many times she could stomach her ideas being energetically talked over in favor of zombies and werewolves as seemed to be his usual habit.

She'd made sure there was time for pleasure included in her schedule.

There were places she wanted to revisit while she was here, places that she'd visited when she had researched the show on the legendary King Arthur, and even though she'd thought she had left little unsaid at the time there was something absolutely fascinating—and undying—about the Grail King. She wanted to revisit Glastonbury first, and climb to the top of the tor on a sunny day. She wanted to look down from the summit and imagine what it might have been like if the land around it had been flooded.

Could the tor really have been the mythical island of Avalon?

Anything was possible, of course, but she was experienced enough to put flights of fantasy out of her head. One thing Annja Creed prided herself on was that she dealt in facts. What the rest of the world didn't know was that there were some facts that it was best they never learned.

"Orange juice?" the flight attendant asked, disturbing her thoughts.

Annja smiled and nodded, then happily let her imagination run away with her while she waited for the captain to turn on the fasten seat belts sign, indicating their descent had begun. She knew that she could spend a month over here and not see a fraction of the places she wanted to visit; the British Isles were a wealth of ruins and history waiting to be explored, of cultures to be rediscovered and ingenuity unparalleled. Her first stop on the itinerary was a place in Wales that had been getting some press on the archaeology discussion boards on the internet.

She'd first heard about the Roman ruins in the small town of Caerleon many years before, but had never had the opportunity to visit. This time she was determined to put that right. Then it was only maybe twenty or thirty miles to Caerphilly, where a wonderfully preserved medieval castle still watched over the town and a number of faithfully re-created siege engines were on display and demonstrated regularly for the benefit of tourists.

What was doubly interesting about Caerleon, though, was that it was also one of the possible sites of Camelot, the fabled court of King Arthur, according to the writing of Geoffrey of Monmouth in the twelfth century. There was also a reference to Arthur fighting a battle against the Romans in the "City of the Legion" according to Nennius in his *Historia Brittonum;* this could easily have been Caerleon, home of the Second Augustan legion. This was why she loved archaeology; it was more than just digging things out of the ground. It was all about sifting through the clues buried in early writings and using them to locate important lost sites. It was more than just history. It was akin to lore and legend in the absolute nerdiest sense.

Annja hadn't even realized her breakfast had been placed in front of her as she had been so caught up in her thoughts. She wouldn't reach the small Welsh town until tomorrow, but she had given herself a few days to stay. She wanted to make sure she saw everything there was to see in case the chance to return didn't come around again.

She picked at the food without any real appetite and drained the orange juice. There would be plenty of time to grab something else to eat later; she'd promised herself a traditional English breakfast of sausage, bacon, eggs, potatoes, beans and fried tomatoes. She knew a great little greasy spoon just around the corner from the station. The locals called the specialty "the heart attack on a plate," but it was nothing compared to some of the stuff they served back home.

She looked through her papers one last time before packing them away for landing, studying the photographs and maps of the area around Caerleon. She skipped past the pages on Caerphilly, slipping those back into her folder. There were another half a dozen folios like this in her case—the other places she planned on visiting on her trip—but they could wait.

When the plane finally touched down she was ready for the shuffle-race to the exit with everyone standing up and crowding the aisles long before the cabin doors were open.

By the time she'd collected her luggage from the baggage carousel, and gotten through customs and passport control, the clouds had begun to break up. It wasn't exactly glorious out, but it was a good morning and it looked like it was going to be a better day, which meant the drive into Wales should be easy, as long as tiredness didn't mean sleeping in a lay-by somewhere near the River Severn.

Annja claimed a hire car from the desk, then went on an expedition to find it. She scoured parking bays that went on forever in a recursive loop of identical hire cars until a click of the key fob resulted in a flicker of lights identifying her ride.

She sat inside the car for a few minutes, trying to familiarize herself with the right-hand-drive position before pulling away. She repeated, "They drive on the left" like a holy mantra as if she really needed any reminding from the minute she hit the open road of the M25.

It felt good to be driving once she got to the motorway rather than crawling through the airport's one-way system. She rolled one shoulder after the other to free it from the kinks that still lay in her muscles from the flight.

The sun was behind her and the steady flow of traffic away from London moved at an even pace with vehicles peeling off and others joining at every junction.

In an ideal world she would have made the journey a little more slowly, but her speed was dictated by the cars and lorries around her. Annja was caught in a stream where each vehicle moved at the same speed as the one in front so she cranked the radio up, choosing volume over taste, and wound the window down. It was summer, after all.

Eventually the discomfort of sitting still for so long after the flight left her with no choice but to pull off at a motorway services area and go in search of coffee and the chance to stretch her legs. The decor was bad, the coffee was worse. She wound up getting back in the car and heading toward the motorway less than fifteen minutes after she'd pulled into the rest stop. The next signpost promised that Cardiff was less than fifty miles away. The turnoff for Caerleon would come some time before that.

4

An engine fired up beside her, gunned quickly into life and was followed by the crunch of tires on gravel as the car pulled away. Awena knew that it was safe to move at last. She'd lain still and silent, listening to the wail of the museum alarm as it carried on into the night air, and then drifted off after it fell silent, one hand on the stone artifact she had liberated from the glass case. She liked to think that she'd saved it from being transferred to some dusty old vault somewhere where it would have been hidden away until doomsday, completely forgotten about. That would have been a bigger crime than anything she'd done.

She hadn't realized what she'd been looking at the first time she'd laid eyes on the exhibit—why would she have?—but there was something about it that had brought her back to it again and again, until she was finally convinced that it was mislabeled. The card had described it as a quern—a hand-grinding stone for grain—but it clearly wasn't; it was too large and too heavy to be one of those. Once upon a time she might have pointed the mistake out to one of the staff to let them know how clever she was and basically how stupid they were for screwing it up. She'd grown up a lot since the days wasted in museums with her easily embarrassed twin, Geraint, who frequently turned a darker shade of red than their flame-red hair while he tried to pretend he had no idea who she was. It never worked. Now, thankfully, she was comfortable with the idea that she was the sharpest person in any given room she walked into. It wasn't arrogance; it was just a fact. It didn't matter who else was there, Awena was ferociously intelligent.

Once the sounds of the car had faded into the distance she eased herself up a little to scope out the lane. A glance through the rear window revealed a blanket of mist across the rugby field, shrouding it with a soft white in the early-morning sun. There was no sign of anyone else around. She'd reached the point of no return. If she waited too much longer to make her move, traffic to the heritage site would increase and it'd be difficult to slip out of the car to stretch the kinks out before getting back into the driver's seat without anyone noticing.

She opened the door.

The air was colder than she'd expected. She used the discarded blanket to cover the stone. A dog came bounding toward her along the lane, its owner calling after it, but it wasn't slowing down. It raced with its tongue lolling between open jaws, full of excitement. Awena wasn't afraid of dogs, but it was the kind of encounter the mutt's owner would remember, and the last thing she wanted was to be memorable. With the dog still thirty feet away, she slipped back behind the wheel and slammed the door. The confused animal stopped dead in its tracks and stared at her for a moment, wounded, like it couldn't understand why she didn't want to stop and play with it, then looked back in the direction it had come from before it took off into the mist-shrouded field.

Awena waited a moment before starting the car, watching the dog's owner shrug helplessly and follow after it into the field, then pulled away.

The streets were dead. She reached the end of the lane, putting on the blinkers to indicate she was turning right. She couldn't see any policemen outside the museum, though she had half expected a guard to have been posted.

Alongside the building where her Land Rover had parked she saw a white van.

She pulled out into the road, driving slowly and straining to catch a glimpse of the writing on the side of the van: a twenty-four-hour locksmith. She smiled. Typical—shut the stable door after the horse has well and truly bolted.

She followed the road as it arced right, curving around a big old Gothic school building, and took her beyond the police station. There was no sign of anyone coming or going. Any panic or rush of excitement at the break-in and the resultant flurry of activity had died down and life had settled back into the normality of its daily routine.

Awena turned left at the end of the street and followed the road through a series of villages that fed one into the next. Eventually, she picked up a faster road and was able to put her foot down on the gas.

She allowed herself to laugh as she felt the rush of speed and the excitement of her plan falling into place. She'd done it. Simple as that. She'd won. She couldn't wait to show Geraint her trophy, even if he still had doubts about what it was that she had stolen. She'd just have to convince him. Awena desperately wanted to call her brother, even though the digits on the dashboard reminded her that it was barely 7:00 a.m. He wasn't an early riser.

She'd almost forgotten that he'd stayed the night in London.

She was going to enjoy the look on his face when he laid his eyes on the treasure.

Like the old commercial said…priceless.

5

The Welsh seemed intent on charging Annja to enter their country—or was it the English charging her for the luxury of leaving theirs? She wasn't entirely sure, but it was the first time she could remember being charged to cross a border. Signs at the side of the sweeping bridge that carried traffic over the River Severn warned that tollbooths lay ahead, clearly marked with the cost for each type of vehicle. *It's highway robbery,* she thought, and grinned at her own dumb joke.

Brake lights glowed in the distance; there was a long queue to the control booths taking the money.

Annja reached for her purse as she joined the back of one of several snakes of cars that had formed and pulled out a crisp ten-pound note fresh from the currency exchange office.

A quick glance to the left confirmed she was already on the far side of the river. To her right she could see the supports of a second, older-looking bridge.

Cars edged forward slowly, and as was the way with queues, some moved faster than others—which really meant all of them seemed to be moving faster than hers. As she neared the front, she realized that some of the booths were actually automated, self-service barriers while the queue that she was in relied on someone giving change.

The guy in the next car flashed a smile across the lanes to her, but Annja was more interested in the car ahead. It wasn't that she didn't like drawing grins from strangers; just like everyone else she found them flattering, and his smile did draw a smile from her, but she didn't want him to see it and think he'd somehow made her day. She was contrary like that. Plus, his queue was moving faster than hers. He'd have another driver to flirt with in a moment.

Eventually her turn came. She smiled to the tired-looking teller, trading money for less money, and he raised the barrier with a snatch of something she didn't understand but assumed was the Welsh equivalent of *Have a nice day* or *Drive safe*.

She pulled away as cars raced into the bottleneck of decreasing lanes, each driver looking to secure one of the three lanes ahead of them before it became a mad scramble. The merging was surprisingly smooth, all things considered, with cars filtering in and drivers allowing one another enough space for safety. It wouldn't have been like that back home, she thought, letting a black Jaguar XJS slip into the lane ahead of her. It was only when the traffic had eased to a steady fifty-five pushing sixty that she realized how tightly she'd been gripping the wheel. Annja relaxed her grip and eased back on the accelerator, signaling to move into the slower traffic of the left-hand lane.

She glanced across to see that the car beside her was the same guy who had flashed her a smile in the queue at the tollbooth. He slowed down and gave her room to pull across in front of him. This time she smiled back.

The off ramp she needed came upon her sooner than she'd anticipated, and almost disappeared into the rearview mirror before she'd seen it. It took a bit of emergency maneuvering, but she managed to cut across the chevrons painted across the road and up onto the ramp before she ran out of room, half expecting the driver behind to hit his horn in protest. But she saw the smiler was still behind her, still smiling.

It was just her luck he was turning off the motorway, too.

Annja followed the brown signs with the outline of a Roman helmet, indicating a tourist attraction, as the road took her through the outskirts of the city of Newport with its run-down houses and seen-better-days factories, before steering the car out into the countryside proper. The short journey from the motorway to the outskirts of Caerleon only took ten minutes or so, but the change of pace with the speed limit dropping by thirty miles per hour made it feel like so much longer.

The approach offered a spectacular view of the town and castle. An old stone bridge too narrow for two cars to pass side by side spanned the River Usk before the road swept right to a wonderful holly-and-ivy country pub. The place had a thatched roof that made it look like something that had slipped through a crack in time from the 1800s. It stood invitingly on the river's bank, promising refreshment and a nice warm hearth. Just the sight of it brought on a sudden thirst and gnawing hunger so Annja decided to take care of both, even though she was only a short distance from her hotel.

The gently swaying sign had the gold-painted words Miller's Arms and a crest. A smaller blue plate on the wall explained that the building was originally a sixteenth century coaching inn and lots of the oldest features seemed to have survived into its new life. It took Annja a few minutes to get used to the landlord's accent as he offered her his very proud spiel, but after a while she found her mind singing along with the rise and fall of his speech.

"You from America, are you, then, me love?" he asked, pulling a bottle of water from one of the fridges behind the bar. She'd never heard anyone call her "me love" before; "my love" was more northern, but the "me" seemed slightly tortured. She smiled as he offered ice by holding a scoop over a plastic ice bucket but she declined.

"For my sins," she said, taking a sip of the water, realizing just how thirsty she really was. The label on the bottle was in Welsh and seemingly unpronounceable, which she thought was cute. "Hope you won't hold it against me."

"We get quite a few of your sort through here over the summer, people coming to take a look at the ruins and stuff. That why you're here?"

"That's me." She laughed. "Just another tourist."

He reached to a dispenser on the side of the bar that was stuffed full of slightly faded leaflets about the various attractions and places of interest in the area and plucked a few of them out for her. "Then you might find these useful," he said.

"You on a commission?" she joked as she glanced through them.

"Well, the museum is free, and so is the amphitheater, so it's not going to make me rich. There's a charge to go and look around the old Roman baths, but hard as I've tried to convince them, no backhanders have come my way." He smiled again, showing he was joking, even if it wasn't a very good one. "There should be one of their leaflets over there." He pointed to another, larger rack that was perched on a low windowsill on the other side of the room.

Annja picked through the stack of leaflets he'd selected for her.

One was for the local museum, which was at the top of her list of places to visit, another about the work of Cadw, the body that looked after ancient monuments in Wales, and the third was a street map of the town. It was a decent selection; she'd already decided to examine them a little more closely while she sat with her drink.

Annja glanced down the small laminated menu on the bar, thought about asking what was good, then remembered something Roux had said about British cuisine—anything was good as long as it was brown. The Brits seemed to have a penchant for brown food, but she didn't fancy a pie or battered fish or anything heavy, so she took a chance on a green salad.

"There's a few tables free down by the river if you'd like to sit outside," the landlord said as he wrote her order on a tiny pad of paper and tore the top sheet off. "I'll bring your food out to you."

"Sounds good," she said, paying for the food and another bottle of water, then heading out into the sunshine. A haphazard arrangement of picnic tables and benches were set out on the grassy bank. There were a dozen large umbrellas fixed through the centers to provide shelter from the sun. Half of them were occupied; some with couples who were oblivious to anything but each other, others with couples who had clearly been together so long that they had little left to say to each other and others with men intent on filling every inch of space with empty beer glasses.

A mother fussed at a wasp that was buzzing around a small child in a buggy beside her. Annja thought that there was something about the scene that was so English but then corrected herself, remembering that Wales was very definitely not England and saying it was tantamount to a hate crime in some minds.

The water in the river seemed low, with steep mud banks on either side. She was staring at some kind of mud-wallowing bird she couldn't name when the landlord appeared with her lunch. "Low tide," he said as if reading her mind. "At high tide the flow slows down and the water level rises as it's being held back."

She'd forgotten how close they were to the sea and yet she knew that the Romans had brought boats up here from somewhere beyond the horizon. It was funny how the journey across the country could disorientate you. The landlord had moved on before she could reply. She saw him work with one swift movement, pulling a glass towel from where it had been tucked into the top of his trousers and flicking the troublesome wasp away from the child, earning a grateful smile from the mother in return. He stacked the unwanted glasses from the crowded table into a precarious tower and headed inside with them.

Annja marveled at him, not for his dexterity, but the way he seemed to be aware of all these different things going on around him and just dealt with them with as little fuss as possible. It was a skill. But then to do a job like this you had to be a master of dealing with the mundane as well as the surprises that might turn up.

From where she was sitting she could see the narrow

stone bridge that had brought her over the Usk. Cars came and went, though the sound of the small amount of traffic didn't disturb the tranquility of the pub garden or drown out the burbling of the river. A bird swooped and touched the surface of the water, snatching something up in its beak and taking to the air again. There was something beautiful about the motion. There was no violence, no brutality in the action; it had more in common with plucking fruit from a tree.

The garden was a little slice of paradise.

Annja spread out the street map that the landlord had given her on the table in front of her. The lightest of breezes tugged at the corners so she weighted the farthest one from her down with the water bottle and the half-empty glass. Back in the car she had a number of printouts she'd pulled off the internet when she'd been prepping for the trip, but here, now, this was so much more real.

She saw the river marked on the map in blue and the bridge that crossed it. The Miller's Arms was also clearly marked on the map. She traced a finger along the road that continued past the pub, picking out the museum, the amphitheater and the Priory Hotel, where she'd booked herself in for a few days. Despite the relatively small scale of the map, she could count the number of buildings between the pub and the hotel on two hands, proving just how close everything was. It couldn't have been more than a couple of minutes' walk.

She'd been eating without realizing or tasting what she'd been putting into her mouth and now her plate was empty.

Annja pushed it to one side, poured the last of the

water into her glass before she folded the map back into its original shape.

A quick glance around her proved that life did indeed go on without one; the young mother with her wasp-fearing child had left, but at least the middle-aged couple still weren't talking to each other. The group of men were working on another empty glass mountain. Time seemed to be passing at a different pace. She could easily have sat there for the rest of the afternoon and just let the world pass her by. After all, it wasn't often life afforded Annja Creed the luxury of just sitting and thinking about nothing in particular other than enjoying what was around her for what it was.

She drained the last of the water from her glass, running her fingers on the outside to wipe the condensation away.

Another wasp fussed around her empty plate. But rather than dive-bomb her, it skirted the edge of her plate, obviously feasting on the sweet tang of leftover dressing, so she let it alone.

A wave of tiredness hit her from nowhere.

She caught her head lolling and realized she'd pretty much blanked out while staring at the wasp. So much for soaking up the warmth of the sun. She should probably check into the hotel and grab a few hours' shut-eye, but if she slept it was unlikely she'd wake up again until the next morning, wasting the rest of the day.

She hated wasting time.

6

The house was silent.

It felt strange to be coming home to an empty house. She was so used to Geraint being there. So used to him just being part of her world it felt peculiar that he'd stay in London even an hour longer than necessary. But he had.

Awena couldn't wait to show him the fruits of her labors and, rather like the eager child she used to be, felt acutely disappointed she couldn't do it straightaway.

They had shared the large house halfway up the mountain—looking down on every other house in the valley—since they'd been children, usually in the care of a housekeeper-cum-nanny while their father came and went.

That she could no longer remember what her mother looked like without looking at the few photographs they still had of her was a constant source of pain for her, but memories were like that. So much so she couldn't be sure if the few she had of the woman were actually true or created from the stories she'd been told by her father. He'd even made her promise not to forget. Could she really remember the trip to St. Davids in Pembrokeshire on the west coast of Wales, when she'd barely been two

years of age? It seemed unlikely, but the memory was
in her head whenever she reached for it. The place was
no more than a village, but somehow had been desig-
nated a city simply because some religious soul a few
hundred years back decided to build his cathedral there.
She'd been there many times since that first visit, of
course, but it was the first visit she impossibly remembered. It didn't matter, really, even if it was an imagined
memory. So were the occasional flashes she got of her
mother smiling down at her. Sometimes the mind was
just being kind.

It had been a few years since the old housekeeper
had lived with them. She'd been replaced by an occasional cleaner who ran the vacuum and a duster over
the place a couple of times a week. And if necessary
she could double as a cook if they wanted something
beyond Awena's culinary expertise—but those occasions were few and far between, with her father rarely
coming home these days.

In the evenings it was almost always just the two of
them, comfortable with no other company and never
needing anyone else. It was how they had been for most
of their lives. It was how she wanted it to stay for the
rest of their days. Her greatest fear was that there would
come a time when one or the other of them would feel
the need for more, for that something their twin couldn't
give.

She wrapped the stone in the blanket that had kept
her warm through the night and carried it into the house
from the car.

It felt even heavier now than it had when she had stolen it from the museum, but then she had been fueled by
adrenaline and urged on by the fear of discovery. Now

there was no strength brought on by the risk of failure, and she was still stiff and tired after trying to sleep in the back of the Land Rover. She wasn't good when it came to sleeping away from her own bed. She was a homebody. Besides being cramped, the back of the car had been stuffy and her sleep had been restless at best.

She felt an overwhelming sense of relief when she placed her burden down carefully on the scrubbed pine kitchen table.

She was hungry and thirsty and in desperate need of a hot shower and fresh clothes. But she was *happy* and that was the most important thing.

She tackled her needs one at a time: first, she spooned coffee into the filter machine, filled the reservoir with water and switched it on, then she headed upstairs for a shower. She knew that she would feel better after that, more alert and ready to face the day. Geraint was unlikely to be back from his trip until at least lunchtime. Like their dad he was always disappearing somewhere, but that was the nature of his job; people needed him to fight their technological fires. It didn't matter if it was their websites, their databases, their security protocols or whatever else he did; if it was to do with computers he was every bit as much a wizard as Myrddin Wyllt. That thought led her to stretching out on her bed without even getting undressed, and pretty soon she'd drifted into sleep, all thoughts of showers and coffee gone.

When she woke it was well past eleven o'clock and the sun was glaring in through her window.

The heat from the shower quickly steamed up the small room. She stripped, shedding her clothes like a snake sloughing its skin, and stepped behind the curtain.

Needles of hot water stung where they struck, turning her skin red and raw, but the warmth made her feel *alive*.

She lathered up, luxuriating in the little agonies of the hot water, suds sluicing off her back to gurgle down the drain, and long after she'd finished washing she stayed beneath the spray, head down, her long red hair sodden and hanging over her face.

Finally, after more than half an hour under the flow with the water finally beginning to turn cold, she switched off the shower and stepped out.

She felt the sudden blast of cold air from the open window, but didn't move for the towel. Instead, she let the air dry her body, then dressed in fresh clothes, her damp hair sticking to the clean T-shirt as she went downstairs.

The hot-plate of the coffee machine hissed as she entered the kitchen, the pot dripping condensation down the outside of the bell jar. She'd put enough water in the pot so that it hadn't dried up yet, but there was only enough for one treacle-thick cup, so she poured it and focused her attention to the bundle on the table.

She didn't unwrap it straightaway. She stared at it, like she half expected there to be nothing inside the blanket. Then slowly she eased back first one corner and then the next.

It wasn't much to look at—a simple piece of stone with a hole in the middle.

It wasn't the kind of treasure that made it on to TV shows. It wasn't sexy enough for any of those. Looking at it, it was easy to see why it had been mistaken for a quern. Although a decent archaeologist ought to have been asking where the second offset hole was. Otherwise, how could they have inserted the stick to rotate the stone and grind grain between this stone and the second lying beneath it?

But it could have been the bottom of the pair, she thought suddenly, angry that she hadn't considered it earlier. Her heart raced a little faster at the mere thought of it. She scrambled to get her fingers underneath and lever it up on its edge. Her fingertip snagged at the rough stone until she realized that she could use the blanket as a cradle to tilt it upward until it stood on its round edge.

With one hand on either side she ran her fingertips over either side, comparing them for differences in texture.

If this had been used for grinding corn, then one face ought to have been worn smooth as it rubbed against its mate. Both were rough. She couldn't find anything resembling wear or weathering that she would have expected on a millstone.

Her hands were trembling as she moved them out toward the very edge of the stone, knowing that this was where she'd find the proof she needed to confirm that the stone had been used the way she suspected.

She moved gingerly at first, with the lightest of touches, then started laughing as she rubbed her hand across the smoothest of surfaces.

This was no quern; it had been used for *sharpening* blades, not grinding down grain. She knew that she was right. The only question that remained was whether this was the stone she was looking for, or whether it was just any old mislabeled whetstone, and she couldn't work that out by touch alone. It would have to wait. Today was about showing her doubting twin precisely what she was capable of.

It had taken a while to convince him that she was

right about the stone, and even then there was that gleam in his eye he got when he was humoring her. Thirteen minutes older than her, he liked to think that he was the dynamic force in their little family of two, but she was no slouch. And this would prove it.

She held the cup of coffee a few inches from her mouth, feeling the heat and breathing in the aroma, savoring every second of it.

BEFORE AWENA WAS able to brew another pot of coffee, she heard the sound of a car approaching.

Geraint coming home.

She wanted to rush to the door and hurry him inside, eager to show what she'd found. It was funny how life didn't change—once upon a time it would have been showing him the new eggs in the birds' nests or foxes in the woods behind the house. Now it was just a different sort of treasure. He'd always humored her then, always followed out to let Awena show him what she'd found and pretended it was the most interesting thing in the world, even if he'd already seen it. He was the perfect big brother like that. Or he had been. He wasn't quite so generous now, a little less tolerant of her whims now they were older and supposed to be beyond flights of fancy. He wouldn't chase her down to the bottom of the garden to hunt fairies anymore, but that didn't stop her wanting to share her tumbling train of thought with him every bit as much as she always had.

"Awena," he called, opening the door.

So many great things in life began with something simple like a door opening, she thought, metaphorical or literal.

"Kitchen," she replied, grinning like an idiot despite

wanting to come across as nonchalant, confident, grown up. She wanted him to walk into the room on his own and see the stone on the table for himself, let him join the pieces together and work it out without her having to spell it out for him.

But he ruined it, walking in blindly and sitting down without even noticing it. He was obviously preoccupied with something he was as every bit as desperate to tell her as she was to tell him. So Awena said nothing, giving him a chance to say his piece, but then he saw the huge stone and whatever he'd been about to tell her was shunted out of his mind.

"What the hell is that?"

It wasn't quite the response she had been hoping for, but it had certainly got his attention.

It was painfully obvious he was unhappy she'd gone ahead and done everything without him, but she didn't care. She'd pulled it off. She'd proved what she was capable of. She'd done it. Not them. Not him. *She* had.

She twisted her lips into a half smile and shook her head, knowing that her eyes were still smiling.

"Don't play games, Awena. There was no need to take stupid risks. We should have planned this out together. There were other ways."

"Were there, now? Like what exactly? Walking up to the museum with a blank check and saying name your price? Don't be ridiculous."

"But I could have paid *someone else* to do it." He thumped the table in frustration, but the stone didn't even move so much as a millimeter. "There was no need to put yourself in danger. What would I do without you? Did you even think about me when you were playing cat burglar?"

"There were no risks," she lied smoothly. It helped that she almost believed that herself. "It was a good plan. Besides, I wanted to do this on my own. I wanted to make you proud of me. I wanted to make *him* proud." She wasn't sure why she said that. She hadn't thought of their father for days, for weeks even. But that was her dad; he was like a specter that loomed over the pair of them, ever present even when he wasn't there. She saw the way that Geraint looked at her when she mentioned him, but let it pass.

"I don't want to know. I don't want to hear about it." He raised both palms in surrender, then walked past the table to join her, seemingly more interested in the coffeepot than her prize. It hurt that he showed no interest in it, but she knew he was just trying to punish her.

Awena was pissed with him. She'd been so excited to share her success with him, but now all she felt like doing was giving him the silent treatment. He always made out that he was the strong one, the rock, but she'd seen how he could be when he thought she wasn't looking. He might not like what she had done, but he wouldn't stay angry with her for long.

She'd give him an hour.

Maybe less.

Then he'd be all over the stone, talking about it, and wanting to hear every audacious word of her heist like it was some grand story.... Still, he'd already ruined it for her.

"So, how was your trip?" she asked, turning the focus back on him. She knew he was dying to tell her now he was over the shock of what she'd done. He shrugged. "Stop sulking," she said. "You know you want to tell me."

"Fine," was all he managed, but nothing more. He still couldn't take his eyes from the stone. She continued to sip her coffee in silence and waited as he started to circle it until finally he crouched down to look at it more closely.

She smiled as he ran his fingertips over the surface just as she had done.

He was hooked.

7

The museum was closed.

Annja had moved her car from the pub to the hotel, checked in, dropped off her bags and, despite the lure of the big comfortable bed, turned around and headed straight back out again. She'd hoped to get a quick look around the museum before it closed for the afternoon, but when she got there she saw a makeshift sign on the door that said it was closed for the day, so it'd have to wait until tomorrow.

She peered through the long window, pressing her face up to the glass. There were lights on inside, and she could just about make out the shadow-shapes of a handful of people milling around. She tried to shield more of the window from the sun, cupping her hands around her brow as though peering through binoculars. She saw a woman talking to a policeman. There was another man—dressed in overalls measuring up the size of one of the display cabinets. The woman saw her face pressed up against the window and mouthed the words *Closed* and *Sorry,* shaking her head before she returned her attention to the policeman with his notebook poised.

It wasn't exactly difficult to put the pieces together: a man measuring up a display case, a policeman taking a statement; there'd obviously been a robbery. It was surprising that a local museum would have any particularly valuable exhibits, though. Normally these rural sites just offered a few fairly interesting treasures dug up from the site, a few battered coins and rings, with the most precious golden torcs and such being spirited away to London for the British Museum's collections.

The brochure the landlord had given her mentioned a cache of small Roman coins, which would be both difficult to sell and unlikely to fetch a great deal of money—certainly not enough to make the effort worthwhile—so the theft was more likely to be a case of petty vandalism, probably bored kids looking for a thrill than any international criminal masterminds at work. Kids would have no idea as to the value of anything inside the collection and probably thought it was all priceless.

Hopefully no one had been hurt.

Annja turned her back on the museum and crossed the quiet road.

A handful of cars had driven by while she stood there. Was the place always this quiet? A woman passed her with a buggy. It took Annja a second to realize it was the same woman she had seen in the beer garden earlier, proving just how small a town it really was. The woman smiled at her, clearly enjoying the momentary respite her sleeping baby offered.

Annja proceeded along the road. An old lady weighted down by straining bags overfilled with shopping nodded at her as she shuffled off toward her home, stockings rolled down around swollen ankles. It was like something out of an L. S. Lowry painting, only she wasn't a matchstick. This was a sleepy little town where strangers smiled at one another in the street. She was from a neighborhood where the guy in the apartment across the landing didn't say hello, never mind a complete stranger. Her commute involved people crowded in on the subway too scared to make eye contact because they never quite knew what was going on in the heads of their fellow passengers. It was a different world. As much as she enjoyed the hustle and bustle of big cities and the anonymity that came with them, there was something special about quiet places like this. She couldn't live here, she'd go out of her mind after a week, but for a couple of days it was a great place to recharge.

A signpost shaped like a finger pointed down a narrow lane, promising her that it led to the amphitheater. She'd followed the same lane to move her car from the pub to the rear of the hotel.

Time to go exploring.

Annja walked past the cluster of cottages on the left and realized that it was in the garden of one that the most recent discoveries had been made. She tried to recall what she'd read. There was some kind of preservation order on the buildings that was supposed to prevent people from digging too deep. But the urgent removal of a tree teetering due to severe storms had exposed earth that had never been excavated and led to all sorts of wonderful finds. Sometimes life was funny like that, in order to preserve one way of life another had been kept hidden for over a century and it had taken a brutal act of nature herself to change that. Annja skirted the gardens, following the lane down toward the ruin.

It wasn't the first time she'd seen an amphitheater, but there was something incredible about seeing it here, right out at the farthest reaches of the Roman Empire.

Beyond the houses the lane opened up, providing

more room for school buses to negotiate the track down
to the ruin. The camber was quite severe, allowing the
rainwater to sluice away without eroding too much of
the track. She saw a row of buses parked on the right
with a cluster of teenagers milling around them, waiting
to board. The kids were full of noise. A few others made
their way to cars parked on the other side, no doubt to
drive home with parents who'd chaperoned the visit.

Annja kept close to the fence, looking for a gate into
the site. What she found looked like a rusty old turnstile
from a ballpark. She slipped through, keen to be away
from the critical mass of teenagers.

She stepped into a huge open field, its grass clipped
as short as a playing field, which maintained the illusion of having entered the ghost of the old stadium. In
the center, instead of a diamond, she spotted an information board. She walked over to it.

As she approached the board, the excavated amphitheater was revealed by the subtle change in elevation. It
was easy to imagine how the remains had been hidden
beneath earth and grass not so long ago. She walked in
the footsteps of history, following a line of Romans and
Britons before her to the excavation, eventually reaching the center. At this point, she imagined the wooden
structure that had once stood above these stone foun-
dations and how it must have towered above anyone
down in the arena.

The acoustics were interesting; the stone sides cut out
the external noise. Despite the fact they were no more
than a couple of hundred meters away, she couldn't hear
the kids who had still seemed so loud before she'd gone
down into the heart of the monument. It was a curiously
intimate moment of tranquility.

Not that it lasted.

Her cell phone's ringtone ended the peace.

She glanced at the display before answering.

"Garin," she said. He only ever seemed to call when it was bad news. That had become the nature of their relationship. Save a girl once, she'd joked, and you think it gives you the right to ruin her life. "What can I do for you?"

"Ah, Annja, sweetheart, how I've missed your dulcet tones," he said, making no effort to hide the sarcasm in his voice. "Not missing me too much, I hope?"

"I've not even been here a day—besides, it's hard to miss you." She checked her watch and tried to work out what the time was where he was, but then realized that she had no idea where he was in the world.

"Well, according to this little gadget I'm looking at you're in Wales of all places."

"Spying on me?"

"Hardly. It's just this new box of tricks we're trying out that tracks back signals when they bounce off satellites. It's a refinement on the old caller ID. You never know when it might come in handy."

"I'm not sure I want to think about why you'd need to know exactly where someone's calling from—mainly because every reason I imagine will probably be suspicious if not illegal."

"Oh, ye of little faith."

"So what can I do for you? Got some relatives you want me to visit?" She looked across the fields at a flock of sheep nuzzling along the barbed wire of the perimeter fence, and pushed a toe against a pile of rotting cigarette butts. She could never understand why people would litter in a place like this.

"Ask not what you can do for me, ask only what I can do for you."

"What on earth are you babbling about?"

"I'm nearby, someplace they call London. Ha! I figured if you were at a loose end I could nip over and entertain you."

"Entertain me?."

"I'm a lover of beautiful women, Annja, you know me. I don't discriminate—black, white, in color— doesn't matter, beauty is beauty. And I like to collect beautiful things."

"And vacuous ones."

"Oh, you wound me…though I will admit to a weakness for the odd dumb blonde. I can't help myself. That isn't a crime. So, let me entertain you."

On a bucket list of wants and desires, that was right down there on the bottom of Annja's bucket along with the dregs. But for all his lecherous ways, Garin was charming, and good company, hence the ease with which he took to womanizing. "I'll give the offer its due consideration, but right now I'm hoping for a couple of days of me time."

"Well, if you change your mind…"

"You'll be the first to know," she replied.

"Excellent," he said. "Have fun and try not to miss me too much."

"I'll do my best," she said, but he'd already killed the call.

A boy peered over the edge of the grassy bank, looking down at her, Roman emperor to her gladiator waiting in the pit. He disappeared back behind the edge without giving her the thumbs-up.

Annja left the amphitheater, climbing the hillside

that would have been banked seating back in the day.
She then spotted her Roman emperor; he'd moved on
to the shelter of a hedge at the end of the field with a
couple of his friends. They were huddled together. She
saw the spark of a lighter, which therefore explained
the cigarette butts.

Behind the boys she could see a lonely spire.

She left them to smoke their coffin nails and went
to check it out.

8

"I don't mean to be difficult—" which of course was exactly what he meant to be "—but what exactly are you are planning to do with this thing now?" Geraint tilted his head slightly, making a show of thinking about it. "I suppose it could make an interesting flowerpot. Maybe you could turn it into a water feature?"

"Or I could hit you over the head with it," Awena said. Her twin was proving more obstinate and much less enthusiastic than she had hoped he'd be, but then it hadn't been his idea to steal the stone in the first place, so perhaps it was all just a case of sour grapes. The important thing was that he agreed with her—the stone wasn't what the museum curator had thought it was. Unfortunately, he didn't agree that it made it any more important than a well-preserved whetstone. That it had been used to hone blades rather than crush grain made no difference to him.

She took a deep breath, refusing to let him wind her up.

"Do I really have to spell it out to you?" She shook her head.

"Spell away, dear sister. I'm clueless."

And he really was. He couldn't see why she'd been

compelled to steal it before it was consigned to some dank storage area in the bowels of the museum, never to be seen again.

She wanted him to be as wrapped up with possibilities as she was, not just humoring her. It might have been her idea, but he was her other half and she didn't just want him to be in this with her; she needed him to be part of it.

"Don't laugh, but I'm ninety-nine percent certain what you are looking at is the Whetstone of Tudwal Tudglyd." She let that sink in. The whetstone was one of their father's obsessions. He'd spent most of his life chasing around the country in search of it.

Geraint stood in silence, running a finger over the stone. "Could it be?" What he really meant was: What makes you so sure that it's one of the things Father wasted his life on?

And it *had* been a waste.

They'd grown up with the stories and knew all about the thirteen Treasures of Britain and their supposed properties. She'd grown up with the myths even if she hadn't grown up with a father, as he'd spent most of their childhood and adolescence chasing shadows.

"Don't do this, Awena," he said finally, not unkindly. "Once you start on this trail it's going to be impossible to stop. You know that, don't you? Don't let it steal your life like it stole his."

"It won't."

"I'm serious. He can't think about anything else. He's obsessed. It's like madness that's worried away at him over the years, removing all trace of his personality. Now all that's left is this compulsive need to prove he's right. Take a good look at this thing, see it for what it really is."

"And what's that?" she asked guardedly.

"A lump of stone."

"Of course it isn't just a lump of stone. We've both read Dad's notes. Look at it. Think about what he worked out…. This has to be *the* whetstone. It was found in the same area where Tudwal Tudglyd's whetstone was last known to have been, and there's no denying it was found with other relics from the same era. It can't be a coincidence."

"Can't it? Or is that just what you want to believe? Dad spent his entire life looking for this. Do you really think he'd have missed it if it was simply sitting in a display case in a local museum? He isn't an idiot, Awena."

She couldn't believe what she was hearing. He *doubted* her. "Certainly it's the real thing," she snapped.

"Is it? Can you prove it? Is it supposed to have some kind of property that no other stone has?"

"If it's used to sharpen a blade and a brave man uses the weapon, then it is guaranteed to draw blood. But if the blade belongs to a coward it won't even sharpen."

"But how do you prove that? Or do you have a convenient coward in mind? And who uses swords nowadays. It's not exactly the weapon of choice, is it?"

"Blade. Not sword. There's no shortage of knife crime in the city, is there?" She shook her head, refusing to be drawn into it. "It's not about proving it and you *know* it. I believe that it's the genuine article and for the moment that's all that matters." She prepared herself for a patronizing response, but surprisingly none came. It had been a while since their father had returned to the cottage, so by rights he ought to be home soon. He'd know just by looking at it and that was all the proof she would need. It was all the proof she had ever needed.

"The question remains—what are you going to do with it?" He still hadn't conceded that it could be the real thing, never mind that it *was*. Awena hadn't really thought much beyond liberating the whetstone.

"I'll keep it safe until Dad comes home."

"*If* he comes home, you mean."

"He'll be back," she said. "He always comes back." Which was true, but there was no way of knowing when. She was planning on accelerating the process by sending a photo of the whetstone to his cell phone. With luck it would be enough to bring him running.

Geraint covered the stone with the blanket. It was as though he didn't want to have to look at it.

Awena decided that it might be for the best if she adhered to the old adage of out of sight, out of mind. If he didn't keep being reminded of it, maybe they wouldn't have to talk about it until they knew for sure she was right.

She tried hard to hide her disappointment by asking, "How was your trip?"

"Not bad," he replied, nothing more.

When he'd come bursting into the house he'd been so full of life, desperate to tell her all about his trip; now it was just "not bad," as though what had happened was suddenly unimportant. The theft had sucked all the joy out of his life. She hadn't for a minute considered the prospect that he'd see it not as the beginning of some grand adventure they could go on together, but rather her catching their father's particular madness.

The sooner the stone was out of sight, the better— that much was clear.

The best place for it was in their father's study.

Geraint never went in there.

He wasn't interested in reading the volumes and volumes of notes that made up Dad's journals, the vast quantities of used and battered books he used as his points of reference for the great hunt, or the huge chart hanging proudly on the wall, tracing back their family tree to the last of the true princes of Wales.

The room contained a lifetime's work, a lifetime's obsession.

Geraint was right, though; she was in danger of following in his footsteps. She really was her father's daughter. She was more than capable of becoming obsessed with the search, even though she knew most of them would never be found. There were worse things that might consume her life, especially now that she'd found one of the lost treasures. And didn't finding one prove the existence of all of the others? In all the years her father had been hunting, he'd never laid his hands on a single one of them. And yet that only fueled his obsession. How would he react now, to actually hold one of them in his hands? To know he'd been right all this time. How would he take that vindication?

What he'd never said on those rare occasions when they'd talked about the quest was what he would do if he ever found one of them. What they did talk about was the history of oppression that was the foundation of Wales, how the English had beaten them down into submission and how these lost relics really were the inheritance of her people. They may have been called the Treasures of Britain, but they belonged to the Celts, not the invaders who came later. These treasures had nothing to do with the Romans, the Danes or the French who invaded their shores. Some of the treasures had their histories in Scotland, but the only documents which recorded their existence were in the *Welsh Triads*.

They were the Treasures of Wales.

Something to be treasured by all pure-blooded Celts like her family.

9

He had tried several times to get a better look at the peculiar pieces of stone during the daylight, but every time he did his presence drew curious looks from visitors and cathedral staff. He tried standing on it again to see if he could replicate that weird voice, but the stone remained silent.

He hadn't noticed the priest he had seen that morning walking across the grounds toward him.

"Can I help you at all?" the cleric asked, a gentle smile on his weathered old face. The heavy crags only served to make him appear closer to God in a literal sense.

The man wrestled down the sudden surge of panic he felt at the curate's approach and plastered a smile on his own face. It was highly unlikely—if not impossible—that the man recognized him from their previous encounter, but if he did, what of it? He wasn't duty bound to accept an offer of tea just to salve the curate's conscience, and walking away was hardly a crime.

"I'm good, thanks," he said, hoping to keep the man at a distance. "Just taking a few minutes to myself. Soaking in the ambience of the cathedral. It really is an incredible building. Inspiring."

"That it is," the cleric agreed, accepting his lie at face value. The curate left him to his contemplation, and as soon as the man was out of sight he crouched down again to take a closer look at the stone he'd been standing on. It was rectangular in shape and stretched almost eight feet in length, but was less than three feet wide, like a grave marker but not. It almost abutted the cathedral wall, stone hugging stone. He ran his fingers across it, sensing there was something strange about the piece of rock, even if he didn't know what. The fact that it was so large and in a single piece was noteworthy, especially in this region, but what really interested him was why it had been placed so close to the wall. That led to a second question he hoped to answer: What was its purpose?

He ran his fingers across the surface, feeling for any irregularities in the sheet of rock, but as far as he could tell it was perfectly smooth. How long had the stone lain in place? Maybe not time immemorial, but it had certainly been there more than a few centuries. Hence the surface was so smooth, as if it had been worn down by the endless shuffle of penitents' and pilgrims' feet. Though given its relative position to the cathedral that was impossible, surely? He lived for a good mystery. They made life interesting.

With one fingertip he found the slightest of indentations. It was so small he almost missed it, but then he found another and knew he was onto something; something had been scratched into the rock once upon a time so long ago that the weather had worn it down to almost nothing.

He reached into his pocket and pulled out a plastic water bottle. It was barely half-full, but that should be more than enough for what he intended. He unscrewed the top and searched with his fingers again, locating the slight indent of the markings, and tipped the contents of the bottle over it.

The water splashed and ran across the surface of the stone; some of it found its way into the shallow indentations. It wasn't about washing them away; the water turned the dirt and grime caught in the cracks a darker shade in contrast to the stone it was ground into. Even without scraping the dirt away he could read the two words that were revealed as if by magic....

Two words that meant he'd found what he had been looking for.

Giraldus Cambrensis.

IT WAS NIGHT when he returned.

It had been so hard to resist the lure of the stone, but he couldn't risk drawing more attention; the curate noticing two men loitering around the stone in one day was coincidence enough, a third time was just downright careless. And carelessness led to questions. And questions increased the risk of discovery.

He'd done his best to scatter earth across the surface, masking the newly revealed writing long enough for the soil to dry out and leave the surface seemingly bare again. The risk was that the curate returned to take a closer look before it had dried out. But even so, in this day and age of heathens who'd forgotten their own history, would the man even know who Giraldus Cambrensis had been? It was a risk he'd rather not run, if he could help it. It was always better to go undetected than trust to blind luck and the failings of the school system.

He had brought a crowbar with him, intending to try

to prize the stone out of its position and reveal what lay beneath, and with luck turning himself into a grave robber in the process. That brought a wry smile to his lips. He was still struggling to believe that after all this time he'd done it…and by chance. Years and years of focused and very deliberate study, years and years of systematic searching, and he'd almost literally stumbled upon Giraldus Cambrensis's final resting place.

He moved slowly around the side of the cathedral, keeping to the shadows as best he could. Nosy neighbors might be a cliché, but it was a cliché born in truth as far as he was concerned.

The section of wall closest to the funereal slab was out of sight of most of the street, but working by flashlight was asking for trouble. Someone would see the beam and, even if they didn't know what it meant, would remember they'd seen it. He needed to operate fast, and as "blind" as possible.

He found the edge of the slab by feel and, on his knees, teased the metal bar down along the edge, pushing at it to feel for its thickness before applying any weight to lever it up. Not that it was going to be easy. The slab had been in place for who knew how long. It was part of the land. It wasn't just going to pop open. He pushed down with all of his weight and the stone shifted slightly. He pushed again, but it didn't budge more than that first inch.

He adjusted his position, trying to get more leverage—it was basic physics. A longer bar would have helped. He slid the tip of the crowbar farther in, forcing it into the dirt and underneath the great stone slab to increase his purchase. Then he leaned into it, putting all of his weight and strength into a single huge push to try to shift it.

For a moment he didn't think it was going to move, then he felt it tear free of the ground, opening a crack no more than six inches wide—but that was all the gap he needed to wedge a piece of wood in place.

His back and shoulders burned from the effort. He could feel the strain in all the muscles around his upper arms and his ribs.

He reached for the flashlight, but didn't hurry. He took the time to recover his breath and give his heart the chance to slow down. He wasn't a young man anymore. He had brought his car jack with him, despite the difficulties of concealing it beneath his coat along with the crowbar and the piece of wood he had liberated from a nearby skip. Now he slipped it into the gap beside the wood and worked the jack's handle until it rose enough to take the weight from the wood, increasing the gap without adding to the strain in his old bones.

He cranked it up another six inches, the jack's feet being pushed down into the ground by the incredible weight of the slab combined with their small surface area.

He wasn't sure how much higher he could risk working it.

The street was still silent. There was no sign of anyone approaching either across the footbridge or from within the cathedral.

He risked turning on the flashlight and angling the beam into the wide crack to try and get a first look at his find.

Beetles scurried for darkness, fleeing the too-bright

beam as it shone inside. Other, slower-moving creatures slithered for safety.

It took him a moment to process what the contours of the darkness and the shades of dirt meant, but soon he realized he was watching something slide through the gaping eye socket of a skull.

There was no doubt in his mind he'd struck metaphorical gold. The only question was whether the stories were true, and if they were, that what he sought was still inside with the remains just waiting for him to find.

They were more "ifs" than he would have liked, but in the grand scheme of things he was closer now than he had ever been, and that was something.

The flashlight's beam caught the glint of something impossibly bright lying on the desiccated remains and his heart raced as everything he'd ever dreamed of became so much more *real*. It was there. He'd found it. He hadn't expected it to have retained its luster after all this time, but there was nothing else it could be. There just wasn't. Not buried with him. It had to be…had to be…

He'd read the letter a thousand times even though it was supposed to be secret, and in it he'd learned the truth about the bones of Gerald of Wales and what they had been buried with. There were countless legends of powerful weapons, great swords, shields, armor, mantles, cups imbued with magic—as many stories as there were weapons to be talked of. Gerald, the letter claimed, had been interred with a weapon of great power, both to keep him safe in the afterlife and to prevent it from falling into the wrong hands.

As with all treasure hunts there were hundreds of dots that needed to be connected, but this was it, the final dot. With the artifact in his hand he would finally know if it truly possessed the properties legend promised.

And if it did…

He slid his left hand into the narrow slit held open by the jack, and eased his arm all the way inside up to the shoulder, imagining the weight of the slab coming down on top of him. His fingers scrabbled against bone and tiny skittering creatures that crawled over the remains, until he found a hand closed around metal.

He intended to ease it free of the bony grasp, but it refused to move, almost as if the dead man was still intent on keeping the weapon safe as he had done for so long.

He took a tighter grip on the weapon, and even as he tried to pull, the inside of the tomb filled with bright blinding light. In panic he tried to wrench it free, but his panic caused the jack to twist and the stone slab to slip. He would have lost his arm but for the fact he hadn't removed the block of wood. Even so, it was trapped, and try though he might, he couldn't pull it or the weapon clear.

He shifted his position, wanting to work the fingers of his free hand under the edge of the stone to ease the pressure on his shoulder, but all he succeeded in doing was contorting his body and dislodging the wood in the process.

He couldn't keep the scream from his lips as the only thing stopping the grave from slamming shut was a corner of the wooden block and his skin and bone.

"Are you all right over there?" came a voice. The damned curate.

He knew any amount of serious struggling risked sending the wood and jack tumbling into the tomb, then there'd be nothing to save his arm. He needed help if he was going to get out of this. "Please," he said. "Help me."

The curate came hurrying toward him, then understanding the heinous crime being perpetrated on his sanctified ground, crouched down beside the grave robber to help him. He asked no questions. He didn't need to. He took hold of the edge of the slab and strained with all his might, slowly shifting it first an inch, then another, gradually releasing the pressure on his trapped arm. The sudden rush of blood through his system and alleviation of pain filled the grave robber with a wave of euphoria.

He drew his arm out of the tomb, bringing the sword out with it.

Its blade still cast a glorious radiance all of its own.

It wasn't enough to prove it was *the* weapon he sought—Giraldus Cambrensis's legendary sword—but he *had* joined together all of the dots, and they had led him to this marked tomb....

The curate lowered the slab, pulling his fingers free at the last moment as the wooden block and metal jack tumbled into the grave.

"What *is* that thing?" the curate asked, unable to take his eyes from the shining blade as he sank to the ground. The grave robber could see the rising tide of panic there behind the man's eyes as he struggled to hold it in check. He gasped for breath, but it was impossible to tell if it was the exertion or the fear that caused it. "What were you doing?"

The grave robber scrambled to his feet, ignoring the searing ache in his arm.

He tried to flex his fingers as though that was all

it would take to restore the circulation. It would take more than that.

He held the sword out in front of him, marveling at the flames dancing along its edge and the pale yellow glow it cast on the prostrate clergyman.

He hadn't wanted this to happen; he'd never intended for anyone to know he'd been there, that the grave had been disturbed, or more importantly that something had been taken from it. But he'd met the curate for a third time. He had no choice. There was no time for regret, even if this morning the curate had proven his kindness by offering a vagrant a cup of tea.

It only took one swing of the burning blade, then it was all over.

10

Annja hit the sack early.

The jet lag had finally gotten to her.

She'd ordered something from room service having learned from bitter experience that while she could have slept through the apocalypse she couldn't sleep through the midnight munchies. She unpacked the few things she needed for the night, her room still light with the hazy glow of the evening sun, and drew the curtains. They didn't quite meet in the middle, leaving a crack of white light in the darkness that she'd just have to live with.

Given the sleepy nature of the village beyond the glass there was nothing else that would keep her awake. Even though it wasn't quite six she was absolutely exhausted. There was no point fighting it, and honestly, it was a fight worth losing, Annja thought as she climbed under the covers and closed her eyes.

When she woke, the crack in the middle of the curtains was still white—or white again; it was impossible to tell. Her first thought was that she'd been woken by something because her head was still foggy and lethargic and her entire body ached. The clock beside the bed said six. That didn't help; she'd either slept about six minutes or twelve hours…but judging by the fact her mouth was sandpaper raw and her eyelids scraped against dry eyes as she blinked, twelve hours felt more likely. She needed a drink, and despite her room service feast, she realized she was starving.

Breakfast came and went. By the time she'd finished, Annja felt decidedly more awake. Jet lag be damned, at least for a few hours until it caught up with her again and sleep came crashing down around her. That was the usual chain of events when she came off a long flight. It would take two or three days to get used to being on the other side of the world. All she could do was roll with it, which meant getting out of the hotel and taking a look at the museum, assuming it reopened today. Not that it would be open for a few hours yet.

But that didn't mean she was going to sit around twiddling her thumbs; that wasn't Annja Creed's style.

She hit the books first, going through all of her papers that covered the village and surrounding countryside, highlighting things of potential interest, then cross-referenced them with the brochures the pub landlord had given her. The lobby carried the same range of brochures. There were enough things to keep her occupied for a few days at least without giving her time to develop itchy feet.

She thought about checking in with Doug, but a quick calculation was enough to know that even a workaholic like him would still be fast asleep.

She thought about reading a novel, but of the dozen they had on the wire carousel in what passed for the hotel's guest shop only one of them caught her eye. The story featured a young aspirant seeking to prove himself by finding the unholy grail. She bought the book, then took a seat in the lobby and started to read. Annja had read three-quarters of the book, drunk three cups of coffee and was on first-name terms with the girl manning the lobby area by the time the museum opened for the day.

The museum was quiet. She couldn't tell if it was closed or not as she walked up the road toward it.

Annja pushed the door tentatively, not expecting it to open.

It did. A small bell rang above the door, announcing what was almost certainly the first visitor this morning. She expected the staff to pounce, only too eager to explain the exhibits in an effort to stave off boredom. She'd visited enough of these places over the years to know there were two poles they veered between; there were those where the staff were just a little too keen, and others where surly staff viewed visitors as an intrusion sent to ruin their shift. There didn't seem to be anything in between.

She saw a youngish girl behind the desk in the main room, probably a volunteer from the nearest university looking to add some summer credits. Behind her there was a display of books with faded jackets, and souvenir racks filled with postcards and faux-Roman trinkets. She smiled and the girl said, "Hello," but that was all.

Another woman polished the glass of the new display case, Annja realized as she circulated around the room.

She came up beside the woman and said, "What happened?" looking down at the obvious emptiness where something had been on display up until yesterday.

"Oh, hello," the woman said, almost dropping her duster in surprise. She seemed to recognize Annja. "Sorry we couldn't let you in yesterday. We had a little trouble, I'm afraid."

"Nothing serious, I hope."

"Anything that keeps us closed for a day is serious for us. We might not charge an entrance fee, but the money we take in for books and stuff makes all the difference in the world when it comes to what we are able to do. School parties, all of that, it keeps us afloat. That someone stole from us hurts because we're all part of the same small community, but it's these other losses that really hurt."

Annja looked into the case and saw that there was a stash of small coins nestling in a terra-cotta pot. "What did they take?"

"Well, between you and me, that's the strange thing. They left all these coins—not that they're worth much, really—and took a grindstone."

"A grindstone?"

The woman shrugged as if to say, *Who knows?* "I know. What on earth would a thief want with an old Roman grindstone? It's essentially worthless outside the educational value, even to a collector. Next to the grindstone those coins are worth a king's ransom."

"Kids? Maybe the whole thing was about breaking in rather than taking any particular relic?"

"Maybe. The ridiculous thing is we were about to put it in storage, anyway. We've got limited space and much more interesting exhibits to take its place, but that's life."

Annja couldn't understand why anyone looking for the thrill would steal something as heavy as a grindstone. It didn't make sense when there were so many other more portable—and resalable—things close to hand, including the slew of coins in the same case, the collection of pins and brooches in the case beside it, even the "cool factor" of the old sword in the display case in the center of the room. It really didn't compute at all, even if it was about the thrill. Maybe it was a dare? Break-in and escape with one of the heaviest treasures to prove their manliness or something? And yet one of the memorial stones or the stone sarcophagus would have been more difficult to remove....

There were plenty of items of interest—some large, some small—but what Annja loved about places like this was that each and every one of them had a story to tell. It was even more special when one considered they'd all been found locally, either in the town or nearby in Usk. Together they offered a fascinating insight into the people who'd lived and died in this area. She could almost hear the ghosts of the Roman legion marching down the street toward the amphitheater, a few good men so far from their own homeland. That was why she loved what she did.

The sound of her cell phone broke the silence of the room.

Both members of staff turned toward her, both smiling as she shrugged *sorry*.

The screen displayed Garin's name. She hit the refuse button to end the call before it began. He could leave a message and she'd return his call—assuming it was anything worth returning—when she was done.

No sooner had the phone fallen silent than he called again.

She killed it on the first ring only for him to call back again.

"Someone really wants to talk to you," the woman said.

Annja answered. "Persistent, aren't you?" she whispered, heading back outside. "Twice in two days? Should I be worried or flattered?"

"You should be moving. Fast."

"Should I now? Why might that be? Thinking of paying a visit, after all?"

"It's Roux. He needs us."

That changed things.

"What's wrong?"

"We've got to get to a place called St. Davids yesterday. I'm picking the old man up. We'll be there by lunchtime." His voice sounded strange and there was a noise in the background she knew should have been familiar.

"What's going on?" She still found it slightly ironic that a man who was more than five hundred years old could call anyone else an old man.

"No idea, but something has really upset him. And you know what he's like. He doesn't upset easy. See you soon." The call ended, leaving Annja with a growing sense of unease. Garin was right; Roux wasn't rattled easily, so if something had got to him it had to be serious. It was equally unnerving that he'd used Garin as a messenger boy. What kind of trouble was Roux in?

11

Annja was on the road again.

So much for being on holiday.

But weirdly, though, the thought of saying no never occurred to her; that was just the way it was. Garin said Roux was in trouble, what else was she going to do? She owed the pair of them more than she'd ever admit, technically everything her life had become. That the older man had recovered every shard of Joan of Arc's shattered sword was down to Roux, and that she'd ever walked away from la Bête du Gévaudan was down to Garin's timely arrival. The man sure knew how to make an entrance.

The manager of the hotel hadn't batted an eye when she asked to extend her stay a week and paid for the room up front. Although he had cocked a curious eyebrow at her bags, she'd explained how she was making an unplanned detour and expected to be back in a day or two tops.

The landscape changed as she traveled. Mile by mile it became more mountainous and increasingly spectacular. She caught the occasional glimpse of the huge white turbines of wind farms as the road curved and coiled toward the urban sprawls of Newport, Cardiff and Bridgend before she reached the industrial landscape of Port Talbot. There she was greeted by a huge gout of flame blazing brightly from one of the chimneys of the steelworks. It was a different world.

Eventually the motorway came to an end and the road narrowed considerably. The cars around her slowed without any warning signs, their drivers used to the slower pace of life and the end of the motorway regardless of the speed limit. She followed the road from village to village rather than town to town; houses were dotted across the hillsides, a few huddled together in small clusters. She had to pull over to the side of the road more than once to double-check the map to be sure she was still on the right road as every few miles it became less and less convincing. The landscape, though, was breathtaking and more than made up for the permanent feeling of being lost. Lots of signposts she saw were in duel languages—English and Welsh—though the Welsh seemed to lack a lot of vowels. At last she skirted the fringes of Haverfordwest and picked up another winding road that would take her to St. Davids.

Her cell phone rang again: Garin.

She pulled over to the side of the road to take the call.

"If you take the second exit at the next island you'll see a small private airfield on your right. If you pull in you can give us a ride."

"That really is creepy, you know."

"What is?"

"Spying on me."

"Annja, it's because I care."

She heard the low drone of an aircraft overhead and, leaning up against her window, could see it coming in to land. It had the name of one of Garin's companies on the side of it, or one of the shell companies his companies pretended to be. She could never really work out what he owned and what he didn't, only that after five hundred years he'd amassed a stupid amount of money. And where Roux was content with his château and pretending it was pre–French Revolution most days, Garin wanted it all—bigger, brighter, shiner, sexier and most definitely more expensive. There was no point berating him; he was just testing another one of his new toys out. Next week it would be some other invasion of her privacy that was merely part of his dubious charm.

They really were the odd couple, Garin and Roux— apprentice and master long gone beyond the original scope of their relationship. She knew how much Garin struggled with the new dynamic and wanting to be seen as more than Roux's former pupil.

She ended the call and followed his directions.

The plane still trundled down the short runway as she pulled the hire car to a halt on the fringe of the strip's hardtop. There'd been next to no security in place, a barrier with an old guard who had been drawing his pension for the past few years. He waved her through without asking for any identification so she assumed Garin had phoned ahead to log her license plate with him. In these days of increased security alerts and color-coded terror threats, this little backwoods airstrip felt incredibly *quaint*.

The facilities were limited to say the least, but given the location it served a purpose. It was unlikely there was another airfield within fifty miles of the place, and even the daredevil in Garin's soul wouldn't have fancied bringing the plane down in a field unless there was no other choice.

Of course, if Roux was in trouble he'd have landed in the middle of Broadway if he had to. But he'd never tell Roux that. Likewise Roux would have done anything in his power to help Garin if he was up to his neck in it, and he'd be every bit as grudging in admitting that Garin was the yang to his yin.

She stayed behind the wheel, waiting for Garin to debark the Gulfstream.

After a moment the seal around the airtight door popped and the door came down, the built-in ladder descending until it reached the ground. Garin emerged a moment later, dressed in a ridiculously expensive suit, jacket slung over his shoulder, aviator sunglasses in place.

Roux came a moment later, gray and grizzled and most of all tired. He looked like he hadn't slept in a week.

He saw her car parked up on the asphalt and descended the steps, waving a hand toward her as he approached. He had an overnight case in one hand and a smaller leather grip bag clutched in his other. Garin carried one in his free hand. They were clearly prepared for this—whatever *this* was—to take more than a day to resolve. She'd expected nothing less, really. Roux wasn't keen on forgoing his creature comforts if it could be helped, so whatever had happened was important enough to keep him away from the poker tables *and* the château. Add to the fact he'd called in both of them, and that spelled trouble with a capital *T.* But at least he was in one piece. She realized she'd been holding her breath, half expecting the worst; hell, if Roux could do one thing well it was get into trouble.

"Annja, you're a sight for sore eyes, girl. Good to see

you. Thanks for agreeing to come," Roux said as she got out of the car to embrace him. Annja decided not to tell him she hadn't agreed to anything, as much fun as being pedantic could be. He knew he'd not given her an actual choice.

"Not a problem," she said, smiling as if butter wouldn't melt as she popped open the trunk. They slung their luggage inside. Roux kept ahold of the leather bag.

Garin smirked. It was the kind of smirk that he thought made him look raffish and debonair but really only made him look like a smug fool. At least he didn't hold out his hands for the keys. She had no intention of letting him drive. He slid onto the passenger's seat without a word. Annja hoped that he was going to stay that way. Every now and then silence really was golden.

She gave it a few minutes, pulling out of the airfield and out onto the main road, before she asked, "Want to tell me what this is all about?"

She watched the older man through the rearview mirror. He stared straight ahead, clutching that leather bag to his chest.

He didn't speak, but neither did he relax his grip on the bag.

Annja couldn't remember the last time she'd seen him like this—half there, half somewhere else. Probably back when he'd been so manfully convincing her to surrender the fragment of Joan's sword, back when Garin would have happily killed her to make sure her reconstituting the sword wouldn't jinx whatever weird curse was supposedly keeping the pair of them alive. The worst of it, she realized, was how frail Roux looked.

She knew him well enough to know he'd talk when he was ready and not before.

"Sorry I had to drag you from your vacation," he said at last. "I know you'd been looking forward to it, but needs must when the devil drives." The road swung away from the last of the shoulder-to-shoulder houses and out into the country again.

"Garin said you were in trouble," Annja replied.

She glanced at him but his eyes were still firmly set on the road ahead.

"In a manner of speaking."

"And what manner would that be?" Annja asked.

"The pretty damn blunt manner," Garin said. "Tell her, old man. No need to dress it up all pretty, she's a big girl."

Roux took a deep breath, like he was preparing to off-load some huge confession. "I shouldn't have involved you…not yet. Not until I was sure." This didn't sound like him; this sounded like a man who had been broken by events.

Annja watched him steadily through the backward land of the mirror, trying to judge just how bad things really were.

She resisted the temptation to press. "Okay, so where am I going?"

"Follow the signs for St. Davids town center," Garin said. "We're going to a cemetery."

"You take a girl to all the most romantic places," she said.

Garin grinned.

"Someone interesting buried in the cathedral?" she asked. She'd read up on some of the tourist literature about the town that was at least a city in name thanks to its cathedral.

"Someone and something, I suspect," Roux offered. "But I won't bore you with that."

"Let's try again—why the sudden rush to get the gang together and visit the boneyard?" Roux may well have been trying to duck the question, but he also had an annoying habit of specificity, so she'd learned to tailor her questions to meet his frustrating personality as best she could. "Something special?"

"Ah, well, there are three things that make this place special to *me*," he began, and she realized she'd unlocked at least one layer of security around the puzzle. She caught sight of Garin leaning back in his seat and she smiled, realizing he knew no more about the motivation for the trip than she did. Roux wasn't one for confiding in people if he didn't have to, which of course was one of the other things that frustrated not only her, but Garin, too; he really hated being treated like an errand boy after five centuries.

"For one, this is the last resting place of Giraldus Cambrensis, or Gerald of Wales to you and me. Gerald was a chronicler of his age. A lot of what we know about Wales from that time comes from his writings, and it really was a different world. But more importantly, just as we know and have seen things that most of our world remains oblivious to, he saw things and knew things in his own time. Only a fraction of the events he witnessed still fall under the gaze of the world, but believe me, there was much more that remains hidden, secrets lost to all but a few...." It sounded like the beginning of a fable, the older man spinning a story for them, but she'd seen enough and lived through enough to know better.

"You have access to his writings?"

"Some," Roux admitted. "A few translations and a

single original illuminated manuscript in my private library back at the château you are free to study when we're through here. That obviously means coming to France, but that's no great hardship, I'm sure."

"I'd like that," Annja said, taking the left-hand turn away from the line of windswept cliffs toward the town proper.

"Gerald was interested in artifacts known as the Matter of Britain, or the Treasures. Even in his day they had attained something approaching legendary status among scholars and knights alike."

"Are we chasing another myth?" Garin said.

"Aren't we always? Given that a myth is just the truth that no one really believes any longer," Roux said quite matter-of-factly. "You could argue that everything we do is rooted in myth, but that doesn't make it any less real."

He had said it in that calm, reassuring manner he had, but Annja knew him well enough by now to recognize that just beneath the surface Roux was seething and it took every bit of self-control he had not to lash out at Garin. That more than anything piqued her interest in the mess she knew she was about to get into. Anything that rattled Roux was going to be interesting and, more likely than not, lethal.

Garin mumbled something she didn't catch over the sound of the motor running.

She glanced and saw that he now seemed fascinated by something he'd spotted through the window. "Okay, that's one. You said three reasons?" Annja asked. She knew a little about these Treasures of Britain, enough to keep up her end in a spirited conversation about them. What she didn't know was what was drawing them to this isolated place, but Roux did.

"Quite right. Well, the second reason is that one of these treasures is buried with Gerald's remains in St. Davids. Believe me, this is not something we want falling into the wrong hands."

Annja nodded, taking his warning at face value. The older man knew things, but coupled with that he wasn't prone to dire prognostications for the fun of it. If he was worried, then they should all be worried. "How do you know that it's there?" she asked, turning to face him and taking her gaze from the road ahead for the first time.

"I know, because I put it there."

12

The old curate looked peaceful.

His skin had turned a pallid, bloodless gray. His hair and beard looked as if it had been combed more in death than it ever had in life.

Annja had no idea how Roux had been able to pull the strings to get them into the mortuary to see the man on the slab. Garin had stayed outside in the car.

"He was a friend," Roux said at last. That changed everything. Roux almost never displayed emotion. It wasn't that he was hard so much as inured to death of all of his friends by the sheer longevity of his own life. The morgue attendant left them alone. Roux didn't need to say any more than those four words for her to understand. In fact, it made perfect sense. It explained why he had been prepared to leave his home, why he'd summoned her, knowing she'd drop everything to be with him, and why he looked like death warmed over.

"How long have you known him?"

"Past tense, dear. Past tense. We'd been friends for forty years, give or take. Long enough for him to decide that I'd stashed Dorian Gray's portrait in the attic, at any rate. He'd worked himself up through the church over the last twenty or so of them, and was a curate at the cathedral here, but my first thought now that he's gone is that I never really paid enough attention to him. I used to come here and see him once a year, but I guess that's what happens in life—you start to take the good things, the good people, for granted."

"He must have been a good friend for you to come to see him every year."

"Good? Yes, but more than that he was a *reliable* friend. He even helped me secure one of the fragments of Joan's sword. He knew of my obsession, and now it may well be my fault that he is dead."

"Your fault? How could it be your fault?"

"He was doing a job for me. I'd asked him to keep watch over the tomb of Gerald of Wales, make sure it remained undisturbed. I should have known we couldn't keep it a secret forever. I should have done more...I should have taken it away from here and put it in a safer place. The police might have this chalked up as a mugging, but he wasn't in the wrong place at the wrong time. He was exactly where he was supposed to be, watching over the sword of Giraldus Cambrensis. The police are simply looking for an easy explanation."

"But what about the tramp hanging around the cathedral? Do you think there's something in that?" Annja asked. On the way in, they'd talked to the mortuary assistant, who had told them the little gossip he'd picked up during the autopsy. That a suspicious vagrant had been seen several times over the past week in the cemetery grounds around the cathedral. It was a straw, but was it one worth clutching at?

She watched Roux tenderly pull back the sheet to reveal the Y-shaped incision that had been stitched postautopsy. "You see those?" He pointed out several burns that had gouged deep into the dead man's flesh and the mess of melted subcutaneous fat. She did, and in truth she'd never seen anything quite like them.

"Those are all the evidence we need to know he wasn't killed by some hungry vagrant," Roux said, then covered his friend up again. Annja couldn't really argue with that. "And there is only one thing I know of that could have inflicted *that* wound. It is all the proof I needed that the burial place has been disturbed and the weapon I had thought safely out of reach has been found. That is why we are here, not to mourn an old friend— there's time for that later. We have to recover Gerald's sword and quickly, before whoever has it causes damage that cannot be repaired." He returned his gaze to the dead man before adding, "Now, I'd like to spend a few minutes alone with him, if I may."

THEY WAITED OUTSIDE beside the car.

The afternoon wore on. Annja was grateful for the fresh air, not least because it purged the scent of disinfectant from her lungs. It also served to keep her awake and alert and jet lag free. The parking lot had a distinctly clinical feel to it, but at least it avoided feeling exactly like what it was, a morgue. It could have been any sort of municipal building. But then, they all shared the same atmosphere of hopelessness, didn't they?

"You think he's gonna snap out of it?" Garin asked, full of sympathy as always.

Annja shrugged. "This is Roux. He's never down— angry, sure, bitter, much, but focused and insanely driven. I'm not used to him like this." She realized that this was the first time they'd been alone since he'd called; could she share the full extent of her anxiety and just how worried she was about Roux?

No, but not for want of trying.

Roux emerged from the building and started walking toward them.

He looked like a shadow of the man he used to be, which was unsurprising, she figured, given the self-imposed weight of the world he was carrying on his shoulders.

"Let's get out of here," Roux said when he reached them. He tugged at the door and got straight into the car.

Annja clambered in behind the wheel and fired up the engine. The car didn't purr so much as growl as it came to life. The sound was in keeping with her mood.

Garin made a call to one of his people. It lasted less than a minute, and when he pocketed his cell phone he said, "That's the accommodation sorted." Annja used the blinkers to indicate right, and pulled out of the car park. "We're a couple of streets from the cathedral, but the same could be said of everything in St. Davids, including the sea."

Annja concentrated on the road ahead—which really wasn't developed enough to deserve the name—until they reached the outskirts of St. Davids, which was small enough to fit on the head of a figurative pin. It wasn't difficult to find the cathedral; the spire dominated the sleepy little town. Garin gave directions from the screen on his cell until Annja finally pulled into the parking lot of a guesthouse. It only had space for three cars and made the hotel she'd stayed in back in Caerleon look like a palace.

It had been a long day already, but it was still less than eight hours since she'd received the summons.

Roux was first out of the car, before she'd even switched off the engine. Head down, he walked along the tight steps flanked with faux-Grecian urns overflowing with near-dead plants that led from the lot down to the main street. They made a particularly sad-looking set of sentinels. Annja and Garin trailed in his wake as he hurried to the cathedral.

He stopped in front of it, keeping his head bowed, as he observed a moment's silence.

"So this tomb…?" Garin said, breaking the stillness.

Annja wanted to ask the same question. She'd not read anything about Gerald of Wales's final resting place in the various pamphlets she'd managed to accumulate, bar the fact he was supposed to be interred somewhere in the vicinity of St. Davids Cathedral. There was nothing more specific about his grave. Meaning it was highly unlikely he was inside the building, and despite their obvious age, none of the gravestones in the shadow of the cathedral looked anywhere near old enough to house him.

As though reading her mind, Roux said, "It's an unmarked grave. Even if you knew it was there it's still unlikely you'd actually realize it was a burial plot. But it doesn't matter. Not anymore. His bones, God rest his soul, were never as important as the sword that lay with them."

"Okay, old man, how about you tell us why this sword is so important. Forewarned is forearmed and all that. I've got a nasty feeling we're about to walk into a boatload of trouble, and you're cryptic crossword stuff isn't helping my mood," Garin said.

Roux scratched at his white beard, then inclined his

head slightly, offering a particularly Gallic shrug that seemed to say, *What can it hurt now?*

"As I told you, this pivots around a fulcrum of the Treasures of Britain, supposedly magical artifacts that possess great power and could be used to cause a great deal of harm in the wrong hands, particularly if someone came into possession of more than one of them. And before you say there's no such thing as magic swords, let me remind you that there are more definitions of the paranormal than there are sticks to shake at them. To paraphrase, any culture sufficiently developed may seem to be in possession of magic. These treasures are from a time of superstition where anything not understood was immediately classified as magical."

Annja nodded.

"I had hidden one of the most potent of these objects here, making sure there was always someone to watch over it. The Sword of Rhydderch Hael."

"Roderick Hail?" Garin mangled the Welsh pronunciation.

"Rhydderch Hael," Annja said, her Welsh pitch-perfect. "His blade was called Dyrnwyn."

"It means nothing to me," Garin said.

"Dyrnwyn had a special blade," she said. "Wielded in battle, it transformed into fire."

"Sweet," Garin said, letting out a low, slow whistle between his teeth.

Even as she said the words she understood why the sight of the corpse had been enough to rattle Roux and serve as proof that the sword had been discovered. That deep wound could quite easily have been caused by something matching the description of Dyrnwyn biting deep into flesh but cauterizing the cut in an instant.

"And very dangerous," Roux said. "Don't think about the Matter of Britain in the abstract, consider it in the collective sense. Imagine what powers might be at play if Dyrnwyn was brought into contact with another of the treasures. Alone, they are strong, but together…together they are unstoppable." He let that sink in. "But all of that pales beside the one unassailable fact we know to be true—a man is dead because I left him to a task I should never have asked him to do. I should have found a safer resting place for the sword a long time ago. This is my fault. The burden of his death falls on my shoulders."

"So, you want us to find whoever killed your friend? I can make a few calls. A guy with a flaming sword isn't going to get far," Garin said.

Roux shook his head. "This isn't about vengeance. Two wrongs do not make one right. No. We need to find the sword, neutralize the threat it poses—that is the only revenge I need."

"So where do you suggest we start?"

"Right here," Roux said, looking at an innocuous patch of ground beneath the shade of a weeping tree.

Annja didn't see it at first; there were no ribbons of police tape to keep people away from the crime scene. Then she remembered what the coroner's assistant had said about the body being found beneath a bridge, which meant it had been moved for some reason. Perhaps that reason had been to keep the grave secret?

They almost missed the simple stone slab; the summer grass had grown across it, though there were fresh signs of disturbance around it where it had been levered up. If she hadn't known what had happened here she never would have guessed from the scene.

"This is it?" Garin asked, his question loaded with

incredulity. "It doesn't look much like a grave. Certainly not for someone who was supposed to have been pretty famous in his day."

"And that was exactly as it was intended to be," Roux said. "There's a certain irony in burying a vain man in a simple grave, don't you think?"

Annja knelt to closely examine the edge of the stone. It was easier to make out the scratches where a crowbar had been used. Even though the grave robber had obviously gone to pains to clean up his mess, he couldn't hide the fact that blades of grass had been trapped when the stone had fallen back into place, nor could he entirely mask where the earth had been disturbed by the crowbar, faint though the indications were now as the ground sought to return to its natural state. There was no sign of any blood on the unmarked grave, but she only needed to turn her head to see the telltale dark stains where a few spatters had hit the nearest headstone. Not much, admittedly, to confirm that the blade had been used to kill the man, but enough.

"We should tell the police," Annja said, standing up at last.

"What good would that do?" Roux asked. "They have a body, and there's not enough evidence here to help them solve the murder. Isn't it better they think of this as a simple mugging gone wrong, not a grave robbing?"

"What the old man's delicately trying to say is, he doesn't want the idiots holding us up if he can help it."

Annja wasn't convinced, but this was Roux's show, not hers.

"What's obvious is our grave robber didn't stumble on the sword by accident," Roux said. "So what led him here? Work that out and maybe we can work our way backward to him."

Annja thought about it for a moment. "If we discount coincidence, that means we're looking for a seeker, right? So he knew what he was looking for. He followed some sort of clue that led him here, which means someone else knew you'd put the sword in this grave."

"Gerald's book," Roux stated. "There are only a handful of copies still known to be in existence. That's the only thing that even hints at the fact he would be buried with the Sword of Rhydderch Hael."

"Then I'd say that narrows down the number of possibilities and gives us a starting point," Annja said.

"What's to say the killer wasn't paid to look for the sword?" Garin asked.

"Doesn't matter. Roux said this is all about finding the sword, not getting revenge."

"It's always about revenge with the old man, so don't let him fool you," Garin told her.

Roux was already walking away, lost in his own thoughts, so he couldn't refute his ex-apprentice's claim.

Not that he would have.

13

Annja ate alone in her room.

Roux had claimed not to be hungry. Garin had said that he needed to make a couple of calls and wanted to do a little digging. She could imagine him huddled over his laptop with his cell phone wedged against his ear, the very model of a modern-day treasure hunter backed by technology and big bucks. The days of getting his hands dirty were very much a thing of the past, but that was what happened when you lived for five hundred years. Everything was pretty much a thing of the past.

She'd had to pry the book from Roux's hands—the one that had been inside the leather bag he had been clutching for the duration of their journey—and even then he really hadn't wanted to let it out of his sight. She offered to wear a pair of pristine white cotton gloves when she handled it. She had no problem with that; she was an archaeologist.

She'd given the words of Giraldus Cambrensis a cursory glance before ordering room service, knowing she'd need to dedicate more than a few minutes to study the text. It was essentially a foreign language, after all, one lost to antiquity at that. Finished with the food, she began a more careful study of the writings, letting her mind wander. It was easy to imagine Roux reading the text while she stumbled over the Latin.

It had taken her more than an hour to find the first reference to the sword, but with it came another clue that might help them in their quest to identify the man who'd taken the weapon from the grave.

The man who had killed Roux's friend.

She checked her watch; it was late and likely Roux would be sleeping. She had no great desire to share her discovery with Garin, at least not until she was sure of it.

She read through the book a second time, cover to cover, taking three hours to slowly pore over the subtleties of the translation. Then she set it aside, carefully returning the ancient volume to its protective bag, and tucked the gloves away with it.

Her memory of the sword's history was sketchy at best—ancient Britain wasn't her specialty—and like it or not certain sword legends all started to blend together eventually. But as she had read the ancient text much of it came back to her, along with new snippets of information that she didn't think she'd seen anywhere else.

She'd been right in remembering the blade of the sword would supposedly transform into flame, and that Rhydderch Hael, the original wielder's name, translated essentially to *generous*. Generous because, unlike many great warriors, he'd always been willing to offer his sword to others, but they all returned it to him as soon as they became fully aware of its properties.

Annja never understood why they'd be so keen to give up the sword, rather than marvel at what the weapon was capable of, but Gerald's book offered an aspect to the legend she hadn't considered before. Dyrnwyn's blade would only blaze if it was held by someone *worthy.* Gerald assumed that worthy meant highborn, but there were other interpretations. Perhaps the fear of looking *not* worthy, or holding dead steel instead of a burning magical sword, was enough to scare them from keeping the weapon....

Annja had seen the evidence with her own eyes that fire had been involved in the curate's death, but how could a grave robber ever be deemed a worthy man? That didn't make any sense...unless he was some sort of highborn man? But that only made sense if the legend was to be believed in full. Not that it helped. Given the sheer passage of time half the people in the country probably had some kind of noble blood running through their veins if they dug far enough back into their family line. But it *felt* important. She couldn't say why, it just did. And she'd learned a long time ago to trust her gut when it came to this stuff. That one line told them something about the man who had taken the sword.

She was still thinking about it when someone knocked on her door.

It was Garin.

"Do you have any idea what time it is?"

"Of course I do, but you're awake so it doesn't matter."

It was hard to argue with his logic.

He grinned as he bustled past her into the room and set his laptop down on the bed. "This is our eureka moment."

"Is it, now? So what am I looking at?"

"The answer. Sit."

She did.

Garin reached over her shoulder, tapping a key to

start a video playing. "Footage from a CCTV camera near the cathedral."

"On the night of the murder?"

"No, a couple of days before." He jabbed a finger at the screen and a man came into shot. "And this handsome fellow is the vagrant that the police are looking for."

She looked at the slightly wild-eyed face and shaggy beard that was seriously distorted by the low-quality image of the recording. "How did you get hold of this?" she asked.

"I stole it, obviously," Garin replied. "But let's not get hung up on that." He fast-forwarded the footage. The view switched to show the man moving from one gravestone to the next, examining each in turn.

"I think that proves it was no accidental mugging. He's definitely looking for something."

Garin nodded. "Now look at this." He moved the curser and called up another window. "This is the night before the body was found."

The quality of the picture was worse, offering a gray and grainy image of a narrow country road lined with thick hedges and brown stone walls.

"Where's this?"

"A couple of miles down the road we came along from Haverfordwest, facing this way."

"And what am I watching for?"

"You'll know it when you see it," Garin replied, and sure enough in the distance she saw the burn of headlights approaching. He touched the keyboard again, slowing down the progress of the car, making it appear as if it was creeping toward the camera, not speeding.

The black-and-white image grew frame by jerky

frame as the car came closer to the camera until Garin paused it with the front seat and driver in the middle of the frame.

"It's the same man," Annja said.

"It certainly is. And let me answer the question I know you're about to ask—never."

"What was the question?"

"When was the last time you saw a tramp driving a car?"

14

Breakfast was a quiet affair.

Annja had been cooped up in her room so long it smelled of her. Sleep hadn't been refreshing, either. It was another bout of tossing and turning and not really sleeping at all, not in any deep and meaningful way. That was what she hated the most about jet lag. It wasn't just that your world turned upside down, it was how it crept into everything, weighing you down, slowing you down. And when you wanted nothing more than to sleep you couldn't. So she went downstairs.

Roux was already sitting at a table by the window, looking out onto a narrow street at the front of the building. He had a copy of a broadsheet open on the table in front of him, but he ignored the paper. Garin joined them after she'd ordered a strong black coffee and told the woman who ran the guesthouse she was good with a bowl of muesli and yogurt; maybe she'd have a full English breakfast later.

As was so often the case, Garin's expression said, *You are in the presence of genius,* but instead of blurting it all out he bided his time, waiting for them to ask why he looked so pleased with himself. Annja knew his game, and Roux had known Garin since he was a boy, which meant pretty much forever. So they made him wait until they'd got their food just because they knew it would infuriate him.

"Come on, then, spill," Annja said finally.

"I wake up every morning wondering what you would do without me," Garin said, keeping a straight face. Annja didn't rise to the bait. "There are only *five* copies of the book in existence, not ten as Roux thought, though there may have been ten once so I'm not saying the old man is wrong…but five is the magic number. There's no record of it ever having been translated, either. So let's do the math. Roux has one copy, another is owned by Jacques LaCroix…."

Annja recognized the name. LaCroix was a Howard Hughes–style billionaire recluse content on seeing out his days beside Lake Geneva in Switzerland. He was a man who liked to own things purely for the pleasure he derived from knowing someone else could *not.*

"Not LaCroix," Roux said. "He is only interested in a book as an object, not for what is written on the pages."

"Even when they might lead him to other objects?" Annja asked.

"Even then. It's a game with him. He's a collector, yes, but he's not interested in the effort of finding something outside of an auctioneer's catalog."

"Maybe he let someone have access to his copy?" Garin suggested.

Roux made a moue. "No. It's not like him. His collection is locked in an airless vault. No one ever gets to see them, not even LaCroix."

"Okay, number three is in the British Museum," Garin said. "According to their records the book hasn't been examined for more than six months, and even then it was only to check on its condition, so that's a dead end."

"And then there were two," Annja said, aware that she was stating the obvious.

"They are both in private hands," Garin said, the smug grin on his face still firmly fixed in place. "One is owned by a minor member of the British royal family, Prince Something or Other. The other is owned by one Owen Llewellyn."

"A Welshman?"

"What gave it away?" he joked, tucking into his fried eggs with gusto.

"What do we know about this man?" Roux asked.

"Not much. His family made their money in coal and steel and have their home somewhere north of Cardiff. There's not a lot about him on the Net. Widowed, two grown-up children—twins, Awena and Geraint— but honestly, there's something a bit off about him. He reckons he's descended from the last of the true princes of Wales."

There was no complicated history of the Welsh being subsumed by the English; that was a tale that didn't need telling.

"I think you should pay him a visit, Annja," Roux said. Before she could comment he said, "A single man is more likely to talk to a beautiful young woman, especially one who happens to work for a television company. Flatter him. Men like that."

"And me?" Garin asked.

"Do what you do best. Stick your nose where it doesn't belong. Maybe Llewellyn is the man we are looking for, but maybe he isn't."

"I can do that." Garin nodded. He told the old man

about the footage he had shown Annja the night before. "I couldn't get anything off the plate, though, typically it was covered in mud. Still, I've sent a copy of the file to one of my people, and who knows what they'll be able to do. But to be honest, without so much as the color, working out who's behind the wheel isn't going to be easy."

"I've got faith in you," Roux said.

"Is it worth checking other CCTV cameras in the vicinity? Maybe the car was caught in better light?"

"Already on it," Garin answered. It was unusual for him to be content doing what amounted to menial work, but stick a challenge in front of him and he'd make sure he aced it. It was just part of his übercompetitive charm. And maybe he'd finally worked out there was more than one way to be the hero.

"I'm assuming you mean you've delegated? Because as dearly as I'd love to be able to do this alone, two minds are better than one," Roux said.

"You need my help, just say it."

"All right." Roux let out a low sigh. "I need your help. Does that make you happy?"

"In ways you can't even imagine, old man," Garin teased. "So what do you need?"

"There are other treasures."

"So we're going hunting? Excellent. Will you be calling out hot and cold as we go?"

Roux ignored him. "I believe one of them is in Caerleon. Isn't that where you were, Annja?"

She nodded.

"What am I looking for?" she asked, feeling a tingle down her spine as if she knew what he was about to say.

"A quern," he said. "Nothing much to look at and easy to hide in plain sight."

"A grindstone?" she asked, even though she already knew the answer.

"It would appear so, to the uninitiated, but no, it is more than that. It is the Whetstone of Tudwal Tudglyd, a treasure in its own right. We need to reach it before the grave robber does."

It hadn't seemed important before, hardly worth mentioning, but now it clearly meant a lot. "It's too late. It's already been stolen," Annja told them.

15

The day had turned gray.

The sky was overcast, weighted down with heavy clouds.

They suited her mood.

Annja anticipated an absolute deluge of biblical proportions. The sky couldn't possibly hold all of that brooding anger in check; it had to rain. From somewhere in the distance she heard the low rumble of thunder. Give it a couple of minutes and the first fat spots of rain would hit the windscreen.

Ahead of her, a lorry made slow progress up the hill. It caused a snake of traffic to build up behind it.

Outrunning the oncoming storm was impossible. Even with three lanes of traffic it would have been unlikely. As it was, Annja was still in the excruciatingly slow tailback of cars when the first drop fell. She'd moved less than a hundred meters.

She'd left Roux and Garin behind in St. Davids; neither had been particularly forthcoming about where they were heading next. Roux mentioned another treasure that needed to be secured, assuming it hadn't already been discovered. He'd been reluctant to talk about what this treasure was and she'd decided against pressing him. Push too hard and the older man would simply clam up.

Their last conversation before parting had been prickly. "There's no guarantee it's the same stone," Roux had said, and she'd wanted to shake him and say, *How naive can you be, of course it is.*

Instead, she'd said, "Too much of a coincidence for it not to be. And can you think of another reason why someone would break into a museum and steal a grindstone? No, I didn't think so. It only makes sense if the thief knows something we don't, like, say, it's not a grindstone at all. It's actually an ancient treasure, priceless, powerful, like, oh, I don't know, the Whetstone of Tudwal Tudglyd. And if we accept that, it means we have to accept that the grave robber's looking for all of them. This isn't random."

"Fine, it isn't random. That just makes it worse. Now stop wasting time arguing with me and go, girl. Do what you're told, this once. Please."

She'd driven away in a mood as black as the sky.

Annja couldn't wrap her head around the fact that the theft of the whetstone and the murder of the curate *must* have happened no more than a couple of hours apart, despite the distance between the two sites. Could the same person really have committed both crimes? Was there even enough time to drive between the two places? It had taken her, what, the best part of two and a half hours to get from Caerleon to St. Davids. Though admittedly she hadn't floored it all the way because she didn't know the roads. Someone who did could probably have shaved ten minutes, maybe fifteen, off the journey. But could they pull off a robbery like that,

evade the law, drive for nigh on two and a half hours
and then kill a man?

Why would they even attempt it?

Surely there couldn't be so much urgency to the hunt
that it necessitated carrying out both crimes back-to-
back like that?

Unless, she thought, maybe it was some kind of challenge, like a grail quest: gather the treasures before the
full moon rises or something. A dare? But kids wouldn't
do something like that, would they? Again, unless it got
out of hand. Annja had seen enough to know that just
about anything was possible.

The road widened up ahead. Cars began to slip past
the huge truck, wipers fighting back the downpour. It
felt good to be moving again, even though she could
barely see beyond the hood. Rain hammered off the
roof, drowning out the radio. She didn't mind; it was
some eighties band she'd never heard of and the crazy
synth just made her nervous. A flash of lightning filled
the sky. She counted out one, two, three, in her head before the rumble of thunder filled the air. Annja thought
about pulling over onto the hard shoulder and sitting out
the storm, but figured she'd be safe enough if she kept
moving. The weather seemed to change so easily in this
small country, and so unpredictably. Hopefully Garin
and Roux hadn't attempted to take off yet—or if they
had, that they were a long way from the eye of the storm.
Garin was a good pilot, but as another spear of lightning split the sky she was reminded of just how powerful and primal Mother Nature was. And as good as
Garin was, she was capable of much worse. Of course,
knowing Garin Braden he'd probably bribed air traf-

fic control to secure a runway slot right as the heavens opened, merely for the hell of it.

As she approached Carmarthen she saw the welcoming bright yellow lights of a supermarket sign and decided to stop. She pulled into the parking lot, finding a space as close to the entrance as she could.

She felt her body relax as she set the hand brake and killed the engine.

In an instant the windshield was a sheet of water that diffused the yellow light from the sign. The drumming on the roof was deafening now the engine had been silenced. It completely drowned out the sound of her cell phone ringing. If it hadn't been for the feel of it vibrating against her thigh she'd have missed the call. It was Garin.

"Didn't make our window. We're grounded for at least the next thirty minutes."

"Thirty minutes? Are you out of your mind, pretty boy? Not even you can fly in this weather."

"No choice. If we leave it any longer, there's no telling how long we'll be stuck in this godforsaken green isle. The runway's pretty much mud as it is. If we're not away soon we'll have to wait for it to drain and the old man's worried we're already going to be too late…so he's basically said now or never. Who am I to say no?"

Even though he couldn't see her, Annja shook her head. "You're mad. The pair of you. You don't need to take stupid risks. Think about it—if you can't move, neither can anyone else."

"You make it sound as if you care, Annja. I'm touched."

"Don't be. I don't have the time to arrange two funerals, that's all." It didn't come out quite as she'd intended, but he got the message.

"I've got people for that, too," Garin said. She couldn't tell if he was joking.

"Do you have guys to scrape you off the tarmac, too?"

"You know I do. No job too big or too small."

Annja was convinced that Garin's belief in his own abilities would get him killed one day—which was ironic considering he'd been knocking around the planet for quite a lot longer than most people, death wish or no death wish.

Lightning flashed again and the call was over.

She tried to ring him back, but her network was down.

Great, she thought, pocketing the phone.

The electrical storm was clearly interfering with the cell tower. There was no telling what it would do to the Gulfstream's systems. Nothing good, obviously.

There was no sign of the storm abating.

She didn't relish the prospect of getting soaked to the bone in the ten seconds it would take to run from the car to the store, but didn't have much choice. The drumming rain alone was enough to drive her mad.

She gave it a couple of minutes in the vain hope that it would ease off a little. It didn't, so she gritted her teeth and clambered out of the car. The rain soaked through to her skin before she'd finished locking up. It was warm, but give it a couple of seconds and it'd chill down, leaving her cold. She sprinted, her feet splashing in puddles of water, splattering her legs and soaking her jeans.

Annja ducked inside the sliding doors, and was glad to see a small café near the checkout. She paid handsomely for a bad cup of coffee and a sugary doughnut. She wasn't alone. The storm meant a dozen or more shoppers had decided they were thirsty enough not to want to venture outside.

Her gaze switched between the rain-streaked windows and the cell phone, which lay on the tabletop beside her coffee, the "no network" message making her feel increasingly nervous about Roux and Garin flying into the storm.

By the time she'd finished her coffee she'd tried to contact him by phone and text repeatedly, but without any joy.

Sitting still wasn't helping her.

There was no sign of the storm easing.

She was ten miles from the next rest stop up by the motorway. Ten miles in torrential rain. It was doable, provided the roads didn't flood. Looking down the slope to the river, it seemed as though the churning water was in the process of breaking its banks. That didn't bode well. One thing this country really seemed to do well was weather. No half measures.

She pocketed her cell and ran back out to the car.

Two minutes later she was on the open road once more.

Spray from other cars was less of a problem as she headed out of Carmarthen. The steep gradient of the hill and the exaggerated camber of the road meant that the rain ran away quickly, and most of her fellow brave hearts drove cautiously. A truck thundered by on the other side of the road as the hill leveled out, sending a torrent of water up against the hire car. The impact was almost as fierce as it would have been if she'd been hit by another vehicle. Annja wrestled with the wheel, cursing the idiot in his eighteen-wheeler. She gripped the wheel much tighter than she needed to, thinking about Garin and Roux up in the air. "Idiots, the pair of them."

Ten miles felt like fifty.

She was more than a little relieved when the signs up ahead finally showed she'd be joining the start of the motorway and promised a rest stop. She pulled off the road and into the forecourt. As she made the turn she caught a glimpse of a bearded face through the rain-streaked window. The beard was every bit as wild as it had been in the CCTV footage.

She was looking at the man who had killed Roux's friend.

16

He saw the woman stare at him.

It wasn't a glance. It didn't end with usual disgust at his appearance and her turning away. It wasn't a casual look.

The rain obscured his view of her, so likewise it must have impeded her view of him, but she'd been staring. Why? Why would she stare at him? She didn't know him. She couldn't know anything about his quest. She had no reason to be so fixated on him. He tried to think…had he left any clues behind? Anything that would lead someone to him here? No.

He'd been careful, thorough; he'd covered his tracks, especially after St. Davids. He'd never meant…no, he couldn't bring himself to think about it. The more he did, the more it ate away at him. He'd shed tears over the holy man. It shouldn't have had to happen. Not like that. He tried to think…he'd left the cathedral…he'd wanted to run straight home. He was that desperate to show Awena what he'd found, but he couldn't risk it, not if someone had seen him, not if the police were already following him. He couldn't risk possibly leading them to his house, so he'd fled into the night, and taken refuge in a small hotel in Haverfordwest.

The do not disturb sign had hung on the doorknob all night, and most of the morning. He preferred solitude when he entered the details of the day in his notebook. Transcribing the events in the cemetery grounds in a way that didn't make him look like a killer was a challenge. Then he'd slept the sleep of the damned for the rest of the day.

He practically jumped into his car, not sure where he was going, just away from here, back out onto the open road and away from this woman. He slammed his foot down on the gas as soon as he rejoined the motorway, weaving into the traffic, carried along with the tide of it like a dirty piece of flotsam.

He hated the woman's look of…recognition.

It was as if she *knew* him.

His first thought was that she must. He'd been so careful to stay out of sight of cameras in and around St. Davids, and it wasn't Cardiff. It wasn't swarming with eyes in the sky looking for crimes from every conceivable angle. It was a tiny little village where the post office robbery had been the crime of the century right up until yesterday.

Even so, he couldn't shake the feeling she'd been focused on him.

And that meant someone must have gotten hold of his picture somehow.

So soon?

No, it had to be a case of mistaken identity. She'd seen his wild man of Borneo getup somewhere else, on someone else. It didn't *have* to be the worst-case scenario.

He adjusted the rearview mirror and caught sight of himself. He barely recognized the man looking back at

him there, unkempt and tainted with madness around
his red-rimmed eyes. Surely that would have been
enough to make a woman stare at him?

But no risks. He needed to put as much distance between himself and her. Just in case.

On the horizon the sky was brighter. The wind was
still fierce, but appeared to be shifting, driving the storm
north. There was markedly less water on the road, too,
and less spray screwing with his visibility. That meant
he could keep his foot down and was soon in touching
distance of eighty—over the limit, but not enough to
trigger the speed cameras—and passing the cars on the
inside lane still crawling along.

It was like he'd developed a nervous tick in the past
half an hour; he kept glancing in the mirror to see what
was behind him.

It was strange—he was more nervous now, after the
woman had stared at him, than he had when he'd carried
the frail and featherlight body of the old cleric through
the graveyard to hide it beneath the wooden footbridge.
He hadn't been afraid of discovery then, despite the
stakes being so much higher, but now he was. His palms
were clammy against the steering wheel.

Every driver he passed seemed to glance across at
him. He concentrated, eyes forward, rigid in his seat.

A car behind flashed its headlights at him once,
twice, three times, before sounding its horn.

He panicked, only to realize that his speed had
dropped and it was no more than an impatient driver
wanting him to move back into the middle lane so he
could pass. Chewing on his lower lip, still rigidly facing forward and urging the car to fly, he pulled across
into the middle of the three-lane highway. He couldn't

calm himself down. He could feel his heart in his throat, the beat resonating through his bones. He was pushing himself too hard. He wasn't concentrating on the driving; rather he relied on muscle memory to do the work for him. He was a danger to himself and others but could not stop again until he reached safety.

But where was safe?

Home?

The sword lay on the backseat wrapped in his old coat but it seemed to be *singing* to him. He could feel it. That was when he thought he was losing his mind. How could a sword demand to be held? Even if it had lain hidden for so many years? There was no such thing as a sentient blade. That wasn't the magic of this weapon. Still, there was no denying the fact that it felt like the ancient weapon was alive and insisting it be held.

What if the other treasures would behave similarly?

His mind raced with the possibilities. They all came together with the same question—how would the treasures react to one another? Would they be amplified? Neutralized? He needed to find another, but he'd spent his entire adult life looking for them and only found this one....

He pulled down hard on the wheel, to the angry blare of horns, until he was on the shoulder. He switched off the engine and turned on the hazard warning lights while he grabbed his journal and wrote down what he was thinking. He couldn't risk losing his train of thought. It took no more than a couple of minutes, then he resumed driving, hoping he wouldn't run into an unfortunate traveler who'd had a blowout or had broken down.

He did not see the car that was in the lane beside him,

not properly. He cursed it for matching his speed and stopping him from merging with the traffic.

Owen Llewellyn looked across, intending to give the driver a piece of his mind, and saw the woman from the rest stop staring straight at him.

She knew.

He floored the accelerator again, forcing his car into the lane even though the gap between her car and the car in front was too close, and narrowing as she gassed the engine to match him again.

So he did the only thing he could think of.

He swung the wheel hard left, making it up onto the embankment beyond the hard shoulder, tires churning up mud, gravel and water as they ripped into the ground. The car slewed viciously, fishtailing as he fought to control it, while no other cars on the road seemed to know what was happening around them. Gritting his teeth, he wrestled with the wheel as it struggled to get away from him. He barely kept control as he pressed the car for more power, more speed, his eyes on a slip of road twenty meters away across a churned field. It was insanity, but he couldn't do anything else but power on now he'd committed to it. Somehow he slid and skidded and churned up mud before he bumped back onto asphalt as horns blared and headlights flashed. He dismissed them all, accelerating again once all four wheels were firmly set on the hard ground.

He glanced sideways, across at the motorway; the woman was still matching him for speed, obviously hoping his evasive maneuver was going to be neutralized by the fact the two roads ran parallel, one obviously a newer replacement of the other, but he knew something she didn't. Even though he couldn't outrun her on the narrower old road, she couldn't follow him where he was going because her next exit was more than a mile beyond where he was turning.

By the time she was off the highway he'd be parked up in the drive at home.

He accelerated. He knew these old roads like the back of his hand. He'd lived here most of his life, despite his travels.

He was free of her.

17

Garin cursed the weather.

The storm had rolled in much more quickly than he'd anticipated. The rain came down in a solid sheet, turning the entire runway into a swimming pool. The surrounding grass was a marshland. Two of the light aircraft parked there looked as though they were sinking into the ground and wouldn't be moving without being towed.

"You're not getting out today," the man said as they approached the office. "You might as well settle in for the long haul—the storm has. We're just not equipped to deal with this kind of weather, sorry." His yellow sou'wester was slick with water that ran freely over its shiny surface.

"It's an emergency," Garin shouted to make sure that his words weren't carried away in the wind. He leaned into the driving gale force, fighting for each step.

"Doesn't really help, I'm afraid," the man called back, then pointed up at the sky.

"It's medical," Garin said.

He glanced at Roux, who looked as if he was having trouble standing up.

"An ambulance will have a better chance of getting through."

"Too long! We need to be airborne. The local hospital isn't equipped to deal with the problem. We need to get to Liverpool." It was the first city that sprang into his head and at least lay in the general direction they wanted to head.

The man didn't press him further. There was no point. Shouting against the storm was just a waste of energy. He waited for them to get closer.

"Chances are you'll miss the worst of it if you head straight north," he said, still shouting even though they were only a couple of feet apart, "but listen...I can't give you permission to take off. I'd be crucified if something happened to you. Sorry, mate, it's not happening."

"I'm not asking for your permission," Garin replied. "To be blunt, all I want is for you to step aside. Don't try and stop me. Write up whatever you need to write up in your logs. I'm going up. End of story."

The man glanced at their Gulfstream plane parked on the concrete apron.

He shrugged. "It's going to take me ten minutes to get back into the control room." The man didn't wait for a response.

Instead, he turned his back on Garin and Roux and headed toward the building.

"And there was me about to offer him a decent bribe." Garin shook his head as though to say, *Some people.*

"Let's just get out of here," Roux spat.

If they were gone before the guy made it up into the tower, then he'd have no choice but to record their departure. Once it was logged, it became real. Until then, well, it was as if they were never here.

They battled their way across to the aircraft, and Garin opened a hatch on the underside to trigger the door and the stairs descended. They boarded quickly, shucking off their soaking coats. "Buckle up, old man, it's going to be a bumpy ride," Garin said, disappearing into the cockpit while Roux went to take up one of the plush leather seats in the cabin. It was nothing like a commercial liner; the Gulfstream was the height of luxury and probably cost more than a third-world country's GDP.

Even though he only had a grace period of a couple of minutes, Garin didn't rush the safety check. Contrary to what Annja might think, he really didn't have a death wish. Quite the opposite actually. He was keen to live forever and suck the marrow out of life and all that. Fly into the eye of a storm, no problem—that was man and machine versus the elements and he'd back this man and this machine every time, but only when the deck was stacked in his favor. He wasn't about to go up in a death trap. Diagnostics run, he fired up the radio and asked, "Anybody there?" but didn't raise so much as a burst of static. The man obviously hadn't reached the control tower yet.

He turned on the internal comms. "Strapped in back there?" He didn't wait for an answer; he flicked a series of switches and the engines roared into life, the sheer power of them drowning out the wind and rain.

The plane turned slowly, edging ever closer to the start of the runway.

Garin pulled back on the throttle, keeping the brake in place so the engines built up power—more and more of it, until he could feel the body of the Gulfstream shivering. He released the brake, quickly gathering speed despite the layer of water on the runway. The plane juddered against the resistance. In response Garin just gave it more power. His eyes flicked backward and forward between the dials and the end of the runway in the distance. "Not enough speed, not enough speed," he kept saying to himself as the end of the runway came closer and closer, but kept pushing until it was too late to stop safely in the conditions and just willed the wheels to lift off the ground. They did, only to bounce back down again. "Come on, up you go. I don't want Annja yelling at me for killing the old man," he grumbled, and this time the plane started to rise as he pulled back on the steering column, lifting the nose in time to avoid a row of hedges that marked the perimeter of the small airfield.

Garin let out a sigh of relief, not realizing that he had been holding his breath the entire time. His knuckles were white from where he'd been gripping the wheel. He relaxed his grip as they started to climb. Through the window there was nothing but gray cloud and rain. He checked the instruments, making minor adjustments to bank them around toward the north. There were no hazards at this height; any commercial flights would be well above the storm or avoiding it all together.

As they leveled up, Roux opened the cabin door and took the copilot's seat beside him.

"In-flight entertainment not up to scratch?" Garin asked.

"I'm not the best passenger," Roux said. "I'd rather be up front."

"Meaning you wanted to keep an eye on me?"

"Something like that."

"Don't worry, I'm not about to get you killed. I like the plane far too much to crash it."

And almost as soon as he said it, the Gulfstream hit a pocket of turbulence that dropped it a hundred feet in a stomach lurching fall. Immediately, it was caught by an updraft and leveled out smoothly, buffeted and bounced from beneath as the wind tried to tip the wings.

"You sure about that?"

"Positive."

"Good," Roux said. "Don't make me regret trusting you."

"Wouldn't dream of it."

Lightning flashed, a sheet of cool blue rippling out through the clouds, too close for comfort. The cabin filled with the sound of thunder.

Garin gripped the controls again, tighter this time, as the vibrations tried to wrench them out of his hands. It took every ounce of strength he had to level off again.

Roux didn't look happy.

He had his eyes closed; his skin had the texture of greaseproof paper and his fingers gouged into the armrests of the copilot's seat.

"You okay, big guy?" he asked.

Roux nodded. That was as far as communication went.

Garin didn't see him open his eyes again until the turbulence was over and the plane had lurched out of the storm.

Beyond them lay sunshine and blue sky.

The Gulfstream had an onboard satellite phone system that rerouted to Garin's cell, meaning his phone was theoretically never out of range. He tried to call Annja, but it went straight to voice mail. No doubt the weather was playing havoc with her reception out in the woolly wilds of Wales.

He would call again before they landed, but for the time being at least he could relax.

"So," he said finally. "Are you going to tell me what we are looking for?" He checked the instrumentation again, making sure the bearings were right for the small airport in Caernarfon that was their destination. He'd booked a hire car that was going to be waiting for them when they touched down.

"In Welsh the word *caer* means *castle,*" Roux said.

"So we're going to the castle."

"A castle, not *the* castle. There's more than one in Wales, but Caernarfon *is* important. It's where the Prince of Wales is given his title."

Garin wasn't about to admit it, but he had no idea that the prince had to be given a title; he had thought that it was simply inherited. "And the treasure we're after is hidden there?"

"There are few safer places," Roux replied. "Including the otherwhere," he said, heading off Garin's obvious response. "You see, each of the relics has certain properties…."

"Sounds ominous."

"These properties manifest themselves in many capacities, not the least in how it interacts with other objects. I wouldn't want to risk it coming into contact with Joan's sword."

"Are you going to tell me what it is?"

"Will it make any difference if I do?"

"Only so much as it'll stop me asking annoying questions," he replied.

He hated it when Roux was evasive. It was just one

of the old man's characteristics that got up his nose. In some ways life had been so much easier when he'd been intent on killing the snooty bastard. Simpler, for sure. Now they were friends, allies, it was occasionally awkward because the old man insisted on treating him like some neophyte. He'd given up trying to argue that he wasn't just a grown man; he was comparatively ancient, all things considered. It was all relative; if he was ancient, then Roux would just argue he was more so.

"The Treasure of Caernrvon is one of the greatest of the treasures that make up the Matter of Britain. One that should *never* leave Wales."

"Okay, now it's getting interesting. What is it? A shield? A sword? The Holy Grail?"

Roux shook his head. "The Mantle of King Arthur."

"The *what* of King Arthur?"

"Mantle. A cloak. Among other powers, the mantle can make the wearer invisible."

"A cloak of invisibility? Seriously? Awesome. I'll buy that for a dollar."

"It's been hidden for a *very* good reason, Garin."

"I'm sure it has, but come on...a cloak of invisibility? Tell me you don't want to try it out."

"I don't. And as long as it hasn't been disturbed, I'm thinking it may be for the best if it remains there."

"Hold on a minute, we're just going to leave it where it is?"

"Is there an echo in here?"

"I don't understand. Why did we just risk our lives if we're going to do nothing?"

"These treasures belong here. All of them. They sustain the country even if people have long ago forgotten their significance."

"Well, if they've forgotten about their significance, then surely they aren't going to miss them. Why risk someone discovering them? We've got plenty of security. Safest place in the country for them is one of our vaults, surely."

"We've had this discussion before. We need to keep the treasures out of the wrong hands."

"You'll get no argument from me. That's exactly what I'm saying."

"Even if yours are the wrong hands?"

"That's low, even for you, old man."

18

Awena could not hide her shock at the sight of her father as he stumbled through the door. She caught herself midscream, thinking he was an intruder. He hadn't shaved in weeks and had the wild-eyed stare of a bum, the same manic intensity to his eyes and the same odd twitches that went with it. He stank. It was obvious he'd been wearing the same clothes for weeks. They were rags hanging off his skeletal frame now. But it was the tangled mass of hair and scraggy beard that transformed him into a different man. He clutched a bundle of rags to his chest, though they were indistinguishable from the clothes on his back. The bundle was long and thin and not like an armful of laundry in the slightest. He clung to them for grim life.

It took her a moment to realize that whatever he was holding was wrapped in one of his old coats.

"Dad?" Even as she said it her brain raced to catch up, processing everything it was seeing, comparing his appearance with how she remembered him.

"Yes, yes, it's me," he said, smiling weakly. She recognized that smile. How could she not? Everything she'd ever done in her life had been to earn that smile. "I've got something to show you, Awena," he said. "Something special. You won't believe it…I did it. I found it. I found one of the treasures. After all this time…I finally found one."

There was joy and excitement in his eyes, in the tone of his voice and in the way he moved. She so wanted to tell him about her own discovery but could not bring herself to take away anything from his excitement. He laid his bundle down on the table, mirroring her first movements when she'd returned with her own hardwon treasure. With the same reverence, he eased back the coat covering it.

"Who is it?" Geraint called from somewhere upstairs. The sound of his son's voice jerked their father from his raptures.

"Geraint, come quickly," Awena called excitedly. "Look who it is!"

The look of shock and disgust on Geraint's face when he entered the kitchen was even more abhorrent than anything Awena could have imagined. How could he feel like that about their father? Why couldn't he just… love him…like she did?

"For the love of God, what have you done to yourself, Dad? You look like a disaster." He shook his head. Awena could see him struggling to overcome his surprise and confusion at the sight of the tramp at their kitchen table.

"How could you let yourself get into this mess?" And then far more accusatory than any of the other questions her brother asked, "When are you going to grow up? You're supposed to be the adult in this family. Not me. Not Awena. *You.* You're not Peter Pan. But you are lost…look at you. Don't you ever stop to think what your obsession is doing to us? Do you even know that Awena is every bit as obsessed with this crap as you are? Have you ever *asked* her what she thinks about your folly? She idolizes you, you moron. She worships the ground you walk on, and now she's got your disease because she thinks it will *please* you! She's still trying to earn your love, and it will ruin her life just as it ruined yours. I'm not going to let it. So go upstairs, shower, shave and then change your clothes and walk out of the front door and keep on walking. You stay away, understand? We don't need you."

Awena had never heard so much anger in his voice, so much venom.

It was staggering.

She didn't know what to say.

How to react?

He was her brother. Her twin. She would run into a burning building for him. But this was their *father*.

She couldn't stand by and let him drive him away forever. She could hear him saying: *But I did it for you...for us....* And knew she'd hate him for the rest of their lives if she let this happen. "Geraint!" she snapped. "Don't. Please. Just don't. This is Dad. Our dad. You can't talk to him like a child."

Their father ignored them. Instead, he turned his attention back to the half-unwrapped bundle on the table and carefully peeled the coat away from the object inside. Slowly, he then removed layer upon layer of clothing that he'd used to protect the artifact until at last he revealed the sword, its blade shining bright.

"Another damn sword. Just what we need in this house. So who conned you into buying this, then? Someone down Cardiff market? I don't even want to ask how much you paid for it. Too much, obviously, because any idiot can see it's worthless. Dad, how can you have wasted your entire life chasing these bloody Treasures of Britain? This thing looks like it was forged yesterday! It has to stop! Please. I'm begging you. Even if these things existed once…even if you find them…can't you see that it isn't going to change anything? It isn't going to transform you into a hero for the modern age. It won't make you king…you'll just be a sad old man who wasted his life in turn for some trinkets."

"Wasted my life?" He shook his head sadly. There was no anger in him despite the barrage he was being subjected to. He simply laid a hand on the too-shiny blade and said, "I haven't wasted my life. This is proof that it was all worthwhile."

Awena heard something in her father's voice…. It wasn't sadness. It wasn't anger. It took her a moment to realize what it was: satisfaction.

But there was nothing he could say that would convince Geraint his search was anything less than a fool's quest.

"This? You think *this* makes it all worthwhile? You're more of a fool than I thought, Dad." Geraint reached across the table to snatch up the sword, but their father beat him to it, raising the gleaming blade aloft.

Awena felt the change in the air as the blade came alive, crackling with a ghostly blue flame that licked along the length of metal.

She struggled to breathe. It was as if all the air had been sucked out of the room.

Her heart beat faster and harder against her breastbone despite the fact she hadn't moved a muscle—faster and harder than it had when she'd struggled to liberate the stone from the museum. The excitement sent a surge of adrenaline through her body. And just this once, excitement was far more powerful than fear.

She *knew* what the sword was. She'd read about it in the books, seen the sketches that her father had made. Even if in her heart of hearts she'd believed they'd never find anything truly mythical, that they'd ever find any of the true Treasures of Britain, there could be no doubting it now. Here was the proof that Geraint was always demanding.

He had to accept it, she thought.

But as though reading her mind, Geraint scoffed and said, "The tricks are getting more convincing, I'll give you that, but they're still only tricks." There was no sign of his anger disappearing. "I've had enough of this. I'm sick of it. I'm sick of Awena always pining for you and us having to struggle to keep this place afloat while you think there's something romantic in abandoning your kids for the promise of adventure. Don't bother with the shower. Just go."

Faced with her brother's point-blank refusal to believe the evidence of his own eyes, Awena saw the twitches intensify around her father's cheek and eye, obviously growing more agitated by the way the confrontation had turned.

And then, before she could scream, he swung the blade so savagely it left a blur of blue light in its wake, just as Geraint took a step closer.

The tip of the blade scorched his shirt.

Smoke rose as the material turned black.

"What are you doing?" Geraint shouted, clutching one hand to his chest, the other arm raised to defend himself.

"Doing? I'll tell you what I'm doing, boy. I'm proving

that I haven't wasted a single second of my life. My life, not yours. Mine. The Matter of Britain is *ours*. All of these treasures belong to every Welsh man and woman. They are our heritage. They are our destiny. We will use them to show the English that we can stand up to them. But that's the problem, isn't it? You don't think there's a problem with us being governed from another country. It doesn't matter to you, does it? You don't care that they treat us like second-class citizens, bleeding us dry while they fiddle their expenses and laugh in our faces."

Awena had never seen him like this. He was always so in control. So poised. Careful.

She had to calm him down before things escalated. Otherwise, one of them was going to be seriously hurt.

Once, when Geraint had broken his arm as a child, she'd felt an echo of her twin's pain, but it had been nothing more than a pale shadow of what he'd felt. She couldn't imagine the pain that searing sword would cause. She didn't want to. She didn't want to feel the ghost of it, either. "Stop it!" she screamed. "Stop it, both of you, before you kill each other!"

There was a long silence after her last word, the two men staring at each other, seemingly ignoring her plea, ready to tear chunks out of each other. And then her father lowered the sword, understanding how close he'd come to doing something he could never take back.

He stood openmouthed and trembling as he stared at the red stain on Geraint's shirt.

He shook his head frantically, all anger gone, replaced by fear and panic.

His arm went limp. Giraldus Cambrensis's legendary sword slipped from his grip, clattering to the tile floor.

He didn't take another breath. He didn't wait for the ringing of metal on stone to subside. He just ran.

Awena wanted to chase after him, to stop him from leaving again.

It was the only thing she had ever wanted.

Though this time it was different, letting him leave now, like this, there was a chance that he would never return.

But Geraint needed the help.

He was the victim.

To help him, though, she had to let her father go.

It was the hardest thing she'd ever done.

19

Annja cursed the guy; he was another one with a death wish. She couldn't believe he'd red-lined it across an open field to get away from her, but it proved one thing beyond any reasonable doubt: he was the man they were looking for.

And she'd let him get away.

She'd tried to call Garin again, but had no luck. And because of that she'd missed the off-ramp, so there was no hope of cutting the guy off from wherever he was going. Looking at the wilderness of this country it could have been anywhere, including a nuclear bunker hidden underground. He was long gone.

But she'd got his license plate, using the voice recorder on her cell phone to dictate it rather than trying to risk writing while driving.

Ten minutes later she saw the blue sign for the next exit and pulled off. She parked up in a small gravel lot and tried Garin again. Still nothing, but at least she got through to his voice mail this time. That was something. The storm was starting to ease off, but it was still a lot more than steady rainfall even if it wasn't the biblical flood. She was about to set off again when the phone rang in her hand.

It was Garin.

The signal was weak and threatened to drop out more than once, but she could hear him.

"You've had me worried," she said.

"I'm indestructible, remember?" She could hear the grin in his voice. He was anything but. The weird curse that involved Joan's sword might keep Garin and Roux around, but just like Shakespeare's merchant, prick them and they doth bleed. None of them had really figured out how it worked, or what had truly happened that day when the two soldiers failed her and Joan of Arc was burned at the stake. All they knew was that instead of dying they lingered. Roux put it down to having unfinished work to do, but maybe it was more than that.

"It was a bit of a bumpy ride, mind you, even for me and you know how bumpy I like it."

"You're an idiot, Garin!" she snapped. It was relief, of course, but that didn't take the sting out of her words. "You could have been killed."

"No need to be all melodramatic, Annja. Once we were in the air I flew *around* the storm, not *through* it. Contrary to popular opinion I'm not actually a moron."

"Could have fooled me," she said.

"And I often do. Roux's a little green around the gills, but he's not a good flier at the best of times. He's more worried about *you*."

"Me? I'm fine," she replied.

"Don't be a hero," Garin teased.

"I've seen him," Annja said, shutting him up.

"Seen *who?*"

"Our tramp," Annja said. "I pulled into a rest stop along the highway, was about to get out of the car, and there he was, larger than life. He made me, and ran. I followed him back out onto the main road, but with the storm and some really stupid driving with him going off-road and nearly killing himself in the process, I lost him." She could hear Garin passing on each snippet of information as she recited it. She half expected to hear Roux tut at her failure. She headed it off with, "But it's not all bad news, I got his plate." She recited the sequence of letters and numbers, and listened carefully as Garin repeated them so Roux could write them down.

"I love you, Miss Creed, you know that? You rock. You roll. And you most certainly make life interesting, and that's the most important thing, don't you think?"

"It's mutual, most of the time. The rest of the time you're just infuriating."

He laughed. "I live to serve. I'll run the plate and get back to you as soon as we touch down."

She heard Roux speaking, then the sound of the phone being passed over.

"Annja," he said, his tone all business. "I want you to stay where you are until Garin's had a chance to run the registration. I don't want you to drive to Caerleon, only for you to have to come back again."

He didn't wait for her to agree. He handed the phone back to Garin, expecting to be obeyed. "Better find somewhere nice and warm," he said. "Give me an hour. I'll work my magic."

Hanging around made sense, as much as she wanted to be on the move. So much for her vacation.

Mercifully, she didn't have to wait long before Garin declared he'd struck gold.

He sounded like a giddy schoolboy as he reported, "The car's registered to one Owen Llewellyn. Yep, that's right, the same Owen Llewellyn that's on the list, owner of one rare copy of the writings of Gerald of Wales. Co-incidence? I think not. We've got our man. I'm sending the address through to you right now, but it looks like you may as well head on to Caerleon and you can make a call on him tomorrow."

"I'm not even going to ask how you can find out those details from a license plate. I just don't want to know." Not for the first time she was glad he was on their side.

"Speak soon." He hung up, leaving her holding the phone to her ear.

"Well, goodbye to you, too," she said, even though he was long gone.

20

He drove away from the house, watching it recede in the rearview mirror.

This wasn't the homecoming he'd hoped for, but how often in this life do you get what you want? It's not all sunshine and roses. It wasn't even open arms most of the time, not for the prodigal father returning at last.

But he had expected better than this.

Maybe it was optimistic to think the boy would be happy he was still alive—still, so much anger? Such hostility? He'd not expected that. Why couldn't the boy just be happy for once? Why couldn't he look at the miracle the sword really was and understand it, see his own heritage in the blue flame that had licked along the blade as he'd held it, and know that it was all true? Everything his old man had ever dared hope, dream. Every story he'd ever told him about his inheritance as the last true son of Wales was true.

And he'd turned the sword on him....

Owen Llewellyn felt sick to the core. He had proved them wrong; he had proved them all wrong, and they claimed he'd wasted his life. How could that be when he'd succeeded? He'd found what he'd been looking for, the first of the treasures; now he would find them all, one by one, and offer them to his children, a gift beyond price.

He'd seen the manner in which the sword responded to Geraint's touch. It called to him. He knew it did. And the other treasures would, too. They'd recognize him. Owen would have to go back and collect it, and the boy, but not now, not yet. He'd have to wait until he'd calmed down. Geraint's Celtic blood was thick and full of fire, but it was full of forgiveness, too, that was what made the Celts such great friends and deadly foes.

For now he would just find somewhere to hole up on his own while his children had the chance to talk to each other. Awena would win the boy over. He knew she would. She always did. He could rely on her.

He turned on the radio as he drove, tuning into Radio Wales expecting to hear reports of the murder in St. Davids.

The curate should have left him alone.

He had done everything he could to stay hidden, looking for the sword at the most ungodly of hours to minimize risk of discovery…the man had brought it on himself. He'd tried to keep him out of it…he'd tried to drive him away, even when he'd saved Owen from himself, but all that had done was hasten a good man's death.

He felt a wave of remorse wash over him as the consequences of his actions started to sink in.

He had killed an innocent man.

Not only that, he'd tried to hide the body so that he wouldn't be caught.

He had been scared stupid when the woman had looked at him, but—paranoia aside—that was all she had done; she'd just looked at him. Meanwhile he could have killed himself trying to get away from her. He couldn't carry on like this. He wasn't thinking straight. He needed to sleep. He needed to clear his head. He needed to weigh the consequences of his actions, and look ahead and not screw up, so close to the end.

He needed to own his actions.

Otherwise, he didn't deserve to possess the sword, no matter how long he had been looking for it. He had almost defied the legend…he'd seen the flames lick along the blade, but when it came right down to it, he wasn't worthy of it. He'd dropped the weapon and the fire had burned out. He wasn't righteous. Not in his own mind.

It had been a while since he had last driven along this particular road, and calling it a road was being generous in the extreme, but he knew every bend, every kink and curve that lay along its path. Some of the cracks had been repaired recently, showing darker black patches where asphalt had been laid, but new cracks and hollows were already beginning to form. It was almost as though the road were a living thing, constantly changing and always needing attention.

The handful of buildings along the roadside were the same as they'd always been, reassuringly so. Though the trees had grown a little larger in the main, a few of them had been cut down. They probably dated back to the time of Giraldus Cambrensis himself. It was Owen Llewellyn who had changed. He did not like what he had become.

It would have been better if he had left the sword in the grave, then at least the curate would still be alive. It would have been better still if Owen had never heard of the treasures, then perhaps he wouldn't have spent so much of his life searching for them and his children would still love him. They had deserved a better father, but he'd never been able to be a better man than he was.

He brushed them away with the back of his hand. He wasn't a sentimental man. That wasn't how his own father had raised him. But he'd sworn all his life he wouldn't be his father, only to go and be exactly that— cold, distant, obsessed with the legends of his people and his own supposed inheritance as the rightful heir of the last true prince of Wales. He breathed in deeply, his vision blurred for a moment as he tried to stem the tears.

He would be a better man.

He would be a better father.

He would make it up to them somehow.

He took the bend without hugging the verge as tightly as he might have done but for the tears and, in turn, took the corner too quickly, narrowly missing a car coming the other way.

Their wing mirrors grazed each other, the sound amplified inside the car as his sprung in toward the car's body, then out again after the obstruction passed.

He glanced in his mirror and saw the brake lights of the other car glowing, then it continued. A close call for both of them, but the other driver had been the one closest to slipping over the edge of the hillside. They'd been lucky. Before he saw the car disappear around the bend, though, another car emerged, following in his wake. This one came on a little more carefully, the driver obviously unfamiliar with the roads. He hadn't seen it there before, but then he hadn't been looking for it, either.

He could not get a clear view of the driver, but didn't need to. He was *sure* it was the same make and model as the woman had been driving earlier.

But how could it possibly be her?

How could she have found him on a road like this?

What was she even doing out at this time of night? He'd lost track of time but it had to be gone midnight.

Looking for him?

Waiting for him?

If that was the case, surely that meant she knew where he lived.

So, was she with the police? That would explain how she'd tracked him down from the rest stop, using his license plate to follow a trail of bread crumbs back to the house. It didn't really matter—she'd found him twice, but he had no intention of letting her catch him, even if he had to keep running.

He didn't want to hear the anger in Geraint's voice again.

He didn't want to hear how he'd ruined their lives.

He couldn't bear it.

Owen Llewellyn blinked again and saw the dead priest, his robes burned black and the flesh beneath still smoldering, standing in the middle of the road. He wasn't there. He couldn't be. He drove straight through the middle of his guilt-formed hallucination. It didn't fade. Neither did the car in the rearview.

He floored the accelerator, even though he knew the road was dangerous; he had the advantage over her. He knew where the bends were. He knew just how sheer the cliffs were and how tight the road hugged them. He knew how high they were climbing and he knew what lay around each blind corner. She didn't.

The conditions were treacherous.

The blacktop slick.

It was a lethal combination.

A thought began to emerge from the darkness, something from deep down that went against every emotion he had been experiencing. He was better than this woman, whoever she was. He was Owen Llewellyn, son of Wales. He didn't have to answer to her. His fear evaporated.

There was no room for remorse. He had killed a man. It had been necessary. He could kill again.

He didn't have the sword with him, but it had awoken something that had been lying dormant and unbidden inside him.

That was enough.

The blood of warriors flowed in his veins.

There was a farm track just around the next bend. He stamped down on the brakes as he reached the narrow turning, pulling off the road just enough to leave her with no choice but to drive past him before coming to a halt a few yards ahead. Metal barriers lined the side of the road. They were the only indication of the sheer drop down to the valley floor below.

Owen Llewellyn kept the car in gear, kept his left foot holding down the clutch and revved the engine, ready for when she got out of her car and tried to talk him into coming in peacefully.

21

Annja could see the driver, but there was no sign of him getting out of his car. She didn't like that he'd engineered the situation, forcing her to drive around him to pull in. It put her on the defensive. She waited for a moment, listening to the rise and fall of his engine and realizing almost too late what Owen Llewellyn was about to do.

She shifted the hire car into first gear, wishing she'd insisted on an automatic, and pushed hard on the gas just as the car behind her started to move.

A split second slower and she would have felt the full force of the car ramming into the trunk and shunting her forward. But since she was already in motion, the laws of physics presided and the impact was reduced to little more than a jolt that nudged the hire car forward.

A jarring pain shot through her arms and into her shoulders, but then the car was moving away.

She took the middle of the road, avoiding being pushed toward the grass verges as she accelerated. She took the hire car from zero to sixty in less time than it took to say, "Watch out!" and even as she hammered into a bend too fast to possibly steer through it, the back end of the car slewed out behind her and dragged across the muddy verge.

Llewellyn closed the gap in seconds, his vehicle so much more powerful than hers. She looked back at him—manic stare, wild visage—in the rearview mirror. Ahead of her a tractor cut straight across her path, lumbering onto the road from the field as it headed toward one of the farm entrances.

She hadn't seen it coming.

Instinctively she moved to hit the brake, but managed to stop herself, knowing it would bring Llewellyn's car right up behind her. Instead, she wrenched down hard on the wheel and accelerated into a swerve that carried her around the tractor. She caught a glimpse of the true nature of the drop, which wasn't a few yards down a steep embankment, but a sheer plummet of a few hundred feet. She couldn't believe how close the farmland ran to the drop-off.

Breathing hard, Annja yanked again on the wheel, sending a spray of dirt over the side as she brought the hire car back onto the asphalt.

She didn't want to think about how far there was to fall.

She hit the horn, hoping the noise would do something, break the moment somehow; it had already gotten entirely out of hand. He shunted her again. The road ahead widened, not much, but enough to give her a few feet either side, and straightened out as the climb became more gradual. Annja turned on her headlights, slamming the gas pedal flat to the floor, and saw the gap widen. She'd bought several precious seconds with the trick; Llewellyn mistaking her rear lights for brake lights and reacting as though she'd been slowing down, not accelerating. It was the kind of trick that would only work once. She needed to make the most of it, control the situation. She had to be the one who decided what the next move was going to be.

In the distance she saw another main road, this one cresting the hilltop. There was a steady flow of traffic. The two roads were going to meet somewhere.

She only hoped Llewellyn wouldn't do something stupid before then. However, considering what had happened on the highway already, she revised her wish: she hoped she'd reach it before he did something stupid.

A quick glance behind in the rearview showed him gaining on her again.

He just wouldn't go away.

Llewellyn bashed into her hard, throwing her forward against the seat belt.

He dropped off behind her again.

His face filled the rearview mirror.

The engine roared and on he came again, slamming into the back of her.

Annja felt the hire car get away from her, fighting with the wheel to keep it on the road. She couldn't think with him ramming her every few seconds.

The phone vibrated in her pocket. She ignored it. She needed to think. Up ahead a tree had fallen during the storm, split by lightning. It had fallen across the metal crash barrier.

Llewellyn tailgated her, shoving Annja toward the fallen tree and the buckled segment of the barrier. She wrestled with the wheel, trying to skirt the debris and *not* look over the edge at the same time. She tried to adjust her grip, mind racing. She needed to do something. Llewellyn came again, much faster this time. It was like looking at her own death in the mirror. She couldn't reach into the otherwhere for the sword to get her out of this. She wasn't any more blessed or special than any other crash victim, and if Llewellyn's car slammed into hers again she was going over the cliff and there'd be nothing she could do about it. Her heightened reflexes wouldn't save her from the fall. Once she went over that edge she was dead.

At the last moment, with Owen Llewellyn's mad face filling her rearview mirror, Annja turned the wheel hard, throwing the hand brake so the turn became a spin—one-eighty, three-sixty and around again. The landscape spun by in a dizzy spiral, and then came the crunching impact that deployed her air bag, powder burning up her wrists as she clung on to the wheel. The momentum threatened to take the hire car up onto two wheels, but it stayed on the road.

The shriek of tires and squeal of metal didn't stop when she stopped spinning.

Metal ground on metal, the two cars locked together like two beasts fighting for supremacy. Annja saw the expression of horror on Owen Llewellyn's face as he fought to maintain control of his car, but he was fighting a losing battle. Even as it tore free of hers, his car slid across the wet grass, unable to get any sort of traction in the thick mud it was churning up. And then there was nothing to grip as, almost in slow motion, the car slipped over the edge and was gone, leaving Annja alone on the road, shaking and scared.

The air bag pinned her in her seat. She reached for the handle and cranked the door open, falling out. She stood, but walked unsteadily toward the barrier and looked down.

She couldn't see the wreck at first, because she wasn't looking far enough down the hillside. The car had gone end over end like a tumbling die. Each impact crumpled the cabin smaller; it was a mess. She couldn't save him—and knew, roles reversed, he wouldn't have given a second thought to saving her. The drop was too sheer for her to get down to him without ropes, the damage to the car too much for him to walk away from, surely.

But she couldn't just drive away even if he had been doing her best to kill her.

She fished her phone out of her pocket and made the call.

By the time she got back into her car, the air bag looked like a sad balloon at the end of an even sadder party.

The ignition didn't bite at first when she turned the key, nor the second or third attempt, then finally the engine sparked to life and she sped away before the emergency services arrived at the scene. She didn't want to answer any of their questions yet.

22

Annja was a good liar.

But even the best liar would have had trouble explaining away the damage to her vehicle. She could have told them she just happened to be on the same road, that she tried to help him, but they'd have to be idiots to buy that. She wasn't looking forward to explaining it to the hire company, either, but at least they wouldn't try and lock her up.

She drove without looking back.

She'd ask Garin for help with the damage. He was always going on about how he had "people." Hopefully one of them was a panel beater.

She merged with the flow of traffic on the main road up ahead, hoping that any road leading south would take her back to the highway, or rather, the motorway eventually. She couldn't get used to the quaint way the Brits called it a motorway, not a highway or a freeway. It was indicative of a bygone age when motors were so much rarer and most people traveled on foot or horse and cart. But then, they called rest stops "service stations," and grilled cheese "cheese-on-toast." They were weird like that, the Brits.

The first sign she hit promised Caerleon and Caer-philly were dead ahead.

It was getting late and she hadn't eaten since break-fast. She wanted to take a walk around the outside of the castle. Hopefully there'd be some sort of takeaway in the vicinity where she could grab a bite to eat and kill two birds with one ravenous stone.

There were plenty of places to park. There was also a sandwich shop in a row of buildings opposite the castle, not that it was open.

Once she'd finally parked, she gave in to the shock. Shaking she reached for the phone. She had to talk to Garin, but she couldn't punch in his number. Twice she triggered the wrong app before getting the dial tone.

"I think he's dead," she said.

"Slow down," Garin told her. "What are you talking about? Who's dead?"

"I saw him again. Llewellyn. We were up on one of those narrow twisting hill roads. He recognized me. I thought he was going to talk…but he tried to ram me off the road."

"Are you okay?"

"Battered, bruised, but yeah, I'm fine. He isn't. He went over the side. It was a long way down, Garin. A long way…"

There was silence on the other end of the line.

Breathing.

Garin was thinking.

"We still need to find the sword," Roux said. She hadn't realized she was on speaker. There was no emotion in his voice, no triumph, no anger. Not even disappointment. "Assuming the sword wasn't in the wreckage with him, we need to go to his house. He has two children, a son and daughter in their mid-twenties."

"I'll go first thing in the morning," she said.

"Why wait?" Garin asked.

"Self-preservation. If the police see my car they're going to put two and two together. Given the state of it, it's obvious it's been in a crash, believe me. I'd rather not explain how my nice new hire car has picked up those dents."

"How bad are we talking?" he asked. "Like broken wing mirror and a few dents bad, or write-off bad?"

"Bad enough. He slammed into me half a dozen times, then I took him side-on and made a mess of the entire passenger's side door panels."

"So more than a few scratches, then. Good job."

"I'm not the one who went off the side of the cliff and down a three-hundred-foot drop, so yeah, I'd say so."

"Kill or be killed," Garin concluded. She wished he'd found a different way of saying it, but he was right. That was the choice Owen Llewellyn had forced on her. And she hadn't pushed him over the edge. Not really.

"Where are you at the moment?" Roux asked.

"Caerphilly."

"*Caer* means *castle,* you know, in Welsh," Garin put in helpfully.

"I know," she replied, surprised at him knowing this snippet of information. "I'm looking at one right now. I am surprised, however, that *you* know."

"I'm full of surprises. I'll make a few calls about the car," he said. "Don't go wandering off."

"Thanks," she replied.

That was it; the call ended. No instructions. She could live with that. She slipped the phone into her pocket and clambered out of the battered door, the hinges complaining as she did. She took another glance at the car; the damage looked much worse each time she studied it. Even leaving the thing parked here, it was going to attract attention.

She crossed the road to the closed door of the sandwich bar. A young guy came wandering down the street with a burrito dripping salsa down his fingers. "Hey, excuse me, where did you get that? I'm starving." He grinned and pointed around the corner to a food truck. "You're a star."

He wiped the juice from his chin and grinned. "No problem."

She got to the truck just as the guy was getting ready to pack up. "What's good?" she called through the window.

"At this time of night, love, it's more a case of what's left," the driver-cum-chef said. He was a big burly bald man with a smile as wide as his apron strings.

"In which case, what's left?"

"Nothing." He grinned, but before she could express her disappoint he said, "But for you, I'll work miracles."

She settled on a three-cheese burrito slathered in hot sauce and a bit of company while she ate.

The thirteenth-century castle in Caerphilly was in remarkable condition; it appeared as if the years had barely touched it. It was easy to imagine it in all of its glory, just how imposing it must have been, and how obvious a symbol of English power it was, lording it from on high over the subdued Welsh. It struck her as ironic that those self-same English conquerors were the descendants of the French who had conquered them in turn no more than two hundred years earlier. They even retained the Gallic names of their homeland.

This castle had been built by Gilbert de Clare. Gilbert's ancestors had arrived in the country from Normandy with William the Conqueror. This same Gilbert de Clare had led the massacre of Jews in Canterbury, but Annja knew that he wasn't alone in having committed such atrocities at the time. Not that that excused butchering innocents for the sake of race, creed or color. But that was the age. His involvement in the Canterbury massacre had led to much of his lands and wealth being seized by the king, and being excommunicated by the pope. He had atoned for his sins by being instrumental in the wars against the Welsh, killing righteously to make up for previous sinful slaughter. When blue blood pumped through your veins, it didn't matter what your crime; it was always possible to regain favor.

Some things never changed.

She was still thinking about the nature of power and greed when her phone rang.

"Okay, Annja, strings have been pulled. You still near the castle?" Garin asked.

"You know I am," she replied.

"Yes, I do. I was merely being polite. I know how you can be about these things. Okay, stay close to your car," he said. "A mechanic's going to be with you in the next twenty minutes. He'll take your car and sort it out. He assures me it'll come back looking like new."

"And how am I supposed to get back to the hotel?"

"It's not that far to walk." Garin laughed. "He'll be bringing a car for you. Enjoy it. My treat."

"Thanks so much," she said sarcastically. No doubt some grease monkey would turn up with a battered old station wagon that would barely get her from A to B, with no guarantee of getting her back again.

She sat on the bench with a bottle of water from the food truck and waited. The burrito had tasted pretty good, and there was no getting away from the revivifying effects of the food. Though she could still feel her body metabolism slowing, such was the climb down from the adrenaline rush of the accident.

"Are you Annja?" a voice asked from behind her, catching her by surprise.

A sudden surge of panic had her hand reaching toward the otherwhere to draw Joan's sword, but she managed to stop herself in time.

The long-haired gangly mechanic looked as if he was barely out of his teens. His overalls hung on his shoulders two sizes too big, making it look as if he were playing dress-up in his dad's clothes.

"That's right," she said, shielding her eyes against the sun to get a good look at him.

"The boss says you've got car trouble," he mumbled, unable to maintain eye contact. He shuffled from one foot to the other, uncomfortable and tongue-tied. Annja took pity on him.

"You could say that," she replied. "Want to take a look at it?"

It was a stupid question. Obviously he wanted to take a look at it. He couldn't do anything *without* looking at it. She screwed up the wrap from her burrito and replaced the cap on her empty water bottle, dropping them into the trash can beside the bench. She led him to the car. Seeing it, he took a deep breath and shook his head, speaking the silent language of all mechanics.

"Nasty," he said. "What happened?"

"Parking lot," she lied. "It was like that when I got back to it."

"Not your lucky day."

She agreed. Garin was a lot of things, but he wasn't a fool when it came to hiding any activity of dubious legality. He'd have picked his man carefully, his ability to keep his mouth shut as important as his handiness with a hammer and torque wrench.

"Can you fix it?"

"Of course."

"How long will it take?"

"More difficult to say. Couple of days, maybe three. It won't be any more than that, though. And trust me, you won't even know that there's been any damage by the time we've finished."

"You're a lifesaver."

"It's a hire car, right? Why don't you just take it back, say you're sorry and pay the excess? Got to be cheaper for you."

"I'd rather not."

The young man shrugged and held one hand out for the keys while he dangled another set from the forefinger and thumb of his other hand. "Better be careful where you park this one," he said. "Wouldn't want lightning to strike twice."

"Where is it?" she asked, looking along the row in search of the anticipated hatchback.

"That one," he said, pointing across the road to where a solitary car was parked alongside the curb, and then to the key fob he'd given her.

"A Porsche? Seriously?" He nodded. "You're sure?"

"Yep. I guess someone likes you."

As soon as the mechanic was gone in her battered hire car, she rang Garin to thank him.

"All sorted, then?"

"A canary-yellow Porsche?"

"Nice. I'm more of a red man. Probably best you don't let the police look at it too closely," he said, and she couldn't tell if he was joking or not.

Annja had crossed the street and was all ready to open the driver's door. "Why?" she asked, but as soon as she had, she regretted it. "No, on second thought, don't tell me." This was definitely going to be one of those cases where she didn't really want to know the answer. Even if there was nothing wrong with it Garin might tell her there was, just to wind her up. She knew only too well she couldn't trust everything he said; that was just part of his charm. And most of the time he was just doing it for his own amusement.

She ran her fingers along the roof of the car as if this was some great temptation placed before her.

She couldn't resist for long.

23

The market stalls were doing a steady trade when Garin and Roux reached Caernarfon. It was difficult to imagine the place ever being busy. Two people probably constituted a rush.

The north of the country had been untouched by the storms that had charged across the south. Instead, it was bathed in sunshine. A Volvo was parked outside the small terminal building. Good old reliable Swedish automotive technology. Safe and sound and good for a bit of punishment if needs must. Plenty of leg room, too. Like a few of the ladies he'd entertained down the years, she was built for comfort, not speed.

They'd not rushed, checking into a boutique hotel in the center of town for the night, then venturing out at first light to get a feel for the place.

The castle loomed over the cobbled square. Rows of stalls sold everything imaginable from fruit and vegetables to costume jewelry, fresh fish to leather purses, sweets to handmade wooden trinket boxes and battered paperbacks. All life was represented here in some way, shape or form. Some of the stalls were clearly intended to milk the tourist trade, others met the needs of the locals who didn't want to live and die by the supermarkets and hypermarkets and out-of-town shopping centers. Garin figured that a market must have existed here for centuries, going back to days when farmers traveled far and wide to bring in their wool and other goods to trade. Just like they would have in so many other market towns all over Europe.

"We've got work to do," Roux said as Garin handed over a few coins for a stick of chili-chocolate-covered licorice. "And I don't know how you can eat that stuff before breakfast."

"You want me to come in with you, or are you going to tell me now that we're here this is something you have to do alone?"

Roux had remained secretive about the location of the mantle, beyond saying it was inside the castle. It bugged him, like they were returning to the bad old sad old days of distrust. Not that he expected the old man to trust him any more than he could trust the old man. That was the very nature of their coexistence these days; like father and son, they'd pretty much die for each other, but that was because of bonds that went beyond the average friendship.

"I will need you with me," Roux said.

Need, not *want.* Garin knew the difference. Sometimes it wasn't bad to be needed, but every now and then it'd be nice to be wanted.

He said nothing.

He followed Roux up to the castle, surprised when the old man came to a sudden halt. In front of the entrance stood two soldiers on guard with automatic weapons.

"What the hell is going on?" Garin whispered urgently. "Guards with semiautomatics? This isn't right, surely? It's a bloody tourist attraction. Something's wrong."

"Wait here," Roux said. "I'm going to play the confused old man, see if I can get them to talk."

Garin did as he was told.

Roux approached the soldiers and glanced around, seeming slightly lost.

The nearest market stallholder wore a look of utter boredom, unsurprisingly, Garin thought, given that he was peddling a collection of what looked to be fake Persian rugs. Hardly the go-to place for the must-have accoutrement. Garin sauntered over to him, deciding to do a bit of sleuthing himself. After all, bored people liked to talk. It was hard-wired into their DNA.

"So, why the soldiers?" he asked, laying on the American accent extrathick. "Expecting trouble?"

"Expecting royalty, more like," the market trader said. "Some special visit the day after tomorrow. The army boys are making sure there's no trouble and that no one tries to sneak in with a bomb before the good prince get here. Back when I was a kid it was flour and eggs, now it's bombs." Which was obviously his standard "What is the world coming to?" speech. Garin nodded.

"Certainly looks like they're taking it seriously."

"You're right, there. They've been here for days. My missus works inside. She reckons they've checked every inch of the place already."

"We're not going to get in today, are we?"

"Not a chance, mate. Sorry. They're not letting anyone inside for the rest of this week." He saw Roux coming back to him, his Gallic shrug saying all that needed to be said. "Well, hope you sell the prince a rug," he offered with a grin. "Take it easy." And he headed toward the old man.

"No luck, then?" Garin said.

"No one's getting in or out for the next four days. Royal visit."

"My friend here was just telling me all about it," he said, inclining his head in the rug trader's direction. Roux looked over Garin's shoulder, but the man was deep in conversation with the neighboring stallholder.

"Doesn't help us. We can't afford to wait that long."

"If we can't get in, neither can the bad guys," Garin said.

"But if they've already got the mantle they get an extra four-day start on us."

"True. Always look on the dark side of life, eh? So what are you suggesting? That we storm the castle?" Garin was joking but he could see that Roux wasn't smiling. "You're not serious? Jeez, Roux, those two guys alone have got enough firepower to protect the castle from a small army."

"Then we'll have to bring a big army, won't we?"

"You're joking, right? Please tell me this is all a big funny. Ha, ha, Roux."

"We have to get in there."

"You can't be serious. It's a royal visit, future king of England. That place is going to be guarded day and night."

"Maybe so. But that doesn't change the fact we have to get access somehow. I need to think. Coffee?" Roux motioned to a small coffee shop with a few tables laid out in the sunshine.

"You scare me."

"Good. That's as it should be. Being scared might help you live another five hundred years."

Garin didn't have any quick put-down for that, so he said nothing, instead cursing the old man under his breath.

All but one of the tables was already occupied. Roux wove through the seated guests and claimed it. Garin joined him, flashing a killer smile at the waitress clearing away the debris left behind by the table's previous occupant. Garin never understood how people could be such pigs when they ate out. They would never have left the same kind of devastation behind at home, so why do it when they were out?

"Two coffees please, as strong as you've got," Roux ordered.

Garin nodded. "Thick enough to stand your spoon up in."

The girl smiled back and slipped inside the café with her loaded tray of dirty crockery.

Garin leaned in so the customers at neighboring tables couldn't overhear them. "Okay, truth or dare time— are you *serious* about trying to get inside?"

"Deadly. I need to know the mantle is still hidden."

"You hid this one yourself, too?"

"Of course I hid them—haven't you been listening to a word I've been saying?"

"I hadn't realized—" Garin started, but Roux waved a hand in front of his face, cutting him off.

"Call me a romantic, but I foolishly believed these treasures *belonged* here. They are the core of the country, dating back to the age of the Celts. I thought that removing them would have meant more than just taking something away, that it would diminish the land some-

how. But I was young and idealistic back then. Things
have changed. The world isn't the same place. Most people have forgotten they exist or have consigned them to
that meaningless place they call fairy tales. Once folks
stop believing in the power of something, they don't
need it any longer.

"The remainder of the treasures ought to be safe,
and even if they are discovered, they wouldn't present
the danger of the other three in and of themselves. The
sword, the stone and the mantle, though, need to be
made safe and secure. It is possible that we are already
too late and that someone has possession of all three.
That is an eventuality that doesn't bear thinking about,
my friend. I should have taken care of this some time
ago, but I grew complacent, preoccupied with the search
for fragments of Annja's sword. I thought that the world
had dismissed the treasures. It is my mistake. I will have
to live with it if worse comes to worst."

Roux paused and then changed tack, switching to
Annja's encounter with Owen Llewellyn, and how it had
ended. "She didn't even check to see if the sword was
still in the car with him," Roux said, clearly exasperated.

"Didn't sound like she even could have. Cut her some
slack."

"She *had* a choice. We all have a choice. Let's be
blunt about this—she didn't *have* to call an ambulance
straightaway. He was a dead man, after all, so it served
no purpose. She didn't *have* to drive Llewellyn's car off
the road. It happened, but she could have confronted the
man, couldn't she? This is Annja we're talking about.
She isn't like other women, and she most certainly isn't
some helpless victim. She inherited Joan's sword for a
reason, Garin—to fight back, not to run away."

"You're being hard on her, old man. It's not like she was running away. She was picking her battles. It's survival instinct, same for you or me."

"Well, she screwed up one way or the other." Roux grunted. "I'm not really in the mood to dissect it all." The waitress returned with their coffees. Garin flashed her another smile, knowing full well the effect it would have on the poor girl. She nearly dropped the little biscotti she was supposed to lay on the side of their saucers. Flustered, she smiled back at him, more than earning her tip. That little smile made his day; what was the point if you couldn't bring a little sunshine into people's lives?

"When did you last check that this mantle was safely tucked away?"

"Not long ago."

"A little more precise?"

"Maybe a hundred years ago, give or take."

"That's a lot of giving and taking."

"There was some restoration being done then to repair the damage caused in the English Civil War. The Roundheads and the Cavaliers hadn't managed to disturb it between them, but there was a good chance builders would. I couldn't take the risk."

"Right, but if the guy who's been searching for these treasures is dead, doesn't that mean everything's good now? He's not exactly going to be looking for this stuff from beyond the grave, is he?"

"Unlikely, I'll grant you that."

"And if he's already found it, then he's going to have it stashed somewhere, so we're going to have to play detective and find it. But given he didn't know we were onto him, I doubt he's hidden it well. Probably left it at home."

"Everything is so simple in your world, isn't it, Garin?"

"That's a bit harsh."

"Is it? Kill it, screw it, steal it—that seems to be your credo. Sometimes life's more complicated than that. The answers don't always tumble into your lap, and a charming smile doesn't get the pretty girl to drop her knickers."

"Jealous?"

"Not at all."

"Keep telling yourself that."

"Oh, I do, every day. Believe me. I go to bed at night thinking I'm really not jealous of your life. There but for the grace of God go I."

"I'm not sure about that, old man. I can't see your smile charming the birds from the trees. Scaring them out of the high branches, maybe."

"I liked you better in 1431. Only marginally, but better."

"Likewise. Funny how we're still stuck with each other after all this time. I would say you must have done something terrible in a past life, but even God would have forgotten about your past lives by now. So, the way I see it, there's no point taking risks. If this cloak of invisibility is still where you hid it, then what exactly is there to gain by trying to get inside? I mean, it's under armed guard. No one is getting in or out. And if Llewellyn had already found it, then Annja's on the case. We can sit back and enjoy the show."

"Which all sounds very reasonable, but there's something you are forgetting."

"Am I?"

Roux nodded. "The laws of physics actually."

"I don't follow?"

"A man cannot be in two places at once. It is as simple as that. It is an impossibility that Owen Llewellyn could desecrate the grave of Gerald of Wales, kill my friend in the process and, simultaneously, be stealing the whetstone from the museum in Caerleon. It doesn't work. Simple physics. Two locations over one hundred miles apart, two robberies only hours apart? No. The CCTV stuff shows Llewellyn was in St. Davids."

"Which means someone else was in Caerleon," Garin finished. "He wasn't working alone."

"He wasn't working alone," Roux agreed. "Now you see the urgency?"

24

Awena decided that it would be for the best if the sword was put away with the whetstone in her father's study. Leaving it out would only make Geraint think she was taunting him with it, trying to rub his face in the fact they'd found not one but two of the treasures, and instead of building bridges between them it would only serve to burn them. That was the last thing she wanted.

The flame had flickered out the moment she'd put the sword down on the kitchen table, barely leaving a scorch mark on the scrubbed pine surface. The steel was cold to the touch a second later when she'd tentatively tested it with a fingertip.

It wasn't until she lifted it by the hilt that it burst back into life, somehow responding to her touch.

She carried the sword nervously through the house, climbing the stairs slowly, and crossing the landing to the study door with the flame licking at the air with each step. It heated the air in front of her. She could feel it.

Awena opened the door.

The whetstone still lay where she'd left it, in the middle of their father's desk.

She still wished she'd had the time to show it to him, to see his face as he realized what she'd found.

She placed the sword on top of her own prize, the flame once again flickering and failing as soon as she released her grip, but this time the sword didn't return to its former inert state.

The steel blade crackled with electricity, blue sparks dancing and fizzing over its surface.

She reached out with a finger, not quite touching the steel. Sparks bridged the gap, tingling her skin and crackling through her body as she felt a sudden surge of energy. Awena wanted to call Geraint, to show him what had just happened, to ask him what he thought was happening…but he'd made his position abundantly clear. She was on her own in this. He wouldn't be joining her in the family business.

She lifted the sword from the precious whetstone, resurrecting the blue fire.

She set it down again, this time on the hearth of the study's disused fireplace. The flue was blocked somewhere up above with a bird's nest.

The flames went out, the blade cold to the touch.

So, it was clearly the combination of the two treasures together that had caused the peculiar effect. Fascinating. And if she needed any proof that the stone really was the Whetstone of Tudwal Tudglyd this was it. Surely there had to be something in her father's notes about the proximity effect of one treasure on the other. But where to begin looking?

Then she remembered the journal he kept in the top drawer of his desk.

Her father was a creature of habit. Whenever he came home he copied the voluminous notes he'd jotted down into a leather-bound journal, detailing where he had been, where he was planning on going next and, most importantly, why. She had her own habits, of course, one of them being that every time he left them again she'd spend ages deciphering his writing. She could rarely make any sense of it, but it was still the right place to start looking for answers now, she was sure of it.

The pages were covered in his familiar spidery scrawl. There were roughly sketched diagrams with what he considered important points ringed to highlight them. It was idiosyncratic, but it was a system. Whenever he mentioned one of the treasures by name he would write it in red ink, making it easy to pick out.

She ran a finger down the spine, fingertip resting on the number twenty-six. There were another twenty-five journals just like this one on the shelves behind the desk.

Awena settled in his chair, deciding to work backward, and started to read through the current book first. Hopefully as he'd come closer to the sword, he'd left a trail of some kind, not back to where he'd found the sword, but more like bread crumbs of thought to where he'd be going next.

She spent a fruitless hour reading through what amounted to her father's life until she reached the last few entries. They offered some hints and more suppositions, but seemed to point toward St. Davids. There was nothing about where he was going after that.

She put the book down on the table beside her and went to the bookshelves to pull down another one and then another after that, burning the midnight oil in her quest to follow her father. At first she looked for any mention of the sword or the whetstone, not expecting to find mention of them together. She would have missed it, too, if it wasn't for a reference to Gerald of Wales. She saw one word in the entry underlined three times—

combine—and a question mark. She read the entry three times before she realized there was nothing in it, though her father had noted "cv. 19" in the margin, which she took to mean "cross-reference with journal nineteen."

She searched the shelves for the leather-bound journal she hoped he was referring to, but it wasn't there. It was the only one in the sequence that was missing.

She was about to give up when she lit onto the safe— it was behind an idealistic painting of Bran the Blessed surrounded by a conspiracy of ravens. Her father had always identified with Bran, telling her how he was the true root of the Arthurian myth, with his cauldron sharing so many of the properties of the Grail, and Bran himself a kind of Fisher King character.

She lifted the painting down from the wall, revealing the fireproof safe where he kept his most valuable possessions. Some men might have used their daughter's birthday or their wedding day as a combination, but not her father. He used 04 03 11, the day the Welsh Assembly gained direct law-making powers independent of Westminster. That was her father through and through.

She spun the dial—four right, three left, eleven right—and turned the capstan lock to a satisfyingly deep click of the bolts disengaging, and opened the safe.

She had only seen inside the safe once, when he'd explained to her the most precious things in his world were hidden inside, and made her commit the sequence of numbers to heart in case the worst should ever happen to him. She'd never been tempted to look inside when he was away. People needed their secret places. To know them all, to know everything about a man, was almost like robbing him of a part of himself, the bit where he could be him and only him, not the person you needed

or wanted him to be. Awena had always respected his
need of privacy, but that didn't stop her looking inside for volume nineteen among the other secrets he'd
stashed in there.

She carried the journal back to the chair and sat beneath the light, lost to time, and opened the book, hoping
that it would open a new window into her father's world.

Her heart sank after she'd turned the first page, the
second, the third, the tenth, twentieth, and realized that
none of the words on the page meant anything to her.

She knew a little Latin, a few conjugations and
phrases appropriated by Shakespeare, but nowhere
near enough to be able to understand the sheer mass of
words neatly inked inside the book. The only thing she
knew for sure was that it wasn't her father's handwrit-
ing and the book itself was far older than anything else
in his collection.

To all intents and purposes, it was another dead end.

She was still searching for something that would help
her, anything at all, when the doorbell rang. She looked
through a crack in the curtains. It was still the middle
of the night. There was a car pulled up in the drive. It
wasn't her father's.

She ran down the stairs, heart in her throat.

Nothing good ever happened in the middle of the
night.

The hands of the grandfather clock in the hallway
had settled on 3:00 a.m.

She'd read somewhere that more people died at 3:00
a.m. than any other time of day.

Awena answered the door.

Two strangers stood on the doorstep. She could feel
the weight of death all around them. They couldn't look

her in the eye as the taller, gaunter of the two asked, "Miss Llewellyn?"

"That's right," she replied as they produced their warrant cards. She wasn't listening as they gave their names. She stepped back inside the house, just a step, but it allowed them to enter, bringing death with them. Until that moment there had been a chance it wasn't happening, that these two men hadn't come bearing news that would change her life forever. And it stayed like that, until they were in the living room and she was sitting down, waiting anxiously for them *not* to say the word.

"Is it Geraint?" she asked finally. She'd heard the door slam earlier. An hour ago? Two? Surely not long enough for anything bad to have happened? But he'd been so angry, and that meant out of control, and that in turn meant his was the name that leaped into her head.

"Geraint?" The two police officers looked at each other for a second.

"My brother."

"No, miss, it's not about your brother," the policeman began. "I'm afraid it is your father."

She listened as they explained that his car had been found on an isolated mountain road through the Brecon Beacons. They mentioned a place name which was vaguely familiar but she couldn't remember why it felt significant.

"I'm sorry. I don't understand. You've found his car? Not him?" She started to hope that there was a mistake, that she had assumed he was dead when really they were searching for him.

The policeman shook his head.

"I'm sorry," the gaunt officer said solemnly. "I'm afraid a body was found near the car. We believe it is your father, but we need someone to make a positive identification. I know this isn't easy, but would you be willing to come to the morgue?"

"Yes, certainly," she started to say, but then she heard the front door open and slam closed.

Geraint was home.

He came into the room, clearly expecting a fight, face still full of thunder from his confrontation with their father. The drive hadn't cooled him down. "Whose car is that?" he demanded, then saw the two men sitting on the edge of the seats, leaning forward. "What's happened?"

The police repeated their expression of sorrow and sympathy, but as she listened to it a second time it sounded hollow. They were just words the officers had learned to say. They didn't mean anything. Maybe they'd had some sort of training course where they were given scripts to learn like telemarketers....

"Can we go together?" she asked. Geraint was as shocked as she was. She could see the pleading in his eyes. She didn't want to go with two strangers to the morgue to stare at the lifeless body of a man she idolized, but she could see Geraint was struggling. She didn't need to be able to read his mind to know he was regretting their fight. She could never make that right for him. His last words with his father would always be filled with hate. He'd have to live with that, but she could be there for him, with him. She could hold his hand and face death with him.

He nodded.

"I just need to freshen up," she lied, and left them long enough to change her shoes and more importantly to make sure that the book was safely stowed in the fireproof safe. She included a stack of notebooks she pulled

hastily from the shelves, before hanging the portrait of
Bran back on the wall to hide the safe.

She hated thinking poorly of her brother, but she
knew him better than he knew himself. He'd come back
into this room before dawn, would see the books on the
shelves and think of the life lived and the life lost, and
was angry enough with their father to do something stupid. After all, for him, destroying those books promised
an opening to get rid of the past, to draw a line beneath
everything that had gone before. All it would take was
one match.

25

They hid his body from her beneath a green sheet.

She waited for the mortuary assistant to draw back the sheet to reveal her father's face.

It was harder than she'd ever imagined it would be.

She reached out to take Geraint's hand.

"Is this your father?" the policewoman asked.

She placed a reassuring hand on Awena's shoulder, but all Awena wanted to do was shrug it off. She didn't need this stranger's platitudes and false sympathy. It didn't matter to her. None of it did. The woman was only doing her job. She was supposed to be sorry. There was no connection between them. They weren't sisters.

"Yes," she said. "It's him. What happened?"

"All indications are that he was driving too fast in treacherous conditions and went off the side of the mountain road."

"Did he suffer?"

The woman didn't look like she wanted to answer, but she did. "He managed to get himself out of the car, but died of his injuries before the ambulance reached him."

"So he suffered. That's what you're saying, isn't it?"

The policewoman didn't answer her this time. Instead, she said, "The car was badly damaged, but we've got our mechanics taking a look to see if there was any mechanical failure."

"Not that it helps," Geraint said. "He's still dead whether it was his fault or the car's."

But it did help, Awena thought. It helped if it was the car that failed him. It meant it wasn't his fault. But she knew his state of mind when he'd left the house. She should have tried to stop him. He was dead because she had let him go instead of making him see sense.

He was their father.

They should have been able to forgive him anything.

But how could they forgive him now?

She looked at him lying there. "Will you clean him up? Shave him, cut his hair. He shouldn't look like this. It isn't how he was." Even thinking this brought a wave of guilt; was she at least partly responsible for what he had become? He'd always said he'd done it for her. For them. For their birthright.

She didn't want to go home, not yet at least.

That was where she'd last seen him. That was where his final words had been in anger.

She wanted time to think.

"Who called the ambulance?"

"A woman who saw the car."

"Do you know who she is? Can I talk to her? I need to know if he said anything...."

"I'm sorry, the call was anonymous. If it helps, I don't think she would have been able to get to your father, or his car. So I don't believe there's anything she could tell you."

Awena wanted to scream and shout, to demand answers that she knew would never come. The police had already decided this was an accident. They had all the answers they needed to make him just another unfortunate statistic. She wasn't prepared to let it be rubber-stamped like that; she wanted to know more. She wanted to know what had *really* happened.

Because if he had gone over the cliff and it was *her* fault...

"It may be a few days before the wreckage can be moved. Specialist equipment will be needed. I'd suggest you don't drive home that way. Seeing it could be quite distressing."

Geraint nodded.

"We have some of his things we recovered from inside the vehicle." The policewoman lifted a plastic bag that was too large for the meager contents—a set of house keys, his wallet, some loose change and most importantly his notebook.

AWENA'S EYES LIT up at the sight of the journal.

Geraint didn't like that look. He'd seen it before in his father's eyes.

Suddenly it was as though nothing else mattered.

She took the bag off the woman and turned her back on her father and brother without a second glance and headed toward the door.

Geraint made his apologies and headed after her. What nobody seemed to realize was that he'd lost his father as well as her, and he'd been the one who had fought with him. That would never change. He replayed the fight over and over in his head, but all he could think of was how the sword had burned in his father's hand and all of those stupid stories he used to invent about those treasures he wasted his life on.

Tears tracked down his cheeks as he left the mortuary.

Awena had insisted on taking her car rather than his. She was in the driver's seat waiting for him. He climbed into the passenger's seat. He couldn't see the notebook. He didn't know whether to be pleased she wasn't already engrossed in their father's madness or frightened by the fact she had so expertly hidden it from his sight.

They drove home in silence.

It was breakfast time and all either of them wanted to do was sleep.

26

It was easier to find the house than she'd expected.

Garin's directions were good.

The winding country road had been eerily empty for most of the journey. For the past four or five miles she'd seen an occasional tractor that had pulled over onto the grass verge to allow her to pass, and that was it. It wasn't exactly the best terrain for a beast like the Porche to handle, but it wasn't quite a dusty track, either.

She swung off the road and onto a perfectly maintained driveway with well-manicured strips of grass on either side and elegant topiaries that had obviously been lavished with some serious tender loving care. The drive ran over one hundred and fifty meters, rising higher up the mountain, before the house came into view.

Built into the hillside the front door was effectively set into the central story, with the garage built into the hillside below. Annja pulled the Porsche to a stop beside a white saloon car that looked in need of a clean. It didn't look like an unmarked police car, but of course that was the point of stripping the decals and lights, wasn't it? It was unlikely it was police, though, as they'd come in a squad car to deliver news of a death, wouldn't they?

She got out of the car, locking it with the remote on

the key fob, and took a glance at where she had come from. The reality of just how high that winding road had climbed sank in; from here she looked down on a great stretch of the valley that felt miles away. "Can I help you?" a rough voice called to her from a balcony.

She hadn't seen the man come outside. "Sorry," she called back.

She'd rehearsed what she was going to say on the way over, but faced with the grief-stricken young man the words seemed trite. What had Garin said his name was? Geraint. "My name's Annja Creed."

"What can I do for you, Miss Creed?"

"I work for an American television show, *Chasing History's Monsters*. I don't know if you've seen it. Anyway, I was hoping to do a feature on your father's work."

"My God," the man said, shaking his head, obviously unable to believe what he was hearing. He pushed away from the balcony railing. "He's only been dead a day and you vultures are circling already?"

This was the part she had to be careful with. She needed to play it right. That meant lying her pretty little heart out. "He's dead? I—I don't know what to say…I had no idea. I'm so sorry for your loss."

"Wait there," he said. His tone shifted. "I'll be right down."

She walked up to the door. When it opened a moment later, Annja was struck by how familiar the man on the threshold appeared. He held out his hand for her to take, and said, "I see you've changed your car."

Annja felt her heart skip a beat. "How did you…?" she started, wondering how he could possibly know she'd ditched the hire car for Garin's bright yellow Porsche.

"We were coming over the bridge at the same time." He smiled sheepishly. "Some faces are hard to forget."

Annja felt the heat rise in her cheeks. The moment he said it she remembered the red-haired guy who'd smiled at her as they queued at the tollbooths.

"Don't worry," he said. "I know that mine isn't one of them." He grinned. "Please, come in. I'm sorry I was so short up there." He nodded toward the balcony.

"I really don't want to intrude."

"It's fine, honestly. Truth be told, we weren't particularly close."

It was a strange thing to tell a complete stranger, but he was obviously doing everything he could to keep any emotions he had over his father's death in check.

She followed him inside.

There were no obvious traces of his father's interests decorating the downstairs. There were plenty of pictures of Geraint and his sister, but only one of the sister with Owen Llewellyn, looking considerably less manic than the man she'd seen. Perhaps Geraint was telling the truth, after all, and it wasn't one big happy family.

Even so, it would have to be one hell of a disagreement for him not to care.

"My sister, Awena, is in the bath. We just had to go and identify his body," he said. "It was hard on her. She was close to him."

"Sorry. This really isn't the right time. I could come back—"

"No, please, stay. It's Awena you really need to talk to. She was far more interested in what he has wasted his life on than I was. She won't be long, but I'd rather just let her soak for a while. Can I get you something?

A drink? And you can tell me all about your show, how does that sound?"

"Coffee, please, and great. Amazing place to live," Annja said, her gaze sweeping around the kitchen, meaning everything, not just the hilltop house.

"I can't take all the credit for it. My grandparents were comfortable, and the house has been in the family for a long time. I've just had to make sure that we didn't lose it while my father was off gallivanting around the country chasing fairy tales and hemorrhaging money."

Annja offered a slight smile. "I'm familiar with the affliction," she said. "I mean, I work on a show called *Chasing History's Monsters.* How could I not be? Your father must have thought it was worthwhile."

"Oh, he did. He was thoroughly obsessed with the hunt. He came back the other day, the first time we had seen him in months, maybe even a year, and he comes walking in as if he'd only been gone a day. That was what he was like. He was all smiles, expecting us to be happy to see him, whenever he showed up. Hell, I think he expected me to give him a pat on the head because he'd finally found something."

"He had?" she asked, not wanting to show too much interest.

"Oh, something and nothing," he said. There was a change in his expression, as if he had suddenly realized that he should be more circumspect. She didn't push it.

"I'm sure that it was important to him."

"Everything was important to him. Well, everything except real life. So are you over here for long?" he asked, changing the topic. She needed to be careful now. She didn't want to seem like she was fishing.

"A couple of weeks' vacation. I'm finally getting to

see some of the places I've always wanted to. A couple of them might even make an interesting segment on the show."

"Really? I wouldn't have thought that there was much here that'd interest an American audience. It's not exactly teeming with life."

"Maybe not, but it's teeming with *history.* I've always wanted to do a feature on the Roman ruins in Caerleon, for instance, and the castle at Caerphilly looks pretty interesting, not to mention that beautiful cathedral in St. Davids." Even as she reeled off the place names she realized she should have been keeping her mouth shut. She'd just named the sites of the whetstone robbery and the curate's murder in the same breath; it went beyond coincidence, and if he knew anything about what his father had been up to she'd tipped her hand. There wasn't so much as a flicker from him. The locations meant nothing to him. Maybe it was more his sister's bag, as he'd said.

"True, I guess if there's one thing we've got more of than America, it's history."

It wasn't the first time she'd heard that crack, but Annja didn't rise to it.

She just smiled, relieved to hear the sound of movement upstairs.

"That'll be Awena. I'll let her know you want to chat about Dad. I'm sure she'll be thrilled."

She heard footsteps on the stairs, and pushed herself out of her seat, ready to spin more lies as a woman in a towel came into the kitchen.

"Oh…I didn't know anyone was here. Geraint, you could have warned me," she said, flustered and trying to cover herself up.

"Awena, this is Annja Creed. She works on an American TV show. She was looking for Dad. She wanted to talk to him about his quest. She hadn't heard…"

"No reason why you should have heard, Miss Creed," the young woman said, adjusting the towel like it was a layer of armor. "But I'm sure that you will understand why we aren't interested in being part of a program right now. People ridiculed our father during his lifetime, so do you mind explaining why you think anyone would be more interested now that he's dead? Or does his being dead make it sexy TV or something?"

"There's no need to be rude, sis," Geraint said.

"It's okay." Annja smiled. "I understand, honestly. If I'd known I wouldn't have called. It's horribly intrusive and terrible timing. But believe me, there are people out there interested in your father's work, even if he didn't know that. I'd love the chance to do a segment on his quest, especially as your brother suggested he found something recently."

"I think you should leave."

Annja nodded. "Let me give you my card in case you'd like to talk about this in the future. I really am sorry for your loss."

"I'll be honest with you, Miss Creed. It's unlikely. This is a very private thing. For you it might be a story, but for us it is our father's life."

"I understand," Annja said.

After no more than the briefest of goodbyes, she headed out to the Porsche.

By the time she had slid behind the wheel the door to the house had been closed.

She could feel the woman looking at her through the frosted window.

27

"Why the hell did you let her in the house?" Awena demanded.

She stood at the door, watching the canary-yellow Porsche drive away through the frosted pane of glass in the center of it. She flicked the business card against her fingernails. "Doesn't it strike you as odd that this American would call on us today of all days? I mean, it's not as if Dad's work was common knowledge."

"She seemed nice," Geraint said.

"She seemed nice?" Awena echoed. "Really? All it takes is a pretty face and a smile and you'll roll over hoping she'll scratch your belly?"

"Of course not."

"Okay, so tell me this—how did she know where we lived?"

"I don't know. It's no secret that we live in this area, though. All she had to do was ask someone in the village to give her directions."

Awena was not convinced. Something wasn't right even though she couldn't pinpoint what it was.

"Fine, then why today?"

"What are you trying to say?"

"I'm trying to say that I don't believe in coincidence. What else did she talk about?"

"Some of the places she was checking out, locations for possible programs. Caerleon, Caerphilly, St. Davids."

Caerleon. She felt a shiver run up her spine. Not good. Not good at all. "I'm not going to fight with you. I'm tired. I just wish you'd think…how could you tell her Dad had found something? Were you showing off for her?"

"It wasn't like that."

"Wasn't it?"

"Look, I know you hate me for sending Dad away… I know you blame me for his death…but it wasn't my fault. He *attacked* me. You saw that crazy burning sword." He crossed his arms over his chest. "I'm not sorry I told him to get out."

It was hard to argue against that and Awena knew it, but she was certain that their father hadn't intended to hurt him. It was a fine distinction, but there was a marked difference between attacking someone and trying to prove a point, and that's what Owen Llewellyn had been trying to do, wasn't it? To prove that he'd succeeded after failing so many times before?

Surely Geraint would understand that, given time.

"Okay, let's not fall out over this," was all she said. "I'm hoping you can do me a favor."

"What kind of favor?"

"An illegal kind of favor," she remarked. "The kind I really shouldn't ask you to do. I wouldn't ask, but I've got this feeling…and if I don't do something about it, it's going to drive me nuts."

Her brother looked at her skeptically. "What do you need?"

"A woman rang for an ambulance. She saw the crash."

"And?"

"And I want to speak to her."

"Surely the police—"

"The police aren't interested. It was an anonymous call and they seem to think that's perfectly normal."

"But you don't?"

"I don't know. But now a woman turns up here asking questions about what Dad was doing."

"What do you want me to do?"

"Find the number of the woman who made the call."

"Do you have any idea of what you're asking?"

"Can you do it?"

"Maybe, but it's not going to be easy, and if I get caught, there will be real trouble. You know that, right?"

"Please." That was all it took. Just one little word.

"Okay, I'll see what I can do," he said. "But only because I love you, not because I feel guilty." He smiled wanly and headed upstairs to the small bedroom he used as an office whenever he worked from home. Maybe he would be able to do it, maybe he wouldn't, but at least he was going try. That was something.

As soon as she heard his office door close she headed across the landing to her father's study, so that she could study his journals in more detail. The answers were in there, she was sure of that. It would tell her about how he found the sword, and why it burned the way it did when she held it.

An hour passed without her even realizing it.

There were comments in her father's working notebook that meant nothing to her, many of them written in a scrawl she could barely read, and plenty of diagrams without any sort of name or label, but there were also several mentions of Gerald of Wales and his final resting place without actually saying where it was.

She retrieved one of the volumes from the safe hoping that between the two she'd find a clue as to where it might be. Even as she turned carefully through the brittle pages something nagged away at her, something her father had told her, but she could not dredge it up from the depths of her memory.

The first reference she found seemed to be saying that the whereabouts of Gerald's mortal remains remained unknown, but she didn't stop looking. Finally, the second reference she found contradicted the first, suggesting Gerald's remains were believed to be in the cathedral at St. Davids.

Awena froze.

The woman had named three locations—Caerleon, Caerphilly and St. Davids. Two of the three were inextricably linked with the treasures.

"You in there?" Geraint called from the other side of the door. He didn't knock.

She had not consciously closed it. Or at least she didn't think she had. Geraint wouldn't come in uninvited, and even then it would be reluctantly.

She slipped the notebook in the drawer before answering him.

"Yeah, just coming." She picked up Annja Creed's card from the desk and pocketed it. Maybe they would have to talk, after all.

Geraint stood outside the study. He had a piece of

paper in his hand but seemed reluctant to hand it over when she held her hand out for it.

"You found her?"

"It wasn't as difficult as I thought it would be actually. I've not been able to access the recording of the call itself. But I've got the number."

"You are sure this is it?"

He nodded. "Certain. It's the only emergency services call that went through the cell tower all day."

"My brilliant brother." Awena kissed him on the cheek and took hold of the piece of paper, but Geraint didn't let go.

"I want you to promise me you're not going to do anything stupid."

"Promise. I just want to talk to her. Whoever she is." Awena took the scrap of paper from him and checked the number. Then she tucked the paper into her purse behind the card that Annja had given her.

It took her a moment to realize that the number was the same.

28

"Annja?"

Annja did not recognize the number on the caller ID. The voice didn't help, either.

"Yep."

"It's Awena. Awena Llewellyn. You came by the house before?"

"Ah, right. What can I do for you, Awena?"

"Sorry if I was rude. It was a hell of a day. I really wasn't myself."

"No need to apologize. Honestly. And you weren't being rude, all things considered. I'm only sorry I added to your troubles."

"You didn't. I was more annoyed with my idiot brother than anything else. You were just in the firing line."

"Let's forget it, shall we? Chalk it up to bad timing."

It couldn't have been easy for Awena to make the call. Harder still for her to ask what she was obviously about to ask. "I know that this is short notice, but Geraint's out this morning and I'm at a bit of a loose end. I've been thinking about Dad a lot, obviously, and, well, if you want to come around I'll be happy to talk to you about my father's work. It would be good to talk to someone who understands what drove him on."

It saved Annja having to find an excuse in order to contact her, though good fortune like this tended to set alarm bells ringing. It was mighty convenient that the woman felt guilty and wanted to chat, but her father had just died, after all, and Annja was offering a tantalizing way of keeping him alive a little longer, with a window for the world to watch and appreciate his grail quest. "Absolutely," she replied. "I'd love to, but you really don't have to."

"Oh, I know, but I want to."

"Okay, then, I'll be over in an hour or so."

"Look forward to it." There was something about how she said those last words that made Annja's skin crawl.

Still, needs must. She had to find the sword and the whetstone. There was a good chance they were in that place, or that clues to their whereabouts were. That meant she had to get into that house, and if a few hours in the company of a creepy young woman was the cost of doing that, then spend a few hours in the company of a creepy young woman she would.

An hour later she drove the Porsche up the long slow incline of the drive once more, still unsure how this was likely to play out.

Awena was on the balcony, waiting for her just as her brother had been on her last visit. She'd almost certainly been keeping watch for her visitor, rather than enjoying the late-summer sun. She waved, then disappeared back inside, reappearing at the door a minute later.

"I'm so glad you came," Awena said, leading Annja inside the house. "I didn't fancy the idea of being alone this morning, you know? Besides, I rarely get to talk about my father's work. Geraint has no interest in it at all. If anything, he blames it for ruining his life and taking Dad away from us."

"He blames it for his death?"

She shook her head. "We lost him a long time before he died. He'd leave us with a nanny and disappear for weeks on end before coming back empty-handed and down. Gradually the trips away became longer and longer. I'd lost track of how long he was away this last time. Maybe a year. Then he just came back out of the blue. He hadn't even phoned for months. He looked a mess. Like he'd been living rough. He hadn't had a shave or a haircut in God knows how long. I didn't even recognize him at first."

"It can't have been easy for you."

"It wasn't easy for either of us, but we just got on with it. Anyway, you haven't come here to talk about my broken home and lonely childhood. Why don't I make us drinks and we can go up to his study while you tell me all about this program you want to make about Dad's work?"

"Sounds great, but I should warn you—it's only a vague idea at the moment, and just a segment, not an entire program."

Awena rattled around the kitchen, setting the kettle to boil and dropping a couple of honeydew tea bags into oversize cups.

"Right, so…I have to admit I've not seen the show… *Chasing History's Monsters?* It doesn't sound like Dad."

"Well, the show's about more than that, obviously. That's only meant to get people's attention. I understand that your father's research was into the Matter of Britain, and Gerald of Wales in particular."

"I would ask how you could possibly know that, but I guess you've got teams of researchers looking for good stories."

Annja smiled. "Something like that, but I do my own research."

"Ah. I should have known that you would.... So where does Dad fit into this?"

Annja decided that there was no point in beating about the bush. She needed to lead Awena in the direction she wanted her to take, and treat this pretty much as she'd treat any other prospective story.

All business, she said, "I heard a rumor he might have discovered the final resting place of Gerald?"

"How could you possibly know that?" Awena asked. Her response came a little too quickly, and a little too sharply, for Annja's liking.

Too far, too quick. She backed down a little. There was no point lying.

"Like I said, it was a rumor. I don't tend to believe stuff like that, hence hoping to talk to him. I mean, finding that grave would be a major archaeological discovery, worthy of a show in and of itself, you know?"

"Ah," Awena replied with a shrug, as though she did indeed know. "Sorry to disappoint, but no, Dad hadn't found any lost graves or anything quite so glamorous." The kettle whistled and she poured boiling water into the huge cups, offering one to Annja. "He did, however, bring something home with him. Shall we go up?"

"Lead the way," Annja said.

She followed the young woman up the stairs, getting a good look at the house for the first time. There were paintings on the wall going upstairs chronicling the history of the place. At the top of the stairs, Awena turned to look down at her, then crossed the landing quickly to open the study door.

Annja saw the whetstone lying in pride of place on the desk in the book-lined room. The room was stuffed to overflowing with papers, maps and promises, but none of them interested her.

"This was his room. He called it the heart of the house. He used to spend hours in here when he was home," Awena said wistfully. She picked up a notebook from the desk and riffled through the pages. "He wrote everything down. Every thought he had about the treasures. Sometimes, when I was younger, he would let me sit with him while he worked. He would show me some of the wonderful old drawings he'd found. He even tried to teach me bits of Latin, hoping I'd follow in his footsteps."

"It sounds like he was quite a scholar."

"He was. The newspapers ran articles on him a long time ago, making out that he was a crackpot, but he wasn't. He took it all seriously. He was dedicated to the search. It was important to him because it was our heritage. It used to upset him that other people just didn't seem to care anymore. But not Dad, he cared. He was Welsh and damned proud to be Welsh. And I wanted to be just like him." Awena smiled, and for the first time Annja could see the truth that she really was her father's daughter. She had that same slightly manic-obsessive gleam to her eye.

"Is that what he found?" Annja asked, inclining her head toward the whetstone. She couldn't resist turning the conversation around to treasure, but Awena put herself between Annja and the desk, obscuring it from her view for a moment.

"I'll tell you anything you want to know, but first, I need to ask you a question."

"Sure. What do you want to know?" Annja asked, thinking it would be something about how the show worked, maybe if they'd be paid for her father's research, something like that.

"Why did you watch my father die?"

It was a simple question.

She didn't have the answer.

Annja felt her heartbeat quicken, convinced that it must have been loud enough for the woman to hear it.

"I don't understand."

"It's a simple enough question, and I don't think you are stupid. Why did you watch my father die? Don't lie to me, Annja. I know you called for the ambulance. And I know you didn't try to help him. So why did you watch him die? Why didn't you at least attempt to save him?"

"I don't know what you're talking about." She started to deny it all, stumbling to find the words to satisfy Llewellyn's grieving daughter.

"Yes, you do. I know it was you."

Annja was torn between lying through her teeth and telling the truth about what had happened.

"It was an accident," she lied, willing the woman to believe her. "He was going too fast. He didn't see me coming in the other direction. He tried to react, but the road wasn't wide enough. It was bad out there. You have to understand that—it was in the worst of the storm. He lost control and went over the edge. There was nothing I could do. Nothing anyone could have done."

"Really? Nothing?" Awena seemed to think about

this for a moment. Tears weren't far away. "What kind of car were you driving? Not that flashy sports car you're in now. Geraint told me he saw you crossing the Severn Bridge. You were in a different car."

"Does it matter?"

"Yes, it matters!" she screamed. The tears she'd been trying so hard to keep in check were of anger and rage, not sadness and sorrow. "You could have *saved* him. You let him *die*. So yes, it matters. You drove away. You didn't wait. You didn't go down and help him. Your car was damaged, wasn't it? That's why you drove away. You didn't want the police asking questions. What did you do with the car? Burn it?"

"It wasn't like that," Annja said, wanting to explain. "Really, it wasn't."

"Wasn't it? What was it like, then? Tell me. I want to hear all about it. Make me feel like I was there."

"I don't—"

"No, I don't suppose you do. So tell me, *Mizz* Creed, what were you doing on that road, anyway? Don't pretend that you were lost. I don't believe that for a second. So how about you do us both a favor and stick to the truth?"

There was a freakish intensity to her now, her words coming with the rhythm of a beat poet, anger making her grow until she seemed to metaphorically dwarf Annja. There wouldn't be any reasoning with her. She was laying all of the blame at Annja's feet.

What she couldn't do was lie her way out of this.

"He was trying to kill me," she confessed. The truth. The whole truth.

"You dirty liar!"

Annja shook her head. "He tried to run me off the road," she said. "It was an accident."

"Don't make me laugh. Dad didn't have a bad bone in his body."

"Really? Is that what you think? Is that what you *really* think? Because if it is, then you didn't know the man he became. A few days ago he murdered someone to get his hands on a sword."

Awena turned to look at the stone on the desk. It wasn't a conscious move; it had happened when Annja mentioned the sword. There was no sign of the blade, but it had to be in here somewhere, she realized. Any sign of hesitation could prove lethal, but tipping her hand and becoming the aggressor would push what she'd hoped would be a reconnaissance mission into a full-on combat situation. And that wasn't why she was here.

Awena left the desk and walked over to the window. She stared out through the glass. Annja watched the steady rise and fall of the woman's chest, waiting for her to say something. To react.

She didn't.

Not for the longest time.

"I don't believe you," she said finally, without turning around. "You are a liar. You want the sword, don't you? That's why you killed him. You want to take it. Well, I won't let you."

Annja hadn't seen her hand move behind the thick velvet curtain, but when she turned, the young woman clutched the hilt of Giraldus Cambrensis's sword, and she looked ready to kill.

"You don't have to do this," Annja said calmly.

"Don't I?" Awena said oh-so-sweetly.

The blade changed as she raised it.

A trail of blue flames licked along the cutting edge until the entire length of the ancient blade was enveloped in fire.

Why does this always happen to me? Annja thought, pushing herself up out of the comfortable leather armchair to face the woman. *Just once it'd be a change to have a nice quiet vacation somewhere. That's not too much to ask, surely?*

The woman trembled, every corded muscle in her arm struggling with the weight of the sword and the implications of what taking the first swing meant.

"You're not a killer," Annja said. "I've met killers. Believe me, you aren't one and you don't want to be one. It does something to your soul."

"You'd know, wouldn't you?" Awena rasped. "You killed my father, after all."

The flame surged, the sheer blue of it intensifying, casting a ghostly glow across everything in the room.

"Don't. You don't have to do this," Annja said, taking a step back, trying to put the armchair between them.

"Do you believe in the nature of balance, Annja?" Awena asked. She sounded calm, but it was a dangerous sort of calm. The calm of a woman on the edge.

Annja still hoped she could talk her down. She didn't want to fight a grief-stricken woman simply because she didn't believe her father had killed Roux's friend and tried to kill Annja.

"Counterparts? Like salt and pepper. Yin and yang. Day and night. Black and white. These things go together. They are natural. One cannot exist without the other, like good and evil, life and death. The world needs balance."

"I can see that," Annja agreed, wanting to sound reasonable.

"I'm glad you understand. You see, there must be balance in all things. Where there is crime there must be punishment. You took his life. That is a crime. You have to face the consequences of your actions to keep the world in balance. You must be punished. An eye for an eye, if you prefer."

Awena planned to kill her. She'd planned to kill her even as she'd made the call to invite her over to the remote hillside house. For a second Annja regretted her own small gesture of humanity; if she hadn't called the ambulance there would have been nothing to trace back to her. However the woman had managed it, that didn't matter: she had and she'd never intended for Annja to leave this meeting alive. It was some sort of righteous showdown in her head. Good versus Evil. Capital *G* capital *E*.

Awena shrieked and launched herself across the room, lashing out wildly with the ancient sword. Annja barely evaded the blow, stumbling in the process as she scrambled backward.

She needed to defend herself.

She didn't want to kill the woman, just subdue her. Disarm her. If her anger evaporated, surely she could be made to understand it was just an accident.

Awena lashed out again, driving her back. Annja's foot came down on an old leather journal that had been discarded, and the pages shifted beneath her weight, sliding out from beneath her. Annja went sprawling across the floor with Awena looming over her every bit as wild-eyed as her dead father had ever been.

As she hit the ground all of the air left her and she gasped for breath.

It's some kind of madness, she thought, feeling the heat of Awena Llewellyn's blade on her arm as she reached out into the otherwhere, willing Joan's sword into her hand. *She's caught it, just like her old man.*

She heard a scream, but didn't realize it came from her own twisted lips.

The pain only lasted a moment as the blue flame scorched her skin.

It was more than long enough for Awena Llewellyn to drop onto Annja's chest, pinning her arms, as she brought the firebrand sword up to rest its burning heat against her cheek. The madness in her eyes was every bit as real as the fire's heat.

There's no reasoning with madness.

And then a second thought: *this isn't going to end well.*

"It's all fun and games until someone loses an eye, Annja," Awena said, pushing the edge of the blade up toward Annja's eyes. The writhing blue flame crept up across her line of sight, filling her vision.

The pain was incredible.

It was beyond bearing.

Annja shrieked and arced her back, trying desperately to dislodge the woman from on top of her. She bucked and writhed, lashing out like a bronco, but the woman clung on, pushing more and more weight behind the blade resting on Annja's face, burning, burning, burning....

"An eye for an eye," she said, and there was nothing sane in her voice now. "I'm a literal kind of girl, Mizz Creed."

Annja felt the pressure ease and the pain diminish from searing to simply agonizing. Then she realized that Awena had lifted the sword intending to pluck out her eye with it or else drive the blade though it into the back of her skull. She didn't have a chance to think; she had to react. The bucking had freed her right hand from beneath Awena's weight, and Annja felt Joan's sword in her hand even as she saw the slashing blade come down. She barely stopped the killing blow inches from her face, metal sparking on metal as the two swords came together.

She saw the shock in the other woman's face, the lack of understanding.

She'd been robbed of her justice.

Annja didn't hesitate; she slammed her left fist up into Awena's face, a clubbing blow that connected with her chin and sent her head rocking back.

Awena lost her grip on the sword. It clattered to the floor.

Annja scrambled to her feet, breathing hard.

Tears stung her face.

Every inch of her skin felt as though it were on fire. Her sleeve was black and smoldering where it had touched the sword. She didn't want to think what her face looked like. She focused on the sword in her hand.

"I don't want to kill you, Awena. This doesn't have to end like this. One death doesn't cancel out another. That isn't balance, that's just two corpses."

"Shut up! I don't want to hear any more of your lies."

"There's already been enough death. Please. Leave the sword alone."

But Awena wasn't prepared to give up on her vengeance. She picked up the burning sword again. She wanted Annja to pay, and lunged at her, slashing wildly. She had no skill with the weapon, but pure rage made her more than dangerous.

Annja parried blow after blow, fending off the attacks, knowing that, like any fire, Awena would burn herself out. She didn't have the stamina to match Annja, even if the blade somehow imbued her with unholy strength. It had to end, eventually.

Beads of sweat streamed down Awena's face.

The room was cramped, the low ceiling making it difficult to fight properly.

There was blood around Awena's mouth, too, from Annja's fist.

Again and again Awena swung, coming at her, but the intensity of the attacks lessened as she tired. Annja felt the strain, too. The muscles in her sword arm burned where it had been touched by the blue flame.

She gritted her teeth and tried to get through again. "I didn't kill him, Awena. It was an accident."

"I don't believe you!" the woman spat, her attacks becoming more frenzied and ferocious as her frustration boiled over. She didn't seem to care if Annja hurt her or not. There was no thought to defense.

"But that doesn't mean I'm lying," Annja pleaded. "Please. I don't want to hurt you."

"Liar!" Awena screeched, and launched another dizzying flurry of blows, all with the sole intention of cleaving Annja's head from her shoulders.

Annja blocked each one, swords ringing out as they clashed.

Tears rolled off Awena's face.

Grief.

Failure.

Annja couldn't kill the woman in front of her.

Awena seemed to shrink in on herself, drawing a single breath before launching the next swing.

Annja knew that this was the moment to strike.

One chance. One opening. That was all she needed. She had to end this now, before one of them was seriously hurt.

She charged forward, leading with her shoulder instead of her sword, and cannoned into the woman. The impact drove the wind out of her opponent even as the flaming sword cut through the air harmlessly.

Awena lost her footing, driven back by Annja, and Annja fell on top of her.

Both of them tumbled to the ground, their bodies so close that a sword was useless—unless it was made of fire and its very touch could burn and blind.

Annja pressed a knee against Awena's forearm, keeping it down, then drove the hilt of her own sword into Awena's wrist, springing her hand open like a trap. Awena howled in agony, the sword spilling from her fingers. The flames failed the moment the contact with Awena Llewellyn's hand was broken. Annja couldn't think about it. Somehow Awena found some final ounce of strength and reached up, grabbing Annja's hair.

She tugged hard, tearing it out at the roots.

It was Annja's turn to scream at the sudden pain.

She swung her left fist as hard as she could, hammering it into Awena's nose, and felt the sickly rupturing of cartilage beneath the impact and the wetness of blood, but the woman didn't release her grip. Instead, Awena writhed and bucked and tore at Annja's hair until she had to shift her balance and release the arm that had been trapped beneath her knee.

They both scrambled to their feet.

Awena kicked out. It wasn't exactly graceful, but her foot connected with Annja's wrist and the sword spun out of her hand. The fabled blade skittered beneath the desk and disappeared back into the otherworld.

Awena grabbed her own sword, the blade reigniting as soon as her fist closed around the hilt.

She looked up, hair falling across her face.

Weaponless, Annja charged, throwing herself at the woman. She slammed into her, driving her back. Awena took the full impact of the charge and stumbled, unable to cope with Annja's momentum.

One backward step became two, became three, and then she was falling, the burning sword flailing in the air.

The room filled with the crash of glass as Annja carried Awena into the window.

And Awena kept falling through it.

Annja stared in horror; she'd been trying to buy herself a second, time enough to reclaim her sword, to disarm the other…but the world slowed down and Awena kept falling. Glass shattered. Wood splintered. The window wasn't strong enough to keep her inside the house.

Annja snatched out a hand, trying to catch Awena's ankle even as Awena clawed helplessly at the air, unable to gain any purchase or stop her inevitable fall.

And then she was gone.

Annja stood in the bay of the broken window and stared down at the body below, Giraldus Cambrensis's sword lying on the gravel driveway beside it.

Annja breathed hard. "It didn't have to be this way," she said, and turned away from the window.

No matter what the woman had done, though, Annja wouldn't abandon her as she had her father.

She wouldn't just leave her to die—if she wasn't dead already. She would stay with her until the ambulance arrived, until the police arrived, whether it was to take Awena Llewellyn to the hospital or the morgue. She would stay with her.

She had no idea how she'd explain it. What could she possibly say that would make any sort of sense to the average person?

She picked up her bag and cell phone from where she'd left them downstairs in the kitchen and headed outside, already dialing 999 to summon the emergency services.

She walked around the side of the huge house to the stretch of driveway beneath Owen Llewellyn's study window. Broken glass crunched underfoot with the gravel.

Annja stopped the call just as the emergency operator was asking which service she required.

There was no sign of Awena.

29

"All I need is for you to get up onto one of the towers," Roux said.

"All?" Garin replied. "There's nothing like expecting miracles, is there, old man? I'm good, but there are special-ops guys crawling over everywhere. We can't even get in through the front gate, but all you need is for me to somehow reach the top of one of the towers. What did you have in mind? Helicopter in and drop me from a great height?" Garin suggested facetiously.

"It's an option," Roux said, all sweetness and light, with a look that could have frozen a penguin in an ice floe. "There's no need to go in through the front gate. There's no need to go *inside* the castle at all."

Garin thought about what Roux was suggesting for a moment, allowing it to sink in, while his eyes traced their way up the outer walls of the castle. He sniffed.

"Which tower?"

There was no point in trying to say that it wasn't possible; it was, obviously. In Roux's philosophy there were only problems and solutions. Some problems needed more thought than others, but there was always a means of solving them. That was how the old man was.

"Walk with me," Roux said, getting to his feet. He

left the table clearly oblivious to the fact that there was still a bill to be paid. Garin slipped a twenty-pound note beneath the saucer of his cup along with his business card—plain black with his phone number and first name in foil, nothing else—and nodded to the girl as she came outside again. The tip was more than the price of the coffee, meaning she was going to remember him for more than just making her blush. With a bit of luck she'd call later. All he had to do was get to the top of the tower, find King Arthur's cloak of invisibility, get back out and give Roux the slip for a few hours. And then maybe he could take her for a drink. Maybe in Paris. That always went down well.

"Try not to look too conspicuous, eh?" Roux said as he ambled across the square to the estuary that was alongside the castle. "Remember, we're just tourists. There are plenty of those—some of them are even taking photos of the guards, but we're just interested in the battlements."

Garin nodded. "Long way up. Or more pertinently, long way *down,*" Garin said, scanning the stonework for natural handholds.

"Do you think you're up to it?"

"With the right equipment, no problem."

Roux shook his head. "No equipment. We can't risk anything that will leave a trace. We were never here, remember?"

"Are you insane? You're asking me to free-climb up the side of a castle in the dark when they've got armed guards waiting to shoot anything that moves?"

"I didn't say you couldn't use a rope, assuming you need one to exfiltrate the castle, but no pegs, nothing hammered into the rock. Nothing that will make a sound. You'd need to be able to self-release the rope, obviously, so we could take it with us. But yes, you are right—you would have to do it in the dark."

"You *are* crazy."

"Never denied it, but I'm not the one climbing castle walls in the middle of the night. Personally, I'm not sure you are up to it."

"Don't try any of your silly mind tricks on me, old man," Garin warned. "I know how you work. Remember, I've known you for a very, very long time. I'm not going to be fooled into breaking my neck simply because you say I can't do something. I don't need to prove you wrong."

"Of course you don't," Roux agreed.

With equipment, in broad daylight, no problem. In the dark, sans gear, that was another story. There was one person who was better suited to make the climb than he was, though he wasn't about to suggest they call in Annja. She had enough on her plate.

"I suppose you're volunteering to be lookout?" he said.

Roux nodded, a wry smile on his lips. He might look like someone's doting granddad, but that didn't mean he couldn't be a right bastard if the need arose, or that he wouldn't enjoy it, either. "I'll avail myself of the shadows down here, yes, and make sure you do not get into trouble."

"Hooting like a barn owl no doubt?"

"If that is your warning of choice, yes. I can do wolves, too, if you prefer."

"Funny. I was more concerned about what happened once I was inside—you know, the whole part about finding the secret hiding place of the mantle, which you haven't actually shared with me. Am I to take it that it is stashed beneath some convenient flagstone on the battlements?"

"Not quite. No. I will give you directions when the time comes. Not that I don't trust you, you understand."

Garin ignored the barbed comment and continued to pace the length of the wall. "Okay, which tower are we talking about?"

Roux nodded to the one that looked out toward the sea. "That one."

"Well, at least there's less chance of being seen by any drunks stumbling across the square." There were boats moored at the quayside. Most of them were small fishing vessels. None of them looked like the kind of place some bohemian would make their home, so the chances of someone spending the night on them were slim to nonexistent. That only left the army to worry about.

Even from this distance he could see that the blocks of stone had cracks between them wide enough to serve as toe- and fingerholds. They weren't perfect or evenly spaced, but they would have been a piece of cake for Annja. The problem was she was at the other end of the country chasing a sword.

Or maybe she wasn't.

Maybe she'd already found it.

The Porsche could do the journey in a couple of hours.

Might as well get his money's worth.

"I'll call her," he said, making the decision himself. "If she's done, she could be here before it's dark."

"Probably wise. Like I said, I'm not sure you're up to it."

"You won't goad me into it, old man. You won't."

"If you say so."

30

Annja felt an overwhelming surge of relief that Awena Llewellyn had survived the fall.

That was quickly replaced by confusion at how she'd just gotten up and walked away.

She *had* to be hurt. Probably even badly hurt.

How could she just walk away?

Annja scanned the ground for some sort of tracks, anything that might give her a clue as to where the woman had gone. She had to find her, and not just for her health; she needed to recover the sword. That was her primary objective here. Get the sword. Bring it home. Roux would kill her if she failed.

She walked a full circuit of the house. There was no sign of her—no freshly trodden path, no trail of blood. Nothing.

When she had reached the far side of the house she heard the sound of a car engine starting.

Annja ran, her arm throbbing as the singed material rubbed against the scorched skin beneath. She gritted her teeth and pushed on through the pain, moving as fast as she could, but she was too slow. She came around the side of the house just as a car disappeared down the drive.

There was no time to waste.

She raced to the Porsche, heart sinking as she saw that one of her tires was flat.

She kicked the tire in frustration; it was a mess. The rubber had been melted away, obviously by the sword. Awena had got one over on her, and split with the sword, so technically she'd gotten two over on her. Annja felt her phone vibrating, but she had no intention of answering it.

She wasn't ready to speak to Garin and admit she'd failed.

No, she'd busy herself with something physical to work her frustration out on, then she'd talk to Garin. Maybe.

Despite the damage, changing the wheel was relatively simple. None of the heat had fused the nuts so it was merely a case of getting her hands dirty.

Done, Annja slipped back inside the house to clean up before leaving.

Entering a stranger's house uninvited, even when it was empty, was strangely eerie; there was nothing but cold silence waiting for her where life should have been. The sounds of her footsteps echoed back to her.

She used the kitchen sink to scrub her hands, then decided to take another look in the study. There was no way of knowing where Awena had gone, or when, if ever, she would return now she knew Annja was onto her. She'd taken the sword, but it was doubtful she'd taken the whetstone given its sheer weight and the lack of time she'd had to move it. One thing was for certain—she had an answer to the puzzle of one criminal doing two crimes at two locations. Awena was keeping it in the family. Owen had found the sword, his daughter the whetstone.

Even though she was partly responsible for it, the sheer devastation wreaked in Owen Llewellyn's study was shocking.

A breeze pulled the curtains through the remains of the window. The material snagged on teeth of broken glass still caught in the wooden window frame.

At first she thought she was wrong and that the woman had somehow come back and recovered the huge whetstone, because it wasn't on the desk where it had been. But then she saw it, lying amid the torn pages of journals and papers on the floor behind the desk.

The Whetstone of Tudwal Tudglyd was larger and heavier than she'd expected. It took all of her strength to lever it up enough just to slide her fingers beneath, never mind *lift* it. Grunting, Annja heaved it up onto the desk.

There was a full-length mirror on the wall behind the door. Annja didn't want to look at any lingering damage the burning sword might have left, yet she couldn't help it; she could feel the tightness of skin across the side of her face and her arm ached bone-deep. She stood in front of the mirror. She looked like she'd been through a small war. Her clothes were singed and blackened from contact with the sword, the sleeve torn and scorched.

The arm itself wasn't so bad—only an angry red welt where the sword had burned her, and it was far from lasting. Her face was more worrying; the skin had already begun to blister and crust across her cheek, but again, it could have been a lot worse. She didn't want to imagine the damage if the sword had been in contact with her flesh for even a heartbeat longer.

On the bright side, she'd recovered one of the artifacts Roux was concerned about.

It was better than leaving empty-handed.

She took a grip of the stone and lifted it again, struggling to find an easy method to carry it as she picked a lurching path through overturned furniture and other debris.

It was only when she reached the door that she realized what she wasn't seeing: the notebook that Awena had been looking at. It wasn't on the desk and it wasn't on the floor amid the other torn papers. There were plenty of journals and books strewn across the floor, but on her hands and knees as she went through them, Annja knew for sure it was gone. Awena had come back into the house for it while Annja was out there looking for her—which meant it was the only thing in the room the woman thought worth saving....

Well, it's gone now, like the sword. No use crying about it.

She struggled with the whetstone, manhandling it out of the house and into the foot well on the passenger's side of the Porsche. It was as secure there as anywhere.

She needed to speak to Roux. He'd know what she was supposed to do with it now she had it. First, though, she wanted to put some distance between her and the house. It wasn't that she expected Awena to return. She was long gone. No, it was about avoiding her brother, Geraint. She really didn't want to have to do the dance again, trying to explain what had happened. It wouldn't go well.

She clambered into the Porsche and drove, and kept on driving until the car had dipped into the valley and climbed back up the other side. There she was back within range of the nearest cell phone tower. She pulled over at the side of the road to make the call while her reception was good.

It still showed that one missed call.

Garin.

She tapped the screen to return the call.

He greeted her quickly. "Too busy for me? I'm wounded, Annja, truly wounded."

"I was a bit preoccupied fighting for my life, nothing personal."

"Given as you're not dead, I take it that went well?"

"As well as can be expected," Annja replied.

"Roux wants to know how you're getting on."

"Good news, bad news time. You pick."

"I'll take the good news first. I'm just that kind of guy," Garin said.

"Tell Roux that I've recovered the Whetstone of Tudwal Tudglyd."

"Excellent. And the bad news would be you haven't recovered the sword, I'm guessing?"

"Good guess. The daughter has it. I lost her."

"How unlike you. This is the fighting for your life part, I suppose?"

"Yep. And it ended with a defenestration."

"That's a little extreme."

"It was unintentional. I can't believe she walked away from it, frankly. She slashed one of my tires so I couldn't chase her."

"You're not having a lot of luck with cars, are you?"

"No idea where she's gone. I do know that she recovered her father's journal, so I think it's reasonable to assume she's following in his footsteps."

"Which would be great if we knew where he intended to go next," Garin observed.

"Exactly."

She heard Garin talking to Roux, but he'd clearly put a hand over the mouthpiece to muffle his words. Then he was back. "The old man says to make your way up to Caernarfon as soon as you can. Forget about the woman. We've got bigger fish to fry. We need you here tonight. I'll sort out a hotel room."

Garin hung up on her before she could agree.

She returned to the hotel to recover her things.

She wouldn't be coming back.

31

Every inch of her ached.

Every cord of muscle was on fire.

Every sinew stung.

Every nerve sang.

Awena Llewellyn felt as though she was alive for the first time.

She had no idea how she'd managed to get back on her feet after the fall. As the impact happened she was sure she was dead, that she'd crushed her spine and shattered her skull, but when the world didn't go out, when she didn't stop breathing, she tried to move. Maybe she'd just been lucky—improbably, impossibly lucky—or maybe it was because she'd clung on to the sword for grim life. It didn't matter. She was alive and in one piece and she wasn't about to look a gift horse in the mouth by hanging around to give her father's killer a second chance.

She was in pain.

While she hurt this much, she wouldn't be able to defend herself, never mind press an attack. That meant running for now.

She wedged the sword between the seat and the passenger's door. It was just out of reach, but she felt reassured by its nearness. All she had to do was glance across while she drove to feel the heat of it even though the flame had flickered and failed, leaving nothing more miraculous than cold steel. She wished she'd been able to bring the whetstone, but given the circumstances beggars couldn't be choosy and she was most definitely the beggar here. Her father had found a far greater treasure. It was a tragedy that he hadn't lived to see what it was capable of. She wished she'd had more time to experiment in terms of putting the two treasures together and seeing what would have been possible.

It could not be helped.

She needed to find someone to study her father's journal where they wouldn't be disturbed. There was more in there about the sword, certainly, but more importantly, there was stuff in there about the other treasures. She'd already found a reference to where he believed another of the treasures might lie, one of the greatest of them all.

If he was right…

If it really was there…

If she could get her hands on it…

She'd be able to do *anything* she set her mind to, including avenging him.

"I promise, Dad. I won't let you down," she told the empty car.

She was still a couple of hours away from her destination. The drive took her through the mountains that lay in the heart of Wales, from the Brecon Beacons in the south to Snowdonia in the north. All she had to do was keep heading north, then eventually she'd see a signpost for her destination. Wales was such a small country that it was possible to make a journey like this without GPS or a map.

She'd call Geraint when she arrived; she'd be in North Wales long before he was due home. She didn't want him coming after her out of some misplaced loyalty or love. There was nothing he could do to stop her. This was her quest now, like it had been her father's before. She really was her father's daughter. And if that meant Geraint washed his hands of her just as he had their father, then so be it. He wasn't afraid of her wasting her life looking for things that didn't exist; he was afraid of her finding them.

What she didn't understand—and had been trying hard not to think about—was how that bitch Creed had been able to pull that sword out of thin air. Had she claimed one of the treasures Awena didn't know about? She couldn't think of any magical swords that could supposedly phase in and out of the material plane. And yet, it was always possible it was Creed rather than the sword that was blessed with strange powers.

Forewarned was forearmed. She wouldn't let the woman reach for her sword the next time.

And she was sure there would be a next time.

Because she was going to make certain there was.

32

They sat in the small hotel bar after dinner, Roux nursing a cognac, Garin sticking with coffee because he was the one about to risk life and limb, not the old man. He didn't fancy being perforated by a hail of a royal guard's bullets and leaking alcohol. It wasn't the done thing.

He'd wanted to wait until the following night, take advantage of tonight to watch the routines and get a feel for where the guards were complacent—assuming they were, somewhere. Roux had insisted that if Annja made it back tonight they were making their attempt. It bought them time for a second chance if things didn't go according to plan. Garin was a fan of second chances, but not necessarily of the circumstances that led to them being needed.

It hadn't taken long to locate an outdoor adventure store that stocked decent climbing rope and a good pair of shoes for the job at hand. "There's one thing I don't understand," Garin said. "If you hid this cloak so well, and never told anyone where, why would anyone even think to look for it here?" It seemed a reasonable question and Garin had wanted to ask it all day. The intimation, of course, was that Roux hadn't been able to keep his own secret. That was akin to walking on broken glass.

"Ah, but I didn't say I never told *anyone*. Just as there was someone keeping an eye on the unmarked grave in St. Davids, there was someone who did the same here."

"And you think he might not have been as trustworthy as you had hoped?"

"She," Roux corrected. "I have not heard from her for some time."

"And you didn't think to contact her?"

Roux shook his head.

"There's something you're not telling me here. I don't know what it is, but I know you, old man. You wouldn't have us charging up here and breaking in to the castle—sorry, the *caer*—in the middle of the night unless you thought there was a good chance she's told someone."

Roux didn't reply.

His attention was focused solely on the last of his brandy he swirled around in his glass.

Garin kept quiet until the silence became uncomfortable. It always worked with Roux. It was simple, really; if the old man changed the subject when he finally spoke, Garin would know for sure he was hiding something. That was the time to push.

"We argued," Roux admitted. "The last time we spoke we argued."

More silence.

There had to be a compelling reason that Roux was holding back. Whatever it was, it wasn't a plain ol' argument. It would come out sooner or later. Sooner would be better, but in the meantime he'd reached his own conclusion: Roux and this mystery woman had been close but kept their relationship from him.

"You need to speak to her. Now," Garin said, spelling it out for him. No disagreement could be bad enough that it was worth the risk of their failing.

"It's too late."

"It's never too late. Be the bigger man. Swallow your pride. Build bridges. Apologize. You can do it, you silver-tongued old devil. How long is it since you argued?"

"Forty years. Maybe longer. Fifty? After a while you start to lose count."

Fifty years? Even as he repeated the words inside his head he knew that the mystery woman was almost certainly long dead, but he wasn't about to voice that thought. Roux knew it, hence his insistence it was too late. There was one question he wanted to ask. "Okay, so it isn't her, but you think she might have told someone?"

Roux shrugged, draining the last few drops from his glass. "I tried to find her a few weeks ago. She spent her last years in a nursing home. She suffered from dementia. She didn't know who anyone was because she was living back in the days of her youth. Believe me, it's the reason why people like us should never get close to anyone. It's too hard watching them slowly die. It was easier to walk out with her hating me than ever go back and say I was sorry. I didn't want to watch her go."

Garin thought that he was capable of being a callous bastard, but he had nothing on Roux.

"Who would she have talked to?"

"No one? Someone? Either is equally possible. She might not even have known she'd said anything. But she had a nephew who was a historian. He worked in the castle. That doesn't mean she told him, but…it doesn't mean she didn't, either."

"Only one person can keep a secret," Garin agreed.

"I should have come back to move it years ago. It's my fault. But I didn't want to be reminded of her."

"You've never thought of finding someone to take her place? Another watch keeper, I mean."

"It didn't seem so important. The world has changed. The whetstone has been unguarded for so long that I haven't so much as thought about it for decades. I'd buried it beneath a site where the law was supposed to prevent excavation, and when they dug it up no one recognized it for what it was. Or so I thought. Someone obviously did."

"The family Llewellyn," Garin filled in the gaps.

"The daughter. The son doesn't appear to share the same familial obsessions. And the more I think about it, the less likely it seems that Awena Llewellyn is in possession of the mantle."

"How so?"

"She would have used it to her advantage. Even Annja would have struggled against a woman capable of phasing in and out of sight."

"And you still sent her with no warning?"

"Would you rather I had sent you?"

Before he had the opportunity to answer the question, Annja walked into the bar.

She did not look happy.

The two men fell silent.

33

"Okay, I'm here. Now what's going on?"

Annja had driven nonstop since picking up her things from the hotel and grabbing a salve from the chemist to treat the burns on her arm and face.

She arched her back, trying to work out the kinks in her spine as she did so. All she wanted was food, a hot bath and the chance to stretch out on a bed for an hour or so. Judging by the older man's face she'd be lucky to get half an hour to gulp down a soda and a sandwich.

"Where's the stone?" It wasn't the most welcoming of greetings but they were the first words she heard from Roux's lips. Not *How are you?* Not *What happened to your face?* Just "Where's the stone?" Priorities established in three little words.

"In the car," she told him. "What do you want me to do with it?"

"Garin, go move it into our car."

Garin looked at Roux like he wanted to slice him up into tiny pieces, but he pushed himself out of his seat and took Annja's keys from her outstretched hand without a word of complaint. She knew just how much he hated being treated like the man's squire, but old habits—really old habits—died very hard indeed.

"What happened to your face?" Roux asked when Garin left.

She told him. He listened carefully, stopping her occasionally and asking her to repeat certain parts in the chain of events, making sure he understood everything that had occurred. He couldn't mask his disappointment that she'd lost the sword, but didn't chastise her, which only made Annja feel like more of a failure.

"How does it feel?" He touched his own cheek. "It doesn't look good."

"I won't be going on camera for a while," she said, "but I'll live."

"Good job you're not vain," Garin said, appearing behind Roux.

"Who says?" Annja teased. "Anyway, as much as I missed you guys, this isn't my idea of a vacation. I'd go so far as to say nearly getting killed means it sucks. So, are you going to tell me why I had to drive like a bat out of hell to be here tonight instead of arriving tomorrow?"

"The old man wants us to break into the castle," Garin said, slumping back into his chair. He dropped her keys in front of her, then added, "With no equipment and under the watchful eye of an elite royal guard."

"Hence not just going in through the front gate, I take it."

"Yep. I don't really fancy being shot down in my prime," Garin said.

"Right, but aren't there huge spotlights illuminating the whole show at night?"

"Yep again. There are some more secluded angles, but how does free-climbing in the dark sound?"

"Foolish, reckless, downright dangerous. Stupid. How many more adjectives do you need?"

"Not even *cool?*" Garin said wryly. He wasn't looking at her; he was looking at Roux as though to say, *I told you so.*

"Why so negative, Annja? It's not as if you're not a superhero, after all. Think of all those women who'd be empowered by your heroics. You can do it." That was Garin's version of a rah-rah pep talk. She almost smiled, purely because she knew he was every bit as vehemently against the break-in as she was.

"I'm not asking you to do something beyond your particular gifts," Roux said, ignoring Garin to look at Annja. "And you don't need to go inside the castle itself, just get yourselves up onto one of the towers."

"And we both need to go up?"

"It's better, yes."

"And let me guess, we're doing it tonight?" She already knew the answer.

"Now."

34

Garin secured the rope to her waist.

She'd free-climbed plenty of times, higher and more complicated climbs than this, but this was sheer. And the heavier the rope was going to feel as it tugged behind her.

Annja rested her hand against the wall.

The stone was slick with moisture.

Not good, she thought.

She'd known that it was a dumb idea the moment the suggestion came out of Garin's mouth. But the reality of just how dumb was only beginning to settle in now she was confronted by the actual climb and their narrow spot where they were out of sight of the guards and the powerful spotlights.

They were estuary-side of the castle, and while there would be no spray from the almost-still water, the air was damp enough to ensure that the stone was never truly dry.

The trick wasn't to cling to the stone face but to even her weight distribution out and maintain three points of contact at all time; less than that and the risks increased exponentially. Even so, the toeholds were treacherously slippery, and more than once as she began the slow ascent she felt the rough grip of the shoe's tread slip, meaning she had to go much slower than she would have liked. It was a long way down should she fall, and she wasn't even halfway yet. There were so many things she was doing here she wished she wasn't. Though Roux was adamant, not so much as a scratch on the castle wall, not so much as the *tink* of a hammer driving in a belay pin. Nothing that might draw the guards, who would almost certainly shoot first and ask questions later.

Great, she thought bitterly, working her way slowly higher. Her arm gave her problems. The muscle beneath the burn couldn't take her weight as well as her other arm, meaning she favored it as she climbed. That presented an entirely new set of problems for the ascent.

Garin waited at the bottom.

Roux was somewhere in the shadows, with a vantage point that included the street and the castle gates.

She had only seen one soldier on patrol, his silhouette moving along the battlements. The rest were no doubt inside watching the football now the gates were secured. After all, they wouldn't expect any sort of insurgency or break-in. This wasn't Egypt on the brink of civil war; this was a sleepy little town in North Wales. Not exactly a hotbed of revolution since the days of Owain Glyndŵr.

The blocks of stone were large, meaning that she had to stretch for each toehold and push herself up for every fingerhold. It wasn't good. It was exactly how accidents happened, but Annja was in the zone. She moved instinctively, choosing the holds without looking at them, without looking down at the drop, and when the slick surface threatened to betray her, she trusted her shoes to keep her on the rock.

Eventually her hand reached out, flexing and stretching, seeking the next handhold, and found a flat surface for her fingers to curl over. She was at the top.

There was no flooding sense of relief; this was the most dangerous part of the climb.

A fall from here would be fatal.

Garin might have bought shoes, but he'd skipped handy safety stuff like a helmet—not that a helmet would have made a lot of difference from a fall like this. The damage caused to bones and internal organs would be too much to survive.

It was hard not to think of Awena and her own fall, though from a substantially lower elevation. She had walked away. A single slip now and Annja wouldn't be so lucky.

Muscles and sinews strained and ached as she reached over the parapet, the rough edge of stone block digging into her flesh through the thin material she was wearing. An extra layer of clothing would have provided more warmth and protected her against this, but would also have made her more bulky and less agile, and right now agility was key.

At last she was over, aching and exhausted with the effort.

She lay on the stone floor on the other side of the parapet, struggling to catch her breath and trying to will the pain away. She could hear Garin down below, hissing like a cat. It wasn't exactly subtle. She rolled over onto her stomach and rose.

The moonlight had been no help when she'd been climbing, but here, on one of the highest parts of the castle, there was nothing to cast shadows. So she stood

in a pool of clear moonlight for all the world to see—
all they had to do was look her way.

There was no obvious mooring point for the rope, so
she wrapped a length of it around one of the merlons,
the solid parts of the defensive wall around the tower.
Between the crenels she secured the rope with a knot
she would be able to release once they'd both climbed
back down. She checked the knot a couple of times before giving Garin the signal to climb.

He scrambled up the wall quickly, with the rope
threaded around his leg and trapped in his feet to serve
as a makeshift harness.

She watched as he climbed, then used her vantage
point to see if she could see Roux, but he was well and
truly hidden.

She glanced over the other side of the parapet down
into a courtyard.

There was no sign of anyone patrolling. Again, she
reasoned, why should they be? The guards might be
there to ensure that no one had planted a bomb inside
one of the main buildings ahead of the royal visit, but
that didn't mean they had to maintain a state of heightened vigilance. There was no reason to assume they'd
come under attack. It was very much business as usual.

She checked back, surprised that Garin was almost
at the top.

She braced herself and offered an arm to help haul
him over the battlement.

It took a couple of minutes to wind the rope up, carefully making sure that it wouldn't snag on itself when
lowered down again. Care was everything. They worked
in silence.

Done, they crouched down. "Time to check in," Annja said.

Garin pressed a button on the Bluetooth earpiece he was wearing and then said, "We're in."

Annja pressed a finger to her lips as the sound of heavy footsteps echoed on the inside of the castle walls. Someone was crossing the courtyard. It might not be a regular patrol checking for intruders, but that didn't mean that the man would not be keeping his eyes and ears open.

She held her finger there until the last echo of the footsteps died away.

It sounded as though the footsteps had been moving toward the tower, but she could not be sure. The acoustics were tricky. She didn't like the added risk that came with working blind.

Garin nodded.

He scrambled away from her, moving like a crab, running his hands over the stone floor of the parapet, until, in the corner farthest from them, he located a dark opening. No doubt the stairwell down the inside of the tower, which would lead either down to the courtyard, the walkway along the inside of the defensive wall or possibly both.

"Found it," he whispered. "Okay." A beat. "Okay." And to Annja, he said, "This might take a few minutes."

He pulled a small Swiss Army knife from his pocket and opened it up. He ran the blade between the stone blocks to clear out the grit and dirt that had gathered and been ground in over the generations. Annja watched him work. It was plainly obvious the stone hadn't been disturbed recently.

If the mantle was gone it had been taken years ago.

He slowly opened the gap around the stone with his knife until the blade slid easily into the dirt. "This is the one."

Annja unhooked a tool that Roux had given to her, a strange piece that turned at right angles. Garin nodded and she worked the hook's bill into the slot he'd levered up. She slowly turned the tool ninety degrees, teasing and twisting it until she could feel the hook grind into position under the slab.

Together, they tugged on the handle, and stone ground against stone as the slab shifted a fraction.

They looked at each other and nodded, timing the moment of pressure, and the stone shifted again, slowly at first. Then the fragments of grit and grime that his knife hadn't been able to shift exploded in a shower of dust. Garin shifted his position and slipped the fingers of one hand into the gap they had created to gain a secure grip.

As the stone slab was lifted, it became obvious that its edge had been cut to create an overlap that sat on a matching shoulder in the stones surrounding it, fashioning a hollow beneath it. Once Garin had lifted the slab sufficiently, Annja could get her hand inside. She expected to find the Mantle of King Arthur, but her fingers closed on nothing.

She felt about frantically, but it wasn't there.

"It's gone," she said.

"It's got to be there."

"It's gone. As in, it's not there."

"Oh, man, Roux's going to lose it. He already thinks this is all his fault. I'm not going to be the one to tell him. He loves you. You get to break the bad news. If he hears it from me—"

"Shh," Annja hissed as she worked her fingertips into the deepest corner of the secret space. She felt them brush over something, something with a different texture. Something that didn't belong in there. She found an edge and pinched it between a finger and thumb and pulled it out. It was a muslin bag and it had obviously deteriorated over time.

Annja sank back against the wall, oblivious to the fact that Garin was beginning to struggle with the slab.

She nodded and he dropped it back into place. He brushed dirt into the grooves, rubbing as much of it in as he could to mask the fact the hiding place had been discovered. Not that they were worried about any would-be treasure hunter, but rather because they didn't want some soldier to come along in the morning and discover that the tower had been breached.

"I take it that's it?" he asked, indicating the muslin sack, but Annja didn't get the chance to respond. They heard the sound of heavy boots on stone steps in the stillness.

"Move!"

Garin didn't need to be told twice.

In an instant he snatched up the rope and threw it over the parapet wall. The rope made enough noise to carry to the courtyard and market square in the quiet night, but the sound of the footsteps didn't quicken. Garin went first, and as he went over the top she pressed the muslin sack into his hand before he rappelled down the side. Annja followed him, wrapping her wrist and waist around the rope, ready to step out into nothing as she heard a voice calling out.

"Who's there?"

The beam of a flashlight shone upward from the stairwell.

In a moment it would be too late. She had to go over the top now even though Garin wasn't on the ground. The guard was seconds from emerging onto the platform and seeing her. It was now or never. She stepped off the wall into thin air, bouncing hard, once, twice, three times, the rope burning as it slid through her hand. She needed to get to the bottom and release the rope before the guard saw it and raised the alarm.

Still thirty feet shy of the ground, she found a hand jam and pulled the quick release on the knot, sending the rope snaking to the ground.

Annja held her position, listening, and willing the guard to move on without investigating any further.

"Must have been the wind, or birds," a voice called back down the stairwell. She willed him to go away. "Nothing up here."

Annja let out a deep breath as the flashlight beam turned around the perimeter wall above her, casting weird shadows through the crenellations, but the guard's face never appeared over the edge.

Hanging there, Annja felt the muscles in her injured arm slowly burn, cramping until her fingers felt like they had to let go to ease the ever-increasing fire she felt inside the wound. All she could think was that there was no way she could make the climb back down again—her muscles and sinews had frozen—but she had no choice. It was that or fall. And she didn't like the odds of survival if she simply let go.

She shifted her balance, taking all of her weight on her toes to relieve the strain on her injured arm. Sweat gathered at the nape of her neck and trickled slowly

down her spine. It broke out on her brow, rolling down
her temples, and threatened to sting her eyes. The fact
she couldn't just wipe it away made the sensation excru-
ciating. She breathed hard, blinking furiously to clear
her vision, and then moved her hands one line of bricks
lower, taking her weight on the fingers of her good hand,
and was moving again with painstaking care. It was
considerably more taxing than the climb had been. She
could feel Garin willing her on, but wasn't about to risk
a misstep.

No looking down. Cheek pressed tight to the stone
so she could feel the roughness against her skin as she
descended, until at last she felt the lightest of touches of
his hands on her ankles. His voice was reassuring and
she allowed his shoulders to take her weight before she
dropped the last few feet.

He nodded toward the opened muslin bag, its contents spilled on the ground. There was a small chamois
leather wrap, which he'd unfolded to reveal a small envelope with Roux's name in careful faded script. What
there wasn't, was any sort of cloak or mantle.

"I know it's supposed to be invisible, but…"

Not good. Not good at all, Annja thought, trying to
process it all. The hiding place had been compromised,
the treasure long gone. All that was left in its place was
some sort of letter to taunt Roux, and now they were
going to have to tell him they'd failed. Again. Today
wasn't a good day.

"Where's Roux," she asked.

"Not here."

35

Awena Llewellyn watched the Creed woman. Everywhere she turned, she seemed to be waiting. It was as if she were haunting her, or taunting her. One or the other. This time she was with two men.

Awena stood in the doorway of a café, masked by shadows as she looked out across the market square toward the high walls of the castle. There was no obvious route inside that didn't involve scaling the walls—walls that had been built with the express purpose of stopping precisely that kind of attack. The market square was derelict, the stalls stripped down to their skeletal remains, the cobbles sluiced down and rotten vegetables swept up.

She had the sword at her side, the blade wrapped in a piece of sacking and clutched tight in her hand. She wore a single leather driving glove and didn't dare touch the hilt for fear the sword would burst into flame regardless of the glove and betray her hiding place.

She had not expected to see anyone moving around at this time of night, let alone the Creed woman. Not here. Not so much farther along the quest than she'd imagined possible. There could only be one explanation, and it confirmed Awena's worst fears. Annja Creed was on a quest for the Treasures of Britain and that was why she had murdered her father.

She shivered despite the lack of cold.

The sky was clear. The moon lit up the square more effectively than the dull amber glow of the five working streetlights along it. The one bright light to match the moon was the castle itself, lit up like a comet on reentry, burning bright. It was both breathtaking and humbling. This was the heritage her father had always promised her, the history that flowed through her veins.

Not that she could claim it today or tomorrow or any day soon with the royal entourage well and truly ensconced. But that didn't detract from the fact she was here, at journey's end. This was the resting place of the greatest treasure of them all.

She watched the three of them separate, one moving off into the shadows to take up a position as watchman, the others appearing to ready themselves to scale the castle wall.

Her father's notebook had been vague, but the sight of them removed every last lingering doubt; the Mantle of King Arthur was hidden in the tower waiting to be claimed. She hadn't understood the sketch of a chessboard with an X in one of the squares when she'd found it. But looking at the cobbles beneath her feet it made perfect sense; he'd quite literally drawn an "X marks the spot" treasure map, no doubt counting out the exact dimensions of the tower and drawing in brick by brick on the grid. But that didn't guarantee that it would be there. Far from it; there had been countless false trails and dead ends over the years. She knew better than to get her hopes up, even at the sight of Annja Creed scaling the wall. All it meant was she'd come across the same line of clues and believed them worth investigating.

But the opportunity for revenge made her pulse quicken.

She wanted to move into a better vantage point that offered an unobstructed view of what they were doing, but that meant crossing the square, which was out of the question. Instead, she waited.

She saw the man move into his own private spot from where he could see the market square and the roads leading to and from the castle.

Creed was already at the top of the tower and the second man was about to follow her up the rope she was lowering for him.

As she turned, Awena saw the watcher seemingly stare straight at her hiding place; her heart hammered against her breastbone as she willed her body not to move, not to breathe.

He stepped from his hiding place and she was sure he was about to stride toward her and unmask her, but he turned his back on her and watched the progress of the other two, until the man was hauled up over the parapet. That meant they were close to finding the mantle. In a moment her chance would be gone forever, and so would her revenge.

It was now or never.

She moved quickly, feet almost dancing across the cobbled square as she made her way back to her previous position. She couldn't worry about the two that had finished their ascent into the tower, not yet. She could deal with them when they came down, but she could deal with their lookout, evening the odds and maybe even gaining some leverage.

She remembered a game she had played with Geraint as a child, a game played outside in the dark with only the moon to provide their light. One of them commanded the flagpole at the far end of the garden where the Welsh flag always fluttered proudly, while the other would attempt to reach the pole unseen. The person would move stealthlike from bush to bush, shadow to shadow. She played the game again, only this time it was more than just a game, mattered more than family bragging rights.

It was only as she drew a little closer, while the man was distracted by his team up on the tower, that she realized just how old he was. This was going to be much easier than she'd thought. Smiling now, she slipped the sword free of the sacking. Stepping right up behind him she pressed the sharp edge of the blade against his flesh and clamped a hand over the old man's mouth.

"Make a noise and it will be your last," Awena Llewellyn promised.

She let go of the blade and took hold of the sword at the hilt. The blade came to life despite the leather glove, its bright blue blush of flame lighting up the old man's face. The sight of it was enough to stop his struggles. He knew what was going on. He knew how much trouble he was in. He knew...

"This way," Awena rasped, steering him from the market square and the castle toward an alleyway between buildings. He didn't fight her. There was no one around to see them. Most would have been tucked up in their beds long ago. No one was going to hear them, not even the pair climbing the tower.

She released her hold on his mouth.

"Don't bother trying to run. It won't end well."

"Look, I don't know what you want, but please…" He fumbled at his wrist to take off his watch and offered it to her.

She laughed. A cold, bitter laugh. "Very good. Play dumb. Pretend you don't know exactly who I am and what I'm holding in my hand." As though in response, the flames licking along the length of the blade seemed to twitch a little more furiously. "So don't try playing the innocent with me."

"Oh, I don't claim to be innocent, my dear," the man said. "But what am I guilty of in particular?"

"You'll find out soon enough," Awena said. "Just keep walking."

"With pleasure."

The narrow alley led to a slightly wider road that in turn led to an open parking lot that was in near-total darkness, save for a single working streetlight. There was a solitary car parked in the darkness on the far side, hers. "Get moving." She pushed him on, every few steps jabbing him in the back to keep him going in the right direction until they reached it.

Awena popped the trunk.

The old man made no attempt to hide the concern on his face.

She liked that. "Don't worry," Awena said, "I'm not going to make you get in. I'm not some barbarian. I wouldn't do that to an old man. Turn around. Put your hands behind your back."

He did as he was told.

The courtesy light in the trunk revealed a scatter of plastic cable ties that Geraint had thrown in there months ago. He used them when he was out doing jobs, organizing cables and the like. Funny how even without being there he was still helping her. Awena needed both hands to secure the plastic tie, cinching it just a little tighter than she wanted to so it bit into his leathery skin. She had to lean the sword against the car. The second she released her hold on the hilt, the flame died out and this side of the parking lot was plunged into darkness.

She almost hoped that he would attempt to get away.

She would be able to stop him if he did. And hurt him. For her father. Because even if it had been the Creed woman who had run him off the road, there was blood on the old man's hands.

"What do you want?"

"The same thing as you."

"World peace?"

"Don't play games with me," she said. "We both know what I'm talking about."

He said nothing, just stared into her eyes.

"You're not what I expected," she said.

"How so?"

"You're old."

"I am. That means I've grown accustomed to living. What do you want?"

"I want to know your name for a start," Awena spoke, snatching up the sword again. It immediately roared into bright blue flame. She pressed it bare inches from his face so it stung and blackened the white bristles pushing through his skin. She expected him to beg for his life. He didn't. That was interesting. Most men would have pleaded or made any sort of deal they possibly could to buy time, but not this man, who had grown accustomed to living. That was very interesting indeed.

"Roux," he said. "My name is Roux."

She opened the rear door of the car and, placing a

hand on top of his head, helped him inside, then slipped behind the wheel. She looked at Roux, her prisoner, in the rearview mirror.

"Roux," she repeated.

"That's my name," he said almost cheerfully.

"You're not dead."

"I'm not."

"You actually exist."

"It would seem so. And I assume you are Awena Llewellyn?"

"So we know each other. Isn't that nice?"

"I'm not sure *nice* is the word I'd use, given the whole hog-tied thing, but it is good to know who has taken you hostage, I suppose."

She turned on the interior light, then pulled her father's notebook out of the glove box. She opened it and found the page she wanted, the one with his name written on it, and showed it to him.

"It's because of you I'm here," she said. "See your name there, in black and white? You led Dad here, and now you've led me here. I suppose I should thank you."

"Manners never hurt anyone," he agreed.

36

There was no sign of Roux.

That was bad.

It wasn't like him.

He wasn't the kind of flake who just wandered off in the middle of a job.

He wasn't some ADD kid who couldn't focus.

If he'd gone he'd gone for a reason.

Annja knew it was out of character. And out of character was never what you wanted when you needed a guy to be his usual unflappable, reliable self.

Annja left Garin to coil up the rope. She followed the edge of the castle wall, looking for any indication as to where he might have gone and hoping to stumble across him just around the corner. But she didn't get that lucky. She tried to think: the threat of discovery had come from inside the castle, not from the market square. She'd assumed he hadn't been needed as a lookout, but what if he *had?* What if someone had come close to rumbling them and Roux had been forced to move to intervene? She continued around the side, toward the moat.

She moved closer to the water's edge. A couple of small boats were moored there. She peered into the blackness.

"You don't think he's fallen in, do you?" Garin asked, coming up behind her.

"We'd have heard the splash," she said, assuming he was serious. "Besides, why would he have come close to the water?"

"Indeed. But that being the case, where's the old bastard gone?"

"Maybe he headed back to the hotel?"

"Unlikely."

"We came down empty-handed."

"He wouldn't just leave, no matter how disappointed he was. It's not like him." And that was what bugged Annja more than anything. Garin was dead right; it wasn't like him. And Garin was beginning to sound concerned, which bugged her, too.

"The man's a law unto himself," she said, wanting to believe that.

"That he is," Garin agreed, still not happy.

"Let's get back to the hotel, regroup. Maybe you can trace him on satellite or whatever it was you did to me from the plane. Anything's got to be better than just standing out here in the dark waiting for him to turn up."

"Agreed. It's not like we can whistle for him as if he were some lost dog, as much as I like the idea. Let's go before someone gets nosy and spots us."

"Right, it's not like we can pull a cloak of invisibility up over our heads, is it?"

"I like you, Annja Creed. Have I mentioned that?"

"Not for at least a week."

"Well, I do. You're the right side of irreverent. Plus you're rocking some killer abs in that outfit. Shame about the whole human torch thing you've got going on." He winked.

She laughed, despite the fact it was the absolute last thing she felt like doing.

The hotel lobby was lit by two table lamps and the faint glow of the emergency exit sign.

There was no night porter, but it was a small hotel so that was hardly surprising. They let themselves into the building with their electronic key card. The bar area was closed, and no one was sitting in reception. The entire place had an abandoned vibe going on.

"You think he's gone up?"

"Dunno, something's not right."

"Could be this old-flame guilt he's nursing," Garin suggested.

"Old flame? I think I've got some catching up to do."

"I'm not sure it's anything. Basically he had some woman looking out for the cloak, like he had the curate watching over the sword, only I guess it was a bit more complicated. They had a fight and never talked again." Garin stepped into the elevator. She followed him inside.

"If he's got someone watching the place, even if they're not exactly best friends, why were we risking our necks back there?"

"Because she's dead. The whole fallout thing was maybe fifty years ago. The mote of dust in the eye of time idea. I don't know if it was pride, or what, but he couldn't bring himself to talk to her again. And now the treasure's gone, I guess he thinks she betrayed him."

"Wow, what a tangled web." She thought about the letter they'd found at the battlements; she'd left it in the car. No doubt it was an apology or an attempt to explain what had happened or build bridges from the afterlife. No wonder he'd gone. She couldn't exactly blame him.

"So we shouldn't start worrying just yet, then?"

"Who knows what goes on in the old man's head? He might have gone for a walk to clear the cobwebs. He might have gone to stand outside her house and look at the windows imagining he could somehow knock on the door and say sorry. Or he might have gone in search of a stiff drink. I say leave the worrying until the morning."

The elevator stopped.

Annja stepped out into a carpeted and Regency-style hallway and started along the corridor. There was no light coming from under Roux's door but that meant nothing. He'd had more than enough time to get back here and into bed, or wander the streets chasing his old ghosts. Garin was right; there was no point worrying until morning. Roux was a big boy. He could look after himself. That didn't mean she had to feel good about it, though.

Garin slipped into his own room without another word, leaving her standing in the corridor alone and unsettled.

She opened the door to her room and went inside.

Annja kicked off her shoes and lay on the bed, intending on heading to the bathroom to wash and clean her teeth before changing for bed, but exhaustion overtook her. She slept the sleep of the damned, dreaming she was climbing a wall that never seemed to end.

High above her she could hear Roux calling out to her, but it wasn't her name.

37

Sunrise began somewhere beyond the horizon.

The old man was asleep in the back of the car. He hadn't caused any trouble all night. Not that she'd expected him to. She'd grilled him after she'd moved the car, finding a tourist lot away from the town with a view looking out over the sea. It had been a frustrating interrogation. The old man wasn't much of a talker.

"The castle was built after the English defeated Llewellyn, the last true prince of Wales," Awena said when she saw him stir. "That's what they called him you know, Llewellyn the Last. Llewellyn, that's my name."

"I'd say that was quite a coincidence," Roux said. He seemed to have aged a decade. It must have been uncomfortable back there all night.

"No coincidence."

"I didn't really think it was. Is that what this is all about? Is this why your father spent all of his life looking for the treasures? Because of some misguided notion that you're descended from Llewellyn the Last and it's your birthright?"

"You knew my father?" It was the question she'd wanted to ask him ever since she'd read his name in her dad's book. "How? What were you? Friends? Enemies?"

"I knew him well enough to know he killed a friend of mine to get that sword you've been waving about."

"He wasn't a killer," she said, full of anger and doubt. "Not like that friend of yours. Annja Creed drove him off the road and left him to die."

She turned in her seat to get a better look at him. His face was impassive. Not so much as a flicker of emotion or surprise.

"You already knew that, didn't you?"

"She told me about the accident."

"It wasn't an accident."

"I suppose not. He was trying to run her off the road. Why do you think he'd do that? Guilt?"

"If she was so innocent, why not just call the police? Why kill him?"

"She didn't kill him. He died, that's different."

She made a face, shaking her head. "You're playing word games. She ran him off the road. That's why she's hidden her car. And that's why you are lying."

The old man shrugged. "It really doesn't matter to me whether you believe me or not. It's the truth. I'll let God be my judge."

She felt like slapping him. An old man with his hands tied behind his back and she still felt like slapping him. That was *nothing* compared with what she wanted to do with the woman. She would make sure that Annja Creed wouldn't have the opportunity to pluck her sword out of thin air the next time they met. She'd break both of the woman's arms first if she had to, but Annja Creed was going to pay for what she'd done to her father. But right now, she wanted the Mantle of King Arthur. That was why they'd snuck into the tower. Well, they might have won yesterday's battle but it was a new day and there was an entire war waiting for her to win. It was time to face them on their level. She needed to wake up.

The phone rang four times before a sleepy voice on the other end answered. "Hello?"

"It's Awena Llewellyn," she said.

Silence.

"Not going to say hello? I'm hurt, Annja. I thought we were friends."

"What do you want?"

"What do I *want?* Oh, that's an easy question to answer. I thought you'd be much more imaginative than that. I thought you'd already know what I want, but I'll help you out because that's the kind of woman I am. I want the Mantle of King Arthur."

There was a pause. She was using the time to construct a lie. "I don't know what you're talking about."

"Is that the best you can do? Denial? Certainly you know what I am talking about, Annja, unless you fell and hit your head on the way down, that is." Awena waited, still no response. "I saw you climbing the tower last night. So let's try again—I want the Mantle of King Arthur."

Annja said nothing. Well, it was harder to find a convincing lie when you'd been caught red-handed. Had she even realized Roux was missing?

"I think you must be mistaken."

"Oh, seriously, stop wasting time. Why don't you go and ask Roux what you should do?"

"Roux?"

"You heard me. Why don't you go and ask your friend what sort of lie you need to tell to get out of this. I'll wait while you go and check his room. I should warn you he won't be there, though, just so you're prepared. Go on, check."

Awena held on as the silence stretched out until the phone she'd taken from Roux's pocket started to ring on the dashboard. She answered it. "Do you believe me now?" she said.

"Where is he?"

"He's safe," Awena said.

"Where are you?"

"Questions, questions. You really are an annoying woman. Don't you get it? I'm in charge here. You don't get to ask things, you don't get to dictate things. I'm going to tell you what happens now, not the other way around. I want the mantle, you will meet me at the ferry terminal at one o'clock and bring it with you. That's the price of the old man's life. I really think you should pay it. I'm not messing around and I'm not the kind of girl who gives people second chances."

"I can't give you what I don't have," Annja replied.

"Please don't lie to me. I like to think we're beyond that now," Awena said.

"I'm not lying. It wasn't there."

"Hmm, that's a problem, then, isn't it? Because if you don't have it with you when you come to the ferry terminal, you won't see Roux again. It really is as simple as that. And needless to say, get the police involved and the old man dies. Be there at one." Awena killed the connection before Creed could object. Likewise, with her own phone. She was in control of the situation. She was giving the orders.

The old man remained passive. He hadn't tried to call out any special message for his companion, and she hadn't demanded to speak to him or any other sort of proof of life.

Awena didn't know if she should be troubled by that or not.

38

The call had woken her from deep within a dream. Traces of it clung on into wakefulness, but by the end of the conversation she was wide-eyed and anything remotely dreamy was long since gone.

When the line went dead the first thing she did was grab the other phone, but that one was just as dead. The second thing she did was call Garin, but his phone just rang and rang, going to voice mail every time. For a moment she thought he was in trouble, too. She was out of her room and across the corridor hammering on Garin's door before his final voice mail kicked in.

A very unhappy-looking Garin poked his head around the door. "All right, all right...where's the fire?"

"Roux has been kidnapped!"

"What do you mean kidnapped?"

It took a while for her to explain everything to him; the words came out in the wrong order, a confused jumble of information, but eventually she managed to tell him everything she knew.

"Well, I guess you were right, then. We should have made sure he was in his room last night," he said. "So much for the romantic brokenhearted version of this story. Five minutes won't make a difference. Go, get a shower and get out of your pj's, because as good as you look in them they're not really rescue attire. Besides, I'm not exactly dressed," Garin said, his modesty hidden behind the door.

She realized she was still in her night wear. She nodded. "Five minutes."

Once she was standing under the hot needles of water she didn't want to step out of it until the water had washed her guilt away. She should have checked in on Roux. She should have called him or sent him a text at the absolute least. Five minutes wasn't anywhere near long enough for that. She'd let the man down. They were a team. You don't leave one of your number unaccounted. Not ever. By the time she had dressed and returned to Garin's room he'd already ordered breakfast from room service and was working at his laptop.

He looked up. "I've got a tracker running on Roux's phone," he said. "He's on the move and best guess is toward Holyhead. Be aware there's no guarantee that it's Roux. Llewellyn's daughter could just as easily have put the phone in someone else's car and be sending us on a wild-goose chase."

"That's assuming she knows you can track it."

"Even a third grader knows this kind of stuff, Annja. It's not magic."

The only relief was that she was heading toward the rendezvous point at the ferry terminal, which suggested Roux was with her.

"Then we'd better get a move on." In every thriller she'd ever read they'd made a point of saying how it was always better to reach a drop point well ahead of the other person, to get a good knowledge of the points of access and exit and control the scene. Awena was already a good hour ahead of them and time was wasting.

"Eat first. You didn't eat last night. I can't remember seeing you eat since we got here. So we're going nowhere until I know you've got some food inside you. No telling when we might get another chance." Garin lifted the cloth from a plate of scrambled eggs, bacon, sausage and fried tomato.

She wanted to argue with him, but this entire thing had always been about being two steps behind the Llewellyns, and without the mantle she and Garin had nothing to trade for Roux's life.

"So, you've met this Llewellyn woman. What's she like? Apart from dangerously unhinged, that is," Garin asked.

"You mean is she capable of doing something stupid? Without a doubt. And given the fact we don't have what she wants, well, stupid seems pretty likely."

"Meaning we've got a couple of hours to come up with some kind of plan to get Roux back."

"Nothing like a deadline to get the blood flowing and the brain working. So, any ideas?"

"Beyond polishing off this plate of eggs and bacon? Nope."

"She saw us climbing the tower last night so she knows there are two of us."

"But she's hardly likely to recognize me. She only saw me in the dark, and from a distance. That might play in our favor."

"It's not a lot."

"Ah, you say that, but I can work miracles with a bit of gaffer tape and a smile."

"That sounds like you're planning on kidnaping her yourself, MacGyver."

"Well, you did say she was pretty, didn't you?"

Annja shook her head. "Do women actually fall for your charm?"

"All the time, especially attractive ones. Now, serious question—is she capable of murder?"

Annja didn't even have to think about it. There was only one answer, and it wasn't the one he wanted to hear. "Yes. She would have killed me if I hadn't been able to defend myself against her flaming sword."

"And Roux can't draw Joan's sword from the other-where." Garin looked at the screen of his laptop, deep in thought. "Okay, well, that sharpens our objectives to a single point…we can't let her get away," he said. "We need to get that sword from her. Whatever the cost, we've got no choice but to pay the price."

"Even if it kills Roux, you mean."

"The old bastard's not going to die," he said. "He's too wily and stubborn for that. And he's been in worse scrapes than this down the years. Don't write him off. We need to focus on what we can control, not what we can't. Let Roux take care of himself. He's been doing it all his life." It was a good, rousing speech, but Annja wasn't sure she believed a word of it.

She wasn't even sure Garin believed it himself.

39

Awena bought limp wax-paper-wrapped sandwiches and lukewarm coffee from a mobile catering van parked on the side of the road. Following that she found a secluded spot farther away for them to eat without risking unwanted attention. She'd considered keeping the old man trussed up and feeding him one bite at a time, but if anyone had seen her they'd remember the sight. She had no real option but to cut him free and let him get out of the car to relieve himself.

"Before you get any clever ideas, I'm younger than you and faster. And I've got the sword. You can run, but you can't run far enough. And look around you—there's no one to see if I cut you down. So let's be grown-up about this. I get the mantle and no one gets hurt. That's our endgame here. That's the resolution that makes everyone happy. So don't go ruining it by trying to run away."

"I'm an old man, Awena. I've got no intention of running anywhere again in my life."

"Good." She felt a twinge of guilt at the sight of his wrists. They were red and raw after being tied for so long, but give him his dues, the old man hadn't complained once. She looked at him. He seemed to have accepted his fate, whatever it might turn out to be. But that felt too easy. He could just be putting it on, wanting to lull her into a false sense of security while he bided his time, hoping the right moment would arrive. Well, there was going to be no moment. She was in control, and she was smarter than him.

He ate slowly. She couldn't blame him; as last meals went it wasn't exactly the height of fine dining. She watched him.

"What will you do when you have Arthur's mantle?"

"What will I do? Well, the very first thing I will do with it is use it to get revenge," she said.

"On Annja? She is an innocent in all of this."

"Innocent?" Awena said, incredulous. "How can she possibly be innocent? By what definition of the word? She *killed* my father. She would have killed me, too."

"Not Annja. You don't know her like I do. She isn't a killer. That's not who she is. It's not who you are, either, Awena. Believe me, if Annja Creed had intended to kill you, you'd be dead."

"Is that supposed to make me feel...what? Like she saved me? Spared me? So I should feel *grateful?* Do you have any idea how powerful this sword is? Do you have any idea what it is capable of?"

"I know that it is perfectly capable of killing old men who have never done anyone any harm."

"I don't want to kill you, Roux. I just want what's mine by rights. I want the mantle. Then you can go."

"I wasn't talking about me. I was talking about an old priest who only ever wanted to help people."

"I told you before that I don't want to hear your lies. My father didn't kill anyone," she insisted. "He wasn't that kind of man. He would carry spiders out into the field rather than crush them. He *never* hurt anyone in his life."

But even before the words had left her lips she knew that she was lying to him. Worse still, she was lying to herself. Once upon a fairy-tale time he hadn't been capable of hurting a fly, but not so long ago, when she was too old to believe in fairy tales, she'd seen him lash out at Geraint, his own son, with the sword and knew he had been capable of much more harm. He hadn't been able to control himself. So if Roux said that he had killed someone it wasn't as out of the question as she wanted to believe.

"I saw his body," the old man said. He didn't push, didn't raise his voice, nor did he lower it to manipulate her into believing him. He simply told her his version of events. His truth. "There was an unmistakable burn on the corpse. You know about the burning, don't you? You know what happens when an heir of the Last wields that sword. So tell me, who else could have done it?"

"It must have been an accident," she said. "Like when your precious Annja ran him off the road. That was an accident, wasn't it?" she sneered. "Or maybe it was self-defense? Have you thought about that?"

"It's possible, of course, but explain to me why he hid the body under a bridge. As you said, why not call an ambulance, why not try and do everything possible to help him, even if he knew that the man was already dead?"

She wanted to lash out and hit him, just to shut him up.

She couldn't stand to hear what he was saying be-cause it was true and she knew it. Until she'd held the sword herself she couldn't have imagined herself ca-

pable of hurting someone, deliberately hurting someone, but that had changed the moment she wielded the
blade against Annja Creed. And that hadn't been self-
defense. She'd planned it. Awena had enticed her to the
house with every intention of killing her. And now she
had a bigger plan, a plan that would right an even bigger wrong.

So if the blade somehow brought out the killer in her
blood, why was it unreasonable to think it had done the
same for her father? The answer, of course, was that it
wasn't unreasonable at all.

"Eat up. We're going." She produced another plastic
tie to restrain him again, and as Roux raised his wrists
for them to be bound she saw again the amount of damage that the first restraint had caused to his wrists. They
were a bloody mess and only likely to get worse left
untreated. She thought about slipping the tie around
his ankles instead. That might stop him running away,
but it wasn't likely to stop him getting up to any dirty
tricks—and with his hands free it was inevitable he'd
make a grab for the sword.

"This'll hurt," she said, but she didn't cinch them as
tightly as before. They wouldn't slip off without him
using the blood to work them loose, though, and that
would hurt plenty. "Try anything and I'll pull them so
tight they cut through to the bone. Understand?"

He stared back at her, holding her gaze unblinking,
then nodded slowly.

Once.

It was enough.

She slid behind the wheel and started the engine. The
drive to the ferry terminal in Holyhead wouldn't take
more than half an hour. She wanted to be there as soon

as she possibly could, though. Every extra minute there could make all the difference. She'd get to see the lie of the land, for a start. There would be places perfect for ambush and other places made for hiding in. But she was interested in the most public of places. Areas where they'd be at low risk of someone doing something heroic, especially Annja Creed. Places where she wouldn't be able to pluck a sword from thin air without being captured on security camera and raising a lot of questions she wouldn't want to answer.

Once Awena had the mantle she wanted to be able to get out of there as quickly as possible. She didn't care what happened to Roux; she didn't need to hurt him. Her plan, when it came right down to it, was to slip away unnoticed once she had the mantle in her hands.

And with something capable of turning her invisible to the naked eye, surely that wouldn't be too much of a challenge....

40

Traffic was backlogged more than a mile as the queue to the ferry terminal ground to a halt.

Annja was glad that they had set off early, not that it looked like it was going to make a lot of difference. She glanced in her wing mirror to see that Garin was still a couple of cars behind her and not moving, just as he had been for the past half an hour. Things would start moving when they opened the ferry doors, no doubt. They'd decided that it would be best if they arrived separately on the off chance Awena wouldn't realize Garin was there. They didn't know how much she really knew about their team; it was unlikely Roux had betrayed them with any meaningful details, but she could have been watching them a lot longer than they'd suspected. There was no telling what precisely there was left in the whole element-of-surprise department, but there was no point simply assuming the worst.

They had two cars, so use two cars. It was as simple as that, really.

She edged forward another car's length in the time it took for the DJ on the radio to spin another track, then another during the news bulletin as the queue slowly eased forward.

It was still going to be a while before she reached the front but at least she was moving.

The clock on the dash flashed 12:03. She had less than an hour until the rendezvous.

She regretted giving in to Garin's demand that they should eat before they left the hotel.

That plate of greasy breakfast could prove to be the difference between a decent recon and going in blind. It was stupid walking into a prearranged meet with no idea what was waiting for you. This was Awena's meet. She'd chosen the place for a reason. Annja didn't know what that reason was, which meant that Awena had at least one trump card if not all of them in her deck. She knew something about the site that they didn't. Local knowledge.

Her phone lay on the passenger's seat beside her. She kept glancing across at it in case it was ringing and for some reason she couldn't hear it. There was a lot of noise around her, not just the incessant blather of the DJ, who seemed intent on proving he was the funniest man alive with the aid of prerecorded skits.

It wasn't a watched pot that would never boil; it was going to ring. And the closer it got to the allotted time, the more likely it was to happen.

Two more songs, a few more yards of ground crept across.

It rang.

Annja snatched it up.

"I can see you," Awena said.

"Hard not to, I'd think," Annja replied.

"Quite. Coward's yellow. Follow the signs to the short-term parking lot and wait for me to call you back." She held on for a response. The phone went dead. She hadn't asked if she had the mantle. Annja had been prepared to lie if the question was raised.

A car behind sounded its horn; the cars in front of her had moved up, opening a gap between them.

Annja raised a hand in apology to the driver behind her, then muted the radio and called Garin, using the hands-free speaker to try and hide the fact she'd made the call.

"She made contact?" he asked.

"Yep. Short-term parking and wait for her to make contact again."

Despite the hands-free precaution, she didn't want to stay on the line too long. There was every chance Awena could see her, not just the car, and talking to herself wasn't exactly normal behavior.

"I'll keep eyes on you. Don't do anything stupid. I won't be far away if you need me."

"Nothing stupid apart from getting out of the car to meet a woman who's just kidnapped Roux and has already tried to kill me once this week."

"Right, nothing stupid." He killed the call from his end.

She followed the sign for the short-term parking. It led her away from the ramps where most of the cars were crawling single file. Cargo bay doors of the ferry that would transport them over the Irish Sea to Dublin were now open.

Rather than take the first vacant spot she saw, Annja carried on to the end of the first row and around onto the second before she reversed into a spot there.

It gave Garin the chance to park close enough to maintain eye contact and put her near the terminal building.

She left the engine running.

She couldn't see anyone in the surrounding cars. She couldn't obviously see Awena on either the roof or observation deck of the terminal building, either. But that didn't mean she wasn't there. She had to assume Awena Llewellyn could see her and knew she'd parked.

So why wasn't she calling?

Perhaps the delay was because she'd moved beyond her eyeline? It wouldn't be easy to find a vantage point that allowed full three-sixty coverage of the lot and the surrounding network of roads and buildings. The place was a labyrinth of industrialization. There were buildings with tall chimneys and buildings sprouting communication masts and others that had huge steel roller doors and transit crates stacked up outside. There were a thousand places she could be hiding; none of them would allow her to see everything.

Annja shut off the engine and picked up her cell phone. Once she was outside of the car she leaned against the canary-yellow bodywork waiting for the woman to call.

The phone rang again.

"Stay where you are. I'm coming to you," Awena said, and again Annja was left holding a dead line.

She leaned against the car, alert for any movement, looking around to see where the woman was coming from.

Garin had parked two bays over, and was facing her.

She tried not to look at him as she swept her gaze around the lot.

Even so, Awena had almost reached her before Annja realized it, clutching what could only be her sword. The blade was wrapped in a piece of sacking.

"Where is it?" Awena asked when she was close enough.

"Where's Roux?"

"Show me the mantle."

"We could do this all day. I'm not showing you the mantle until you prove to me that Roux's unharmed."

"You'll just have to trust me."

"Uh-uh, not going to happen. Where is he?"

"Fine." Awena reached into her pocket and pulled out a ticket. "He's on the ferry, fast asleep in the trunk of my car. You're going to have to be quick if you're going to get to him before the ship sails. This ticket is for you once I have the mantle. I told you, I've got no intention of hurting him."

Annja snatched the ticket from her hand.

She didn't hesitate; she ran between the parked cars, straight to where Garin was clambering out of his car. It wasn't the smartest move tactically—she thought about disarming the woman, taking her down and making sure she couldn't use the sword—but the cargo bay doors would be closing any minute and they needed to get to Roux.

"He's on the ferry," she told him, thrusting the ticket into his hand. "Get him. I'll deal with her."

Garin didn't waste any time. With a squeal of tires on asphalt he reversed out of his space and cut across the lot, angling for the front of the snake of cars.

"You double-crossing bitch!" Awena screamed as she ran toward Annja, lips curled back in a feral snarl. "Where is it? Where is *my* mantle?"

"I don't have it. I told you, it wasn't there."

"Don't lie to me!"

Awena was right up in her face, inches from her, so

close she could taste the sour reek of teeth that hadn't been cleaned in a couple of days.

"Where is it?"

Annja said nothing.

"Where is the mantle?"

"I don't have it," Annja said again. "Look in the car for yourself. Go on. I haven't got it. There was no cloak." She stepped back to let the woman get through, but instead of leaning in to check the backseat for the treasure, she leaned in and brought her right arm up. She slammed her forearm into the burns on the side of Annja's face and, as Annja stumbled back, shocked, drove a fist hard into the side of her head that sent Annja to the ground.

Awena stepped over her and delivered a rib-crushing kick.

It was a small mercy that she didn't drop the muslin sacking from the sword and plunge it into Annja. Gasping for breath she struggled to get up as Awena ran off between the cars. Dazed, Annja crawled to the end of the car, only to be greeted by the blare of a car horn as she very nearly stumbled straight into its path.

She scrambled back to her feet, leaning on the nearest car, and scanned the lot for Awena Llewellyn, but there was no sign of her.

Instinctively, Annja's gaze went to the wheels of the Porsche as she reached it, but they hadn't been slashed.

As she stood there, a car roared past so close the wing mirror clipped her arm. Annja wrenched her arm away, wincing, and turned, catching a fleeting glance of the driver and the white-haired passenger in the backseat.

The passenger turned to look at her back through the rear window, face unreadable.

Roux.

41

"She tried to *trick* me!" Awena screamed, slamming her fists on the wheel, then lashing out at the dashboard. Rage seethed through her. She wished she'd hit the woman harder, breaking something in her skull or chest, or just run her down. That would have been poetic. Annja could lay there in the street, her lifeblood leaking out, waiting for someone to come and save her, just like her father.

"Did she?"

"You know she did. You are in this together! That was the plan, wasn't it? Fool stupid Awena...take advantage of me to get what you want. I should cut your lying tongue out. That would show you."

"Honestly, what did you expect?" Roux asked.

"I expected her to be honorable. To do the right thing. I expected her to save you."

"But think about it, Awena, if she's telling the truth, how could she bring the Mantle of King Arthur with her if it wasn't there?"

"Stop trying to confuse me, Roux. No one knew it was there. It had to be there."

"People knew it was there, Awena. I knew it was there, you knew, your father—that's three of us right

there. And someone else knew. A friend of mine. It's
long gone. I should have known."

"So where is it, then? Where is it if you're so clever?
Take me to it and I'll spare your life."

"I don't know where it is, and the woman who I think
moved it has been dead for years, so we can't ask her.…
It is lost to the world."

"No!" Awena slammed the steering wheel hard, im-
pact-pain shooting up her arm.

"I'm sorry, but that's the truth."

"You lie so much you don't even remember what
the truth is," she spat. "It doesn't matter. I don't need
it, anyway."

"Don't need it for what?"

She ignored his question, accelerating into the road
and cutting straight across the line of traffic taking her
away from the terminal.

"Your choice. If I tell you I will not be able to let you
go. So, decide. I tell you my wicked plan, and you don't
get out of this car. Is that what you want?"

"No, that's not what I want, Awena. I want everyone to walk away from this while they still can. There's
been enough dying to last a lifetime as far as I am concerned. Believe me, if Annja had the mantle she would
have given it to you to free me, even if she knew that I
wouldn't have wanted her to. She's like a willful child—
she never listens to me."

"You would rather die than let me have it?"

"Don't take it personally," Roux said. "I'd rather die
than anyone have it, but then I've been alive a very long
time, so that's less impressive than it might sound. You
need to understand, girl, these treasures are *dangerous*. They affect people, they change them. Look what

they did to your father. You know he killed my friend, but you still remember the man who couldn't hurt a fly. There's nothing good that can come out of this. These are weapons from a bygone age. A time of blood and death. You shouldn't wield that sword. No good will come of it."

"I see things more clearly."

"Do you? Are you sure about that?" Roux pressed.

She knew he was just goading her to put doubts in her head. She had no room for them. She was doing the right thing. She was righting a wrong that had festered for far too long.

She glanced in her rearview mirror. The canary-yellow Porsche was unmistakable. It wove in and out of traffic trying to get closer to them.

"She's gaining on us," Roux said.

"Then I'll drive faster."

"Not forever you won't. You're in a tortoise, and she's in a hare."

"So what, then? I just pull over and let you out? Or maybe I should jam the brakes on and let her rear end me, then get the sword and finish this once and for all, right here, right now. Is that better?"

"No. Slow down enough for her to get close. Stay near the verge. Let me jump. It'll look like I'm escaping."

"Are you out of your mind?"

"I'm giving you a chance to end this. She'll stop to pick me up, and she won't come after you."

"She won't come after me," Awena repeated. It was a statement, not a question.

"Sooner or later you're going to have to kill me or let me go. There's no other conclusion to this. We all

know that. So you may as well get it over with. I don't
think you want to kill me, so why not use me? Use my
escape to buy you an advantage."

"Why are you helping me?"

"Because I want to get out of the car alive. Does there
need to be another reason?"

He was right. She'd gambled and failed. He wasn't the
key to getting the mantle because Annja Creed didn't
have it. She believed him when he said that the woman
would have used it to save him. Why wouldn't she? He
was an old man. She'd come running the moment she
thought he was in trouble. It wasn't Roux's fault. He
could have made things considerably more difficult if
he'd wanted to. He hadn't tried to escape. He hadn't
fought her in any way. He'd been docile, waiting to allow
the scene to play itself out. He had acted according to
rules when there should have been none.

"Are you sure that she'll stop for you?"

"I'll make sure that she does. I'll buy you time. I can't
promise that she won't come looking for you, but you'll
have a head start. You have my word."

"What about the sword? Are you just going to forget about it?"

"I already have," Roux said.

For the very first time since she'd taken the old man
prisoner she wasn't sure she could believe him.

There was a bend up ahead as the road swept around
to the right before leading to a junction. Beyond that
there was a choice of several roads, meaning the opportunity to lose Annja Creed. She just wanted this over.
It was never meant to be like this.

This wasn't the life she'd always dreamed for herself.

But that life wasn't gone for good.

She could still claim it, even if she let the old man go. She touched the brake, slowing slightly.

"Be ready to jump," she said. "And pray for a soft landing."

42

Her jaw still stung from the forearm and punch. The coppery taste of blood hung heavy on her tongue. She couldn't allow herself to be distracted by that. She'd misjudged the woman even though she'd seen her behaving like a sword-wielding maniac once before. She shouldn't have given her the chance to take her out; she should have just reached into the otherwhere for Joan's sword and put an end to the whole thing right there and then.

But there had been an upside, too.

Awena had tipped her hand early, undoing her own lie. Roux wasn't on the ferry at all.

And now Annja knew that, which meant she wasn't about to throw herself between the closing doors and be cut off from the mainland right as things were racing to a head.

While it was still slow going back to the terminal and the ferry, it was basically open road heading the other way with all of the arrivals from the Emerald Isle long since dispersed into the Welsh countryside.

Annja laid a thick coating of rubber on the road as she peeled out of the lot. She was almost half a mile behind Awena, but thankfully there were no other roads until she hit the intersection at the exit ramp. But after that it was anyone's guess as there were maybe a dozen possible intersections and side roads and crossroads that would eventually fan out all over Wales. It was imperative she catch the woman before she reached the intersection and those opportunities opened up for her.

Mercifully the only other car on this side of road was Awena's beaten-up station wagon.

The road up ahead began to bend gradually. She closed the gap between them, more so because Awena seemed to be slowing down rather than accelerating into the corner. Annja was close enough to be able to read the decals on the bumper. Brake lights flared red. The station wagon slowed alarmingly. Annja didn't understand what was happening until she saw the white-haired Roux bundle out of the car and hit the grass verge bone-jarringly hard.

Torn, Annja slammed on the brakes, knowing it meant the woman was getting away, but as she saw his bruised and bloody body come to rest she knew she had to stop. Awena was gone.

"Roux!" Annja yelled, two of the Porsche's four wheels up on the verge and churning up dirt as she skidded to a halt. She scrambled out of the car and raced to his side. Horns blared at the suicidal maneuver, but were silenced at the sight of Annja helping an old man to his feet. He moved unsteadily, not saying anything until he was buckled into the passenger's seat.

"What happened?"

Roux was clearly shaken as she helped him into the car. She fumbled in the bottom of her bag and found a tiny pair of nail scissors that were sufficient to free him from the plastic tie around his wrists. The damage was bad. She could see where the plastic had bitten into the tendon. It was going to be a slow, painful healing process. He looked gray and ashen. No sleep, little food. It hadn't had a flattering effect on him. In fact, it was almost possible to forget he was a soldier and had been all of his incredibly long life.

He shook his head. "Nothing I didn't intend. Get back into the car."

"It's too late. She's gone. There are a dozen different routes she can take from here."

"But only one will lead her to where she's going."

"Very zen, Roux, but not very helpful."

He smiled. "There's only one route where life is concerned, Annja. It's a river. It flows from birth to death."

"What are you rattling on about? Did she hit you on the head, Roux?"

That smile again. "I know exactly where she's heading."

"Well, why didn't you just say so?"

"I did."

Annja gunned the engine and the Porsche roared to life. "So where to?"

"Back to Caernarfon."

"The mantle isn't there. She knows that, right?"

"Absolutely. But it's not about the Treasures of Britain anymore. It never truly was. It was always about what they represented."

"Okay, I'll bite. What did they represent?"

"Her birthright."

"Again, a little more clarity. Some of us weren't just locked up with a lunatic for twenty-four hours and don't have the advantage of having them spill their fiendish plan to us, right before we escaped."

"Her name is Awena Llewellyn. Her father was Owen Llewellyn."

"Yes? And?"

"Llewellyn is an old name. It's an old bloodline. It dates back all the way to the last true prince of Wales, Llewellyn the Last."

"So, what, she's related to this true prince?"

"Without a doubt. The sword is the clue, the way it reacts to her."

"The flame?"

"Yes."

"I've been meaning to ask how that works. Is it some kind of trick?"

"Not really. Purely scientific, actually, if you understand the forces at play. I'll explain it all, I promise, but now is not the time. Now we need to stop Awena Llewellyn from claiming what she sees as her birthright."

"And how do we do that?"

"By preventing the murder of the Prince of Wales," Roux said.

"You're kidding me, right?"

"Llewellyn the Last was killed by the English when Wales was subdued. Her father, Owen Llewellyn, believed that the English should be forced out of Wales and control returned to the Welsh. She has inherited his... zeal. I don't know if the treasures are magnifying what was always there, but I believe she intends to claim her birthright as heir of Llewellyn the Last."

"Wow, she really has lost her mind."

Roux shrugged. "Grief can undermine the strongest of us. Her father just died, and she believes he, like their ancestor, was murdered. These are thoughts she's no doubt harbored since childhood when people kept telling her she was special, that she had the blood of Celtic kings flowing through her veins. And with the recent trauma coupled with the fact that her father's death coincides with the recovery of not one but two of the lost treasures of her people…it's not surprising she is fragile."

"That's a nice way of putting it."

"I am nice, most of the time, Annja. Ask Garin. He'll tell you what I can be like when I'm not being nice." They had history, of course, the master and student, that extended to the fields of France and the shattering of Joan of Arc's sword after the two men failed her. Something had happened back there that neither of them understood, though it didn't really matter.

As long as those fragments of Joan's sword remained scattered to the four winds they'd been immune to aging—that's different to immortal, a very fine difference, but different. They could die, brutally and bloodily; they could succumb to poison and any other nefarious means but not time—the one thing that killed everything couldn't touch them. And when it had become clear to Garin that Roux intended to reforge the sword and thus end the curse that kept them breathing, he'd done everything in his power to kill Roux. What existed between them now was an uneasy sort of truce. It wasn't trust-based. They were two of a kind. And despite the fact several years had gone by since Annja had set that final piece of the blade in place reuniting Joan's sword, neither of them appeared to have aged a day. So for the time being, at least, that was a fight they no longer needed to pursue relentlessly. That didn't mean they entirely trusted each other, either.

"Most of us have black thoughts we allow to fester because we know they will never come to pass. But what happens when we're suddenly in a position to bring them into reality? Do we suddenly discard them? Probably. But in the right set of circumstances perhaps we embrace them. Awena's father is dead, murdered in her mind by you, but he brought her the sword. That was his sacrifice. It's more than just a symbol. It is the last sword of power, and now she is wielding it, feeling it resonate to her touch, feeling it respond to her. She has started to understand the sword is more than just a weapon. It is a tool to bring about her destiny. It is the key to claiming her birthright."

"All she has to do is kill the prince," Annja said, finishing the thought for him.

She concentrated on her driving as they approached another junction, double-checking the sign to make sure she wasn't on a road to nowhere. There was no sign of Awena's station wagon on the road ahead, but Roux's reasoning made sense.

As though reading her mind, Roux asked, "Where's pretty boy, did you lose him?"

Annja had completely forgotten about Garin. "He's probably halfway to Ireland by now," she said.

"Do I want to ask?"

"He's looking for you. Probably one trunk at a time in the hold of that ferry."

"And neither of you wondered how she'd have been able to board and then just walk off the ferry without triggering some sort of alarm? We live in a world of terrorists, Annja. They don't just let people on and off ferries these days, not when they could stow a car on board with a bomb in it."

He was right, of course, but that didn't make her feel any better. "Let's just say I was more concerned about trying to find you than thinking of the logistics of how she spirited you away, okay?"

"Sometimes you have to think beyond what you're seeing and hearing."

"I know that."

"Good, then we'll say no more."

Well, he didn't need to. It was a long drive and it was all she could think of.

They would be back in Caernarfon in less than half an hour. She would call Garin then if he hadn't been in touch.

"So," Roux asked after a while, keeping his voice light. "There was nothing in the tower?"

So much had happened in less than a day, Annja had almost forgotten they hadn't spoken about their failed attempts to find the Mantle of King Arthur.

"It looked as if the stones hadn't been disturbed for a very long time," she explained, not that it helped.

"I see." Roux fell silent, just as he had done on the drive to St. Davids.

"But it wasn't empty," Annja said, opening the dashboard for the envelope she'd taken from the muslin sack and chamois leather wrap. She'd almost forgotten about it. She handed it across to him. "This was in the bottom."

He took it off her and with a thumbnail broke the seal, pulling a single sheet of paper from inside.

"What is it?" Annja asked after a while.

"An explanation," he said. She didn't press him on the matter. The letter was clearly personal, no doubt from the woman he had entrusted the safekeeping of the treasure to. He would tell Annja more if he wanted to, in his own time. Roux slipped the piece of paper back into the envelope and returned it to the glove compartment. "You're welcome to read it for yourself later, when I'm not around. All I ask is you don't judge me."

Which guaranteed she would read it, of course. Curiosity was like that; bait it well enough and it couldn't be resisted. Annja wondered why he thought she'd judge him. What could he have done? What could be so bad about his falling out with the mystery woman?

"And the mantle?"

"Who knows? Destroyed perhaps? Given so few people are aware of it, it is unlikely to fall into the wrong hands at least. That is a small mercy."

"And you still think that Awena will try to kill the prince?"

"She has nothing to lose and everything to gain in her mind, so yes. I do. Both of her parents are dead and her brother appears to want to have nothing to do with her as long as she is on the same fool's quest that consumed their father."

"But she could still go home, couldn't she? It could still end happily ever after. If we could take the sword from her, she could just go home. She hasn't gone beyond the point of no return. Right now, she can turn back. She doesn't need to be punished. There can be a positive ending for her."

"The woman is troubled, but she isn't a monster," he agreed. "The sword has done this to her. It has turned her into something she is not, just like I suspect it did to her father."

"But she stole the whetstone before she came into contact with the sword. Something drove her to that."

"Simple. The need to please her father. There's no arcane magic behind that. How many children live to please their parents? How many want to do things that prove they are praiseworthy?"

"I wouldn't know," Annja said. "I never lived to please the nuns." Which of course wasn't true. There were plenty of occasions she'd done something or hadn't done something because she believed it would please one of the holy sisters who cared for her in the orphanage.

Roux raised a skeptical eyebrow.

"The break-in was reckless, but no one was ever in any danger."

"The same couldn't be said for Owen Llewellyn."

"Indeed," Roux mused. "But I doubt he had ever hurt anyone until after he took possession of the sword."

"It sounds like you almost feel sorry for her."

"I do. But more importantly, I think there is time to save her. If she tries to kill the prince, though, then it can only end badly."

"Save the prince, save the girl," Annja said, paraphrasing a television show slogan. Even just thinking about television made her feel guilty. She needed to check in with Doug and tell him there was nothing doing with this whole Wales research-vacation trip. What a disaster! It had turned out to be nothing like the quiet, relaxing trip she'd planned. The frown on her face deepened when she thought about the armed soldiers guarding the castle gates.

That had been prior to the prince's arrival. Security would be tighter than her expense account once he was in residence. If Awena tried anything, then the men who fired first and asked questions later would be already at the question stage before Annja had parked the car.

Awena might think that the sword had saved her when she fell from the upstairs window. That was the kind of delusion that went hand in hand with ancient treasures and quests for birthrights, but it was wrongheaded thinking. A sword couldn't stop a hail of automatic gunfire—well, a normal sword couldn't. Annja had turned aside a few bullets with Joan's blade, but that was different, wasn't it?

They had to find Awena first and do everything they could to stop her.

43

"Thank you for your call. Your call is important to us. Please hold on while we wait for our operative to get his head out of every stinking trunk in every stinking car on this godforsaken ferry."

"Sorry," Annja said. Garin was in a foul temper.

"Just tell me how long you've known he's safe?"

"Half an hour. Maybe."

"And in all that time you didn't think to call me? Meanwhile I've been cavity searched by security and hauled off to Guantanamo as suspicious dude number one."

"Don't exaggerate."

"Who says I'm exaggerating? I'll be walking with a limp for a week."

Annja couldn't help it; she laughed. "Okay, look, I said I'm sorry." They were back in the hotel and it was considerably longer than an hour that she'd known Roux was safe, but she wasn't going to admit that. "Roux's safe. That's what counts. There was nothing you could have done."

"Apart from avoid the strip search. What about the woman?"

"She gave us the slip."

"So she still has the sword?"

"She still has the sword."

"How is he?"

"Sore. Both of body and pride."

"Ha! That won't hurt him too much. So, any idea of where sword woman has gone?"

Annja glanced across to Roux before speaking. He nodded. "He's made a pretty convincing argument for her being back in Caernarfon tomorrow."

"Is being out of her tiny mind part of the argument?" Garin scoffed. She could hear him shaking his head. "Why would she ever go back there? The smart money's on getting as far away as possible now that she knows the cloak of invisibility's lost." He paused a beat. "Unless she's got another line of investigation... Does she know where it is?"

"Roux? You want to field that one?" Annja said.

"She won't know where the mantle is," he said confidently. "It's gone. Off the table. Awena Llewellyn has no hidden knowledge about the Treasures of Britain, only what her father unearthed, and he never got as far as knowing who was watching the tower. Think it through—if she had known, she wouldn't have been so adamant that Annja had the mantle." That made sense.

"Okay, so what's crazy lady's next move?"

"She's going to try to kill the Prince of Wales during his visit to the castle."

"Uh, back up a second. I'm lost. Suddenly we're not looking for some flaming sword but instead stopping an assassination? Why the hell would she go off the deep end like that?"

"Because Awena Llewellyn holds the English responsible for ancient wrongs done to her family," Roux explained. "Suffice it to say, she believes that Llewellyn the Last was the last true prince of Wales and she is his heir."

"Okay, so we're definitely into the realm of crazy. Fine. I can handle that."

"She's not in her right mind," Roux agreed. "Possession of the sword has changed her. The situation is this—we've got to stop her before she attempts to kill the prince. That's our endgame. Fail and someone dies. I don't need any more blood on my hands. How soon do you think you can get back here?"

"No problem, once I break out of Guantanamo, negotiate my freedom from the FBI watch lists and pray they let me back on the next ferry—that won't be until dawn tomorrow. I could abandon my car and have the pilot bring the Gulfstream over to make the short hop if things are desperate. That being the case, probably five hours, give or take. Meaning the middle of the night. Oh, how I love night flying instead of sleeping."

"Take your time," Roux said. "I don't think she'll make her move tonight, so get here tomorrow, fresh."

"Roger that, big guy."

It was still only late afternoon. Roux wanted to take a walk through the town center to get his bearings. Preknowledge could be the difference here. It wasn't that he expected or even hoped to encounter Awena. He just wanted local details. He wanted to know where she might run, where the procession would travel, where she could hide and where if she got that close she could make her move. The castle itself was always going to be tightly controlled, so what alternatives were open to her?

She wasn't getting inside with a sword. That was obvious, unless she had some stupid idea about fighting through the cordon of soldiers defending the prince.

A few market stallholders were in the last throes of packing when she and Roux reached the square.

Two soldiers were once again on sentry duty. They kept a close eye on everything that was going on in the vicinity, but they'd become so much a part of the scenery over the past week, the stallholders were ignoring them.

As she and Roux strolled by a café, a waitress was clearing cups from one of the tables in the street, but she paused for a moment to give them a smile.

"Hi," the girl said, clearly recognizing Roux. "Not got your friend with you today?"

"Sorry to disappoint you." Roux offered a rueful smile. "He's taking an unexpected day trip," Roux replied. "He'll be here tomorrow."

"Just in time for the fun and games, eh?"

Annja had been so wrapped up in thoughts of Awena that she'd forgotten that this was a big deal for the town itself. She forgot how gung ho the Brits could be about their royal family.

"I hope so," Roux said.

Annja knew that the girl was almost certainly thinking the same thing, but for a very different reason. Garin had that effect on women. Well, some of them, anyway. And this one in particular, obviously.

"Why don't we grab a couple of coffees?" Annja suggested.

They sat at a table while the girl disappeared inside.

"She's pretty," Annja said as she sat down.

"Aren't they always?"

"Well, yes, I'll give you that. But she's a bit young for Garin."

"Every woman alive is too young for him," Roux said. She saw the smile on his face, but there was no laughter in his voice. It wasn't like Roux to be maudlin, but clearly the past was weighing on his mind. She wondered what was in that letter, what explanation could have affected his mood so badly. She'd do as he asked, and read the letter in good time, but not yet. If he wanted her to know what it said he'd have told her himself. She could wait.

The girl returned with two coffees, all smiling and happy with herself.

"Busy day tomorrow, then?" Annja asked.

"For everyone except the stallholders," she said. "They aren't happy, but they've been shut down until the visit's over. Busiest day the town has seen for years and they can't trade."

"My heart bleeds for them," Roux said wickedly, earning a grin from the girl.

"They want to bring the cars through the town this way," she explained.

Annja cast her gaze up and down the cobbled street. So now they knew which route the cavalcade was going to take and the direction the cars would approach the castle from.

"You expecting a lot of people?"

"For sure. This place will be packed. I remember getting a day off school the last time there was a visit like this. We made flags and banners and stood at the side of the road to wave as the car went past. Him and Lady Di—God rest her soul—stopped outside the school and got out to say hello. She was lovely…I'll always remember that."

Annja wanted to interrupt the girl and ask which

school she was talking about, but Roux was a step ahead. "So, you're not part of the anti-English brigade, then?"

"Me? Oh, dear, no. I bleed red, white and blue on my mother's side." She offered a smile. "But I grew up speaking Welsh at home and chat to the regulars like that. I know there was a time when the English tried to stop all that, but that was ages ago. Things have changed a lot since my grandmother's day. Besides, it's no better having people in charge in Cardiff than it was when they were in London. People are people."

No matter where in the world Annja went, there were always people who wanted things to be exactly as they had been once upon a time; no matter how far back in their history they had to look, there was always some mythical better day and age. For some people, change wasn't always for the better.

Annja's mind was racing. Security would be tight in the town square, most likely sweeping the prince straight into the castle. But if they had a scheduled meet-and-greet at an earlier point along the route, surely that was the time to make a move?

"Are you thinking what I'm thinking," Roux asked when the girl had finally left them to their coffee.

"Do you think she's so far gone that she would make her attempt to kill the prince in front of a load of school-children?"

Roux nodded. "It's the perfect place for it. People will be expected to step out of the crowds, kids will be curtsying and delivering bouquets of flowers. They'll be cheering. So much noise, so many distractions. The problem is that if we go to the school to stop her and we're wrong…" He didn't have to say any more than that: *if they were wrong*.

"So we have to ensure she makes her move where we want her to," Annja said.

"And how do we make that happen?"

"I have an idea."

"If anyone else had said that, I'd be worried. Because it's you," Roux said, "I'm terrified." He was only partially joking.

44

They were back in Annja's room. Afternoon had moved on into evening. They had eaten. Then Roux called Garin on Annja's phone, using the speaker.

His voice was faint; his answers rote. "Garin," Roux said. "Do you have your laptop with you?"

"It's surgically attached," Garin replied.

"Good. I need you to do a few things for me. First, I need you to check to see if my cell phone is still in Awena's car. If it is, track the signal tomorrow. I need to know where she is."

"Easy enough, even if she's turned it off. Only a problem if she pulls the battery out."

"I doubt she's even thought about turning it off, but I don't want to spook her by calling it."

"Okay. What else?"

It was Annja this time. "Leak some information to the local radio station. We need to make sure that they report that the prince's party will be stopping at a high school just outside of town before they arrive at the castle."

"Is he?"

"No idea. I don't even know the names of any schools in the area. That's up to you."

"So you're luring her into a trap? Nice. I approve. I take it the next thing on my roster of jobs for the day is to make sure the children are evacuated before the madwoman with a sword turns up?"

"Should keep you out of trouble for a while."

"Okay, leave it with me. That it?"

"For now at least."

Roux hung up but Annja had a question. "Why are we letting things take their course like this?"

"What's on your mind, Annja?"

"I don't like it. Garin can track her through your phone. We should find her tonight and end this while she's asleep. No fuss, no bother."

"Good in theory, but what if she slips away?"

"There are always 'ifs.'"

"Here's one for you. What if she realizes we are expecting her to try to kill the prince? What then? I'll tell you what—she'll realize there was only one way we could know where she is and she'll get rid of it. We don't want that."

"That's what I'm saying. Why drag it out? Why risk her disappearing with the sword? She can try and kill the prince anytime. It doesn't have to be tomorrow, it doesn't have to be here."

"We need to try to control things. Get her alone. Get her away from her car. Get the sword away from her. That's your job in all of this. You have to stop her."

Annja had known that was his plan all along, one swordswoman against another.

It was always going to come down to that.

It was one thing to go into a situation knowing the risks, knowing you might have to fight for your life, but quite another going in knowing you were fighting for someone else's. She wasn't comfortable with that.

"You do realize I'm supposed to be on vacation, right?"

Her phone rang again before Roux could answer.

It was Garin.

She put him on speaker. "Just to let you know I got a ping from Roux's cell phone. It's moving. She's still in the area, but the signal's weak. She's on the edge of tower range. Once she goes beyond that, she's gone."

"How's the battery?" Roux asked.

"How could I possibly know that?" Garin fired back.

"I don't know, you're the tech wiz. I'm just an old man."

"Just do what you can, Garin," Annja said, putting herself between them.

Annja ended the call.

Tiredness lined Roux's face. He couldn't have slept much in the past few days, if at all. But the stubborn old fool would never have admitted he was close to exhaustion, even if he couldn't stand on his own two feet. "We need to be fresh tomorrow. I'm hitting the sack." It was for his benefit; she wasn't that tired, but Roux didn't need any further prodding. He nodded and headed to his own room.

Annja was glad of the time on her own, a chance to freshen up and clear her head before settling down to sleep. She understood Roux's desire to bring the woman in without hurting her, but when it came right down to it there was every chance that trying to neutralize her

was only going to make things so much more dangerous than they needed to be.

And it was Annja who was going to be on the pointy
end of Awena's sword, not him.

45

Morning arrived with brilliant sunshine and a cloudless sky.

Workmen were out fixing bunting along the streets leading to the market square and the castle, sweepers out sluicing down the roads and clearing every visible scrap of litter. The entire town was being given a scrub down before the red carpet was laid out over the cobbles. And it was a literal red carpet. Annja liked that. It felt very regal. She decided she needed to clear some of the cobwebs from her mind and went out for a dawn run, pounding the streets hard, pushing herself. She missed working out in the gym and would have killed for a good sparring session with one of the guys back in NYC. For now she had to content herself with the bite of the early-morning Welsh air, as she gulped it down until her legs burned and her mind raced with endorphins. It felt good after spending so much of the past few days cooped up behind the wheel of a car.

Her jaw still ached from the double hit she'd taken, but the burns were surprisingly painless. A quick look in the mirror revealed that most of the worst of it had already faded. She had no idea how the steel could burn like that, but Roux insisted it wasn't some sort of alchemy but rather a very natural phenomenon. She'd just have to trust him—and make certain to avoid the sword the next time it swung for her. Right now it was all about putting one foot in front of the other and maintaining a steady pace. Nothing else mattered. It might not have begun as an exercise in pushing her limits, but it became one.

Barriers were being erected to keep the anticipated crowds back from the road when the cars finally arrived. It would only be a few hours before the streets were lined with people waving. The police force had already begun to gather in the square, ready to be put in position. Each of them was armed with nothing more than an expandable baton instead of the old-fashioned truncheon. It wouldn't stop a woman with a sword.

Annja was aware of a couple of the officers watching her as she ran.

They weren't suspicious. They were lecherous.

She didn't dwell on it.

She ran straight through the middle of their ranks, focusing on the ground at her feet. Another day it might have been different, another day she might have done a lot of things differently. But not today. Today she kept her head down and ran, doing a full circuit of the town before turning back eventually toward the hotel.

Roux waited for her in the lobby.

He didn't look pleased.

"Where have you been?"

She looked down at her sweats and then back up at Roux. "Isn't it obvious?"

"I've been trying to get hold of you. Garin's been trying to reach you, too." It was a rebuke and she knew it.

"Sorry."

"He called me on the hotel number in the end."

"Good for him. If at first you don't succeed and all that. So, what did he have to say?"

She walked toward the elevator. Roux reached it first and hit the button. He waited until they were inside before he spoke.

"He's been monitoring the signal from my phone all night. The battery died a few hours ago, but not before Awena started to move."

"And?"

"She took the bait. She's relocated into the vicinity of the school."

"Score one for the good guys," she said. "What about the kids?"

"Reported a gas leak in the area, so the school is closed for the day. The prince has been diverted, too."

"Garin has been a busy boy, hasn't he?"

"Unlike some of us," Roux said. It was a dig. She didn't rise to it. He wasn't the one about to go toe-to-toe with a maniac. She was. If she had to blow off some steam first, then that was what she had to do. Some people did yoga to unwind; Annja pounded the streets or went six rounds in the gym.

"There are already police in the square and barriers are being put in place to keep back onlookers," she said, reporting what she'd seen on her run. "There's a red carpet leading to the castle gate, which makes me think that the car will be stopping outside and they'll enter on foot. It does mean that there will still be a moment when the prince is in full view if Awena changes her mind and decides that the school isn't the best place to make her attempt."

"Be ready to leave in fifteen minutes," he said.

Breakfast was obviously an optional extra she wasn't going to enjoy.

She returned to her room and took a quick shower and wasted a minute chewing down an energy bar. She downed plenty of water, too, replenishing her electrolytes.

She checked her phone as she rubbed her hair dry with a towel. Four missed calls. All from Garin. Only one message. She played it back.

"It's Garin," the voice said. "I've managed to get hold of Roux. Guess you're out for a morning constitutional. Anyway, just wanted to make sure that I managed to take care of everything, but it's going to be tight to get to you before the show goes on. I'll head straight to the castle just in case things don't go according to plan at the school. Good luck, Annja. Break a leg. Preferably hers."

So Roux hadn't told her everything, after all.

It didn't make any difference, but she wasn't a fan of being kept in the dark. It screwed up the whole trust thing. It left you wondering what else you weren't being told. Like why wouldn't Roux tell her she couldn't rely on Garin's guns for backup? It was the kind of thing it would have been good to know going into a fight, not finding out halfway through one.

She was barely dressed when Roux came knocking on her door.

"Come on, time to go."

She grabbed a second energy bar to eat on the move.

"I'm trusting you, Annja. No mistakes. If you can't neutralize her, get out of there. Understood?" he said as they went directly to the car.

"Trust me, I've got no intention of getting hurt."

"Not just you. She's ill, she's not evil—there's a huge

difference. Our win scenario here is simple—retrieve the sword without hurting the woman."

"And if it's not that easy?"

"No risks. You can't allow your own safety to be jeopardized. That sword is dangerous. She can't walk away with it. No matter what. I don't want anyone else to be killed because of my mistakes. Look after yourself out there. I'll be seconds away. I promise. I've got your back. You can trust me. I swear."

She nodded, but that was all.

She remembered the letter in the glove compartment. Was that why Roux was so fixated on her knowing she could trust him? He'd already earned her trust a thousand times over. Surely he believed that.

46

Awena ached.

Every inch of her body, every muscle, every tendon. She felt that ache in her soul.

It was the second night she'd slept in the car, but the first one alone. Not that it made much difference to the comfort, but at least she hadn't had to stay alert to make sure Roux didn't slip away.

She reached out to touch the sword.

Still wrapped in sacking she felt its comfortable shape beneath its bindings and drew strength from it. Every touch reminded her that it was a quest she had ventured upon, like some knight of old, and that gave her renewed strength. She would not fail her father. She would make him proud of her. That was all she had ever wanted. She would make the world sit up and take notice of the Llewellyn name once more. She would reclaim what was hers by birth.

She cradled the sword in her hands. In the night she'd imagined she'd heard it calling to her, whether in some half dream or some half wakefulness it didn't matter. It banished any doubts that still lingered.

This was right.

She was on the side of the righteous.

The school gates had been locked as she'd approached them, but a side street off the main road had brought her around to the playing fields at the rear.

She'd been woken by the sound of car doors slamming and engines starting as early risers set off for work. She sat hunkered down in the car, watching them come and go. None of them turned onto the track she'd pulled onto. She listened to the car radio, careful to only tune in for short bursts so she didn't drain the battery. The news reports had filtered through that the prince would make his traditional visit to the secondary school, and it had been enough to convince Awena to change her plans. There was a wonderful symmetry to it. This was her school. This was where she had curtsyed to the Prince of Wales and presented him and Lady Diana with a bunch of sunflowers. That was the day her father had first told her the history of the treasures and her own role in the rule of their country. She'd cried thinking of how she'd been tricked into bending her knee to the false prince that morning.

Well, no more bending and scraping now.

This time when he came to the school he'd get a taste of Welsh steel.

Awena drove past the school three times before deciding on her current position. It was unlikely he'd have the army here, a few bodyguards, maybe. She couldn't remember what it had been like the last time. As long as she stayed at the back of the crowd to begin with, no one would think of her as a threat.

According to the radio report the prince was due at the castle around ten-thirty, which meant the school visit would take place within an hour of that. She wanted to be in place well before nine-thirty. It was unlikely they'd arrive before that.

She played the permutations over and over in her head.

She didn't want to arrive too early only to find herself standing there alone, but neither did she want to run the risk of missing him.

She watched the seconds tick by on her watch until it reached nine o'clock.

She'd timed the walk just before dawn. Even if she took it slowly it wouldn't be more than ten minutes before she was by the main gates.

In the daylight the playground looked more run-down than it did when she'd been a schoolgirl there. The chains on the swings showed signs of rust toward the top of the frame and the grass was in desperate need of cutting. It was a sad sight—a playground without any children in it, neglected and unloved.

It should have been full with children playing, but there was nothing but silence, not even the sound of traffic moving along the main road.

Awena clutched the hessian-wrapped sword a little tighter as she walked the final stretch to the gate.

She knew that there was something wrong.

The street was deserted.

Not just that, there was no bunting. No flags. Nothing.

Biting her bottom lip, Awena glanced up and down the road, then turned to scan the schoolyard. There wasn't a single parent in sight, no teachers' cars in the parking lot, either. None of it made any sense.

The radio had said that the prince was going to be

stopping at the school, but the school wasn't even open. Why would he come here if it was closed?

She hugged the sword even tighter, trying to work out what was going on.

The world felt as though it were spinning around her, faster and faster.

She had to lean against the fence for support, steadying herself.

Where was the prince?

Why wasn't he here?

Surely…he had to come here before driving into the town center. The radio had promised he was coming here….

And it had been lying to her.

Anger flared inside her.

She felt like *screaming*.

The world was conspiring against her.

But it wouldn't win.

She would claim her inheritance. She would avenge her forefathers. The blood of the prince would flow. She gripped the sword tighter still.

Awena heard footsteps walking toward her.

A voice called her name.

47

"Hello, Awena," Annja said as the young redheaded woman emerged from the lane alongside the school. There had been a long moment where she worried Awena wouldn't arrive. It had been a gamble, because once she got here it was impossible not to see the radio broadcast had been a hoax.

Awena stared at her, clearly confused.

She fumbled with the sacking, until the hilt of Gerald of Wales's sword was exposed. She grasped it. Smoke filled the air as the sacking began to smolder and shrivel away from the blade as it responded to her touch.

Awena screamed and scythed the air with the blade, showering Annja with the last few scraps of burning rag.

Annja rocked back on her heels, the tip of the blade slicing though the air a whisker away from her cheek. She didn't so much as flinch. She reached out with her right hand and smiled. "I'm really glad you did that, Awena," she said as Joan's sword crystalized in her grasp. "Now, that should even things out."

She took the next swing on the sword, the impact shivering down the length of the blade. Flames and sparks cascaded as the two swords made contact; Annja felt the full force of the blow through her shoulder. She grunted and winced as her injured arm took the brunt of the attack.

Awena was stronger than before, faster, and obviously more in tune with the sword's power. That was how it had been for her, too, back when she'd first drawn Joan's blade. She'd felt the sudden rush of strength flow through her veins and not been able to control it. It had taken time to contain it, to master the weapon and learn how to turn it on her enemies. Awena was obviously a fast learner.

That wasn't good.

She came at her again, driven by a rage that burned so furiously bright inside her the sword seemed to blaze twice as blue in her grasp. Annja barely held her off, blocking high, twisting her wrist and trying to yank the blade out of Awena's hands, only for the woman to sweep her feet out from under her. Annja hit the ground hard and rolled, coming up to her feet again before the woman could press the advantage. She was breathing hard, the flame dancing spectrally across her face as she moved. The entire street was silent but for the clash of steel.

Annja backed up under a fresh assault, hoping the woman was too far gone to realize she wasn't fighting back, just holding her off. The longer she kept her here in the street, the less chance she had of getting into the town before the prince arrived. It was as simple as that. Someone in the row of houses overlooking the schoolyard would see and call 999.

All Annja had to do in the meantime was stay alive, which for one treacherous second looked in doubt. Awena leaped, launching a spinning roundhouse kick that slammed into Annja's jaw and sent her sprawling, the sword skittering away across the yard as she lost her grip on it.

Awena came in, running, sword raised.

Annja rolled over and rammed her hand upward, fist closing around the sword as it reappeared in her hand.

Awena Llewellyn barely avoided being impaled on it.

She stood there, gasping for breath and staring at the sword that had impossibly reappeared in Annja's hand.

"Don't make me kill you," Annja said.

"You killed my father."

"It was an accident."

Sword clashed against sword again, metal against burning metal. The blaze threatened to blind Annja with each sweep and cut as the swords came together close to her face.

Awena was relentless.

There was a difference this time, though. The rage that Awena had harnessed when they'd faced each other in her father's study was missing. She was more controlled. Less erratic. But that meant she was more containable, too. Maybe that would change if Annja backed her into a corner and gave her no choice but to fight for her life. As it was, she still had the illusion of control, the choice of flight. But that couldn't last.

Roux's request that she shouldn't be hurt if possible rang inside Annja's head.

It was easier said than done.

She needed to get the sword out of the woman's hands.

Awena backed up a step, then another as Annja moved onto the front foot. She dropped her shoulder and whipped in a quick low swing toward her ankles, which had Awena darting another few feet. Annja pressed the attack, bringing her sword up fast in a vicious arc that would have gutted Awena if she hadn't managed to bring the burning blade to bear in time. As it was the sword shrieked in protest and, for one heart-stopping second, felt as though it was going to shatter beneath the sheer ferocity of Annja's strike. But that scream only intensified, and Annja realized the blades had long since ceased to resonate and the scream came out of Awena Llewellyn's mouth.

It was a bansheelike howl that sent shivers to her very core.

The swords broke apart and Annja staggered away.

She'd backed Awena into the mouth of the narrow lane running parallel to the yard. She followed her.

"Come on, Awena. It's over. Give me the sword and go back home to your brother. It doesn't have to end badly."

"Are you scared? You should be. I owe you for my father's death. Blood for blood. I'm going nowhere," she said. Backing down the path, she waved the sword in front of her to keep Annja at bay.

Just keep her talking, Annja thought. That made her less of a threat. Maybe she could talk her down…

The burning sword brushed against the dry leaves of a bush that encroached on the alley and sent a shower of burning leaves into Annja's face.

She was sure that Awena hadn't done it deliberately, but the woman was smart. It didn't take her long to realize she could use the fire and dry foliage to her advantage.

Another shower of sizzling leaves came at her as Awena slashed forward through the bushes. Annja stayed back. Another cascade of leaves and smoldering ash filled the air, Awena's sword rising and falling slash after slash, until the low-hanging branches of several trees lining the narrow path were ablaze. The flames crackled and spat, spreading with alarming speed as they fed on the brittle vegetation.

Annja sliced through the burning vegetation with her own sword, bringing a mass of it crashing to the ground. It wasn't enough to stop the spread of the fire, and it blocked part of the path. She hacked at the overhead branches again, but it was obvious there was nothing she could do to stop the fire.

She really hated fire.

It made her skin crawl.

It blazed in her darkest, deepest nightmares.

She could feel its phantom heat bite into her flesh.

Annja rocked back on her heels and launched herself over the burning branches, and saw too late that Awena had spilled a blazing pile of cardboard across the pathway, which she came down in the middle of.

Raging flames licked out across the path. Through them, Annja caught a glimpse of Awena looking back over her shoulder as she bolted.

Flames tore at the asphalt-coated fence that separated the path from someone's garden. The stench was foul. The rising heat battered her back. She felt the burning cardboard sear at her ankles, the heat coming up through the soles of her feet even as the branches overhead dripped fire down on her.

Getting through the cordon of fire wouldn't be easy.

She tried to kick as much of the cardboard away from the fence and stamp the fire out even as more flames tore up the fence and raced down the path. The acrid smoke stung her eyes. She really felt it where her face was burned, as though the sores that had begun to scab the day before were opening up again to welcome the fire into her flesh.

She lashed out in frustration, but the flames battered her back.

Awena had used her time well, lining the alley with garbage and everything imaginable that would burn, knowing she might need a path of fire to make her escape.

Annja heard the sound of a car's engine roaring into life.

Dizzy and reeling, she staggered away from the flames back toward the mouth of the alley.

Coughing and spluttering, she emerged by the school gates. The fire raged behind her. There was every chance it might make the leap from the trees to the roof of the school if the wind picked up.

She fished her cell phone out of her pocket and dialed 999. "Fire," she said when the operator asked her which service she required. She read the name of the school off the sign beside the gate and explained that the entire alleyway running beside the schoolyard was ablaze. She could hear the wail of the sirens before she hung up.

She'd parked the Porsche in a side street a little farther down the road, knowing Awena would recognize it if she saw it anywhere near the school. She started to run toward it, but even as she did the bright yellow car swept toward her, Roux behind the wheel.

She hadn't even realized she was still running with the sword in her hand until she saw a woman standing in a doorway across the street staring at her. That was one reliable eyewitness report the police were going to have. *A woman with burn marks on her clothes and clutching a sword got into a new yellow Porsche driven by a white-haired old man and fled the scene of the fire, Officer.* You didn't get many of those to the dozen.

"In," Roux snapped, not stopping the car.

He slowed just enough for her to pull the door open and throw herself into the vehicle. She simply let go of the sword, knowing it would return to its one safe place in the otherwhere.

Even before she'd slammed her seat belt into place, Roux floored the gas and roared away, the engine complaining that the gear needed shifting in less than two seconds. The sheer force of the acceleration pressed Annja deep into the passenger's seat. Awena may have had a couple of minutes' head start on them, but the Porsche was chewing up the streets in seconds. As Roux ramped up through the gears, it was a matter of seconds rather than minutes before they were closing the gap on her fender.

"Roux, Roux," Annja said as the Frenchman powered on remorselessly. "Roux, you're going to hit her!" Visions of the mountain road and Owen Llewellyn's car going over the barriers flashed before her eyes.

"Enough people have died over this sword. It ends here," he said. She couldn't tell if he intended to ram the car in front of them off the road or not. There was something deeply troubling about the intensity of his gaze as he stared straight ahead, foot flat to the floor.

He pulled out to overtake at the last second, shifted gear and accelerated, pulling up side by side with Awena's station wagon.

A car horn blared frantically.

Annja saw almost too late that another car was com-

ing around a bend ahead of them, hurtling straight toward them.

There was no chance it was going to be able to brake
in time.

Fifty yards.

It was a sports car.

Forty.

Thirty.

Roux wasn't stopping. He wasn't pulling over. He
was driving straight at the car bearing down on them.

"Roux!"

She grabbed the wheel and yanked it sharply, pulling
the car across the front of Awena's station wagon. The
sudden move meant their momentum threatened to put
the Porsche on its roof.

It entered a gut-churning three-sixty, tires screech-
ing, Annja screaming as she braced for impact as the
cars tangled in a type of spin with the oncoming car.
One carrying the other around and around in an endless
dance of rubber, glass and buckled steel.

When the car finally slowed into the final arc of
its wild spin, she saw Awena's station wagon had left
the road and come to a halt at an angle with one wheel
caught in a ditch.

Annja had released her seat belt and was out of the
door even before the car had come to a complete halt.
She sprinted toward the car as fast as she could. Smoke
billowed up from the radiator grille.

She heard an ominous ticking coming from deep
down inside the wrecked station wagon.

48

"Awena!"

A strong smell of gasoline filled her lungs.

She grasped the door handle and pulled at it, but the door was locked or the impact had buckled it so much it wouldn't open no matter how hard she pulled at it. The engine was still running and one wheel continued to turn even though it was off the ground.

"Awena," she called out again, hammering on the glass. *"Get out of there!"*

Awena was slumped over, barely stirring as Annja hammered on the window.

There was blood smeared on the inside of the glass where her head had hit it hard.

The air bag had deployed and the inside of the car was filled with the mist of propellant.

Annja banged on the glass frantically, but no matter how hard she did, Awena wasn't coming around.

The first sign of a flame licked out from under the hood.

She knew that she had only moments to spare.

"Get back," Roux called, running toward her.

The engine ticked alarmingly. The station wagon was seconds from bursting into flames; Annja knew that, but she couldn't leave the woman to that fate. She couldn't let her burn. No one deserved that. Ever. She had to get her out of there one way or another.

Without thinking about it, she reached into the otherwhere, her fingers closing around the reassuring grip of her sword as she pulled it into existence.

She stepped back and hit the rear window with the pommel. One single rock-hard blow with every ounce of strength she could muster behind it.

Glass flew in every direction, shards gouging into the fleshy parts of her hand even as she dropped the fabled blade and reached inside to unlock the driver's door. She heaved it open. Awena gave out a groan and shifted. She wasn't coherent. She wasn't helping herself.

Annja pushed the air bag aside and reached across to release Awena's seat belt.

As she did, Awena opened her eyes and reached out viper-fast, grabbing a tangle of hair and slamming Annja's head against the steering wheel.

The impact filled her ears with ringing and left her blind and dizzy and reeling.

Somehow the clasp on the belt released and Annja lurched away from the car dazed and confused by the ferocity of Awena's attack.

"Get out!" Annja shouted, clutching at the side of her head.

Part of her wanted to leave the woman there, let her pay for her crusade with her life just like her father, but Roux was right—too many people had died for this sword.

Annja stumbled forward again, determined to drag her out of the car even though Awena was still hell-bent on killing her.

She grabbed Awena's arm and pulled her until she started to tip out of her seat.

Awena struggled against her, obviously in serious trouble.

The flames climbing out from under the hood grew higher and higher by the second, the explosion gathering, ready to blow. It could only be a heartbeat away. Two at most. Annja pulled with all of her might, and Awena tumbled out of the car. The sudden shift in balance betrayed Annja and sent her tumbling backward.

In an instant the woman was standing above her, half of her face covered in blood, eyes bulging with the effort of standing, screaming, the sword of Wales swinging down toward her face.

The air was filled with the sound of thunder that wasn't thunder.

The explosion ripped through the car, tossing huge twisted metal parts of the frame into the air and down the street.

Awena fell on top of Annja, blown forward by the force of the blast, and inadvertently shielding Annja from the worst of it.

The world fell silent.

Annja struggled to push the woman off her, rising painfully to her feet. She could feel the heat of the fire against her face.

Frantically she looked around. She saw Roux running toward them. His mouth was opening and closing but she couldn't hear anything.

She bent down to see if Awena was still breathing. The woman was stubborn. She clung to life every bit as tenaciously as she clung to the sword, but now its flames barely flickered along its length, dimmed as though in response to the strength and vitality leaking out of her body.

Awena shifted, and for a sickening moment Annja thought she was going to lash out with that damned sword, using her dying breath to take her down. Annja had had enough and instantly Joan's sword was miraculously in her hand as Awena struggled to get to her feet.

It seemed impossible that Awena could survive the blast but then she had fallen out of a second-story window and walked away. She seemed capable of enduring any amount of pain. She lifted her sword once more, meeting Annja's gaze head-on. But she couldn't maintain the stance and sank to her knees even as the sword seemed to be spilling out of her hands. With one colossal final effort she drove the blade into the ground in front of her to act as a support and lowered her head.

Annja felt Roux's hand on her shoulder.

It was over.

It had to be over.

The emergency services would be there soon. She could hear the sirens. It was the only thing she could hear. Faint. Muffled. The paramedics would give Awena all the help she needed. They had to pry the sword from her hands, but at least they weren't cold, dead hands.

The woman's mouth moved silently.

A smile spread across her face.

Annja saw someone walking toward them. The driver of the other car.

It was no random stranger; it was her brother, Geraint Llewellyn.

Enough of Annja's hearing returned for her to hear him calling his sister's name.

49

"You did this?" Geraint demanded.

He grabbed the sword from Awena's hands. There was no flame when he held it.

"No, she didn't," Roux said. "I did. But in my place you would have done the same."

"The hell I would."

"I couldn't let her do it."

"Do what? What was she going to do that was so bad you had to just about kill her?"

"She was going to kill the Prince of Wales," Roux told him flatly. His voice betrayed no emotion, no judgment.

"I don't believe you. She wouldn't do something that stupid…I mean…why? Why would she?"

"Because of what they did to our family," Awena whispered. She sounded weak. She needed help and she needed it quickly.

"What are you talking about, Awena?" Geraint said.

"We are the last Llewellyns," she said. "The heirs of the Last…we are the children of kings. You're the true prince, Geraint, not him…I was doing it for you…for all of us. For every Llewellyn who lived without what was theirs. Rightfully. For every one of them who lived in the shadow of England."

"You're crazy," he said, shaking his head. "You've lost your mind. You sound just like Dad."

"It's not her," Roux said. "It's the sword. It changes some people. It gets into their heads and makes them do things. Things they wouldn't usually do."

"This sword? It's just a stupid piece of metal. There's nothing magical about it. Nothing that can screw with someone's head. It doesn't make you a princess or me a prince. My father wasted his life looking for it."

"Let me take it," Annja said, holding out her hand for the sword. "Let me make it safe."

"What will you do with it?"

"Put it in a place where no one will ever find it," she promised.

In the distance the sound of sirens grew louder. Annja had no idea if this was an ambulance, the police or a fire engine on its way. It could well be all three responding to her call.

"Give me the sword. If the police arrive and find it, there will be more questions. A man died in St. Davids. This is the murder weapon. Let me dispose of it and all we have is a car accident."

Geraint held the sword up and examined it for a moment, but there was no obvious sign that he was being enthralled by its glamour. It was nothing to him and he was nothing to it. He tossed it up into the air.

Annja snatched it.

"No!" screamed Awena as Annja took hold of it. There was no flame this time. She looked at Roux.

"Magnesium in the metal," Roux said. "It reacted to something in her skin, their DNA," he said. "It had been buried so long it had become volatile. The flame could never have lasted. It was burning itself out."

"No," Awena repeated. She was weeping. "It is mine...it knows me...it burns at my touch. I am worthy of it. It's my birthright."

"Awena," Roux said quietly. His voice was enough to break the sword's tentative hold on her and she fell to her knees.

It was over.

An ambulance approached. Geraint stood in the middle of the road waving frantically for it to stop. "Please," he said to Annja. "Take the sword and get out of here. This is my problem. She is my sister. Let me look after her. I won't let her hurt anyone, I swear."

Annja believed him. She passed the sword to Roux and hobbled back to the car.

Roux fired up the engine and they pulled away before the police arrived.

Annja took a single glance back in the mirror and saw a brother and sister embracing, backlit by the flames from her burning car.

They looked like they'd been to hell and back.

Back. That was the important part.

50

The square was deserted when Annja, Roux and Garin finally sat down outside the coffee shop that evening.

The cobbles were littered with the debris of the day; flags and bunting trodden underfoot looked sad and not a little tragic. The council workers were emerging to clear it all away. The police had long gone and the barriers had been stacked and removed, freeing up the roads.

Garin had arrived about an hour after the fun ended. Just in time to meet the young waitress as she finished work.

"So how did you make sure that the prince didn't roll up in the middle of it?"

Garin grinned that raffish grin of his. "No prince wants to walk into the middle of a protest by a Welsh Nationalist group. I put an amber alert out. Easy. They simply changed the route for the prince's car. But there's bad news, I'm afraid," he added. "The Porsche needs to be back in Caerleon tonight. Your hire car will be waiting for you good as new."

"Unlike the Porsche," Annja said.

"I don't want to know."

"You really don't. But it wasn't my fault."

"Right, two cars wrecked in less than a week. One is

an accident, two is downright careless. Still, good job you didn't hang around waiting for the police. You might have had to answer one or two awkward questions."

"Not much of a vacation," Roux said.

"Oh, I don't know—fast cars, sword fights, even a royal prince at the end of it. A girl could do worse." She smiled.

Once they had finished their coffee she walked back to the hotel with Roux to collect his belongings, leaving Garin to deal with the waitress, who seemed far too eager to serve him.

They said their goodbyes, Roux assuring her that he was going directly home to the château in France.

Home. That sure sounded good to her.

It wasn't until she was cutting through the gorge this side of Caerleon that Annja remembered the letter lying in the glove compartment. Sure, it would still be there when she reached the hotel, but the hotel was a long way off and with each mile that sped by, the urge to finally read it increased. Roux had been so enigmatic about its contents and wanting her forgiveness and trust. How could she not read it?

She pulled over onto the side of the road.

Annja turned the envelope over in her hands a couple of times, running a thumb over Roux's name. Whoever had written this had expected him to find it. But had they expected anyone else to read it? She felt strange teasing the single sheet of paper out. Her heart beat a little faster than it should as she opened it and started to read.

My dearest Roux,
Yes, you still are, after all this time, after all these years and all the silences.

If you are reading this it is almost certain that you have returned to remove the treasure you have entrusted to my care, but that you have not come to see me. After so long apart, I suppose that pride has come in the way of you getting in touch, but I hope that once you find this you will come and seek me out.

Over the past few years I have seen a change in you. Every time you have come you have insisted on trying on the cloak and I have watched as you have disappeared before my eyes. Each time you kept it on a little longer, each time you emerged a little different. The mantle was turning you into something different, I am sure of it—someone I was growing to like less even if I never stopped loving you—but when I told you this you would not listen.

To begin with, it was the cloak that brought us together, but eventually it was the cloak that tore us apart.

I am sorry. I am so, so sorry.

After our argument, I knew that you would be unable to resist its call, that you would return to wear it one last time, and then spirit it away. Once that happened I knew there would be no hope of reconciliation. I still think about seeing you again. But not if you claimed the cloak. I couldn't bear to see what it would finally turn you into, dear Roux.

So in my anger and my sorrow, I turned to my brother and told him about the miraculous treasure and what it had done to us. I do not believe that he will tell anyone about it, but I cannot dismiss the possibility. I am sorry that I have broken your trust. You deserve better than that. But no one shall find it. I know the trouble it can cause in the heart of even the best of men, so I have moved the cloak to a new hiding place where it will be safe from the world and where you will be safe from it. It is better that way.

I will always love you, believe me, always and into death, because you are the owner of my heart.
Anna Llewellyn

There was no date on the letter, no indication of how long ago it had been written, or how many years it had lain waiting to be found. What it did was cast light on a part of Roux's life she'd never known existed and explained how he was aware that Awena was being influenced by Gerald's sword and why he was so desperate she shouldn't be hurt.

Annja read it again.

She didn't think less of him.

In fact, it made him more human and she loved him for it.

That was the thing about baring your soul; people loved you for your weaknesses, not despite them. She put the letter back in the envelope and the envelope back into the glove box, then fired up the engine.

The road and her old hire car waited for her.

She cranked up the radio as an old Alarm song came on: the lead singer imploring to give him love, hope and strength. It wasn't a bad message to take into the last few days of her vacation. She'd call Doug Morrell when she reached the hotel, not that he'd believe a word she had to say if she started trying to explain what had happened to her. Scratch that, he'd have her turn around and go looking for the mantle.

After reading Roux's letter, that was the last thing she wanted to do.

Some secrets were best left hidden, some treasures best left lost.

* * * * *

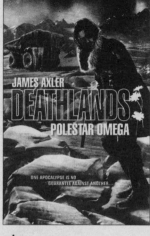

The Executioner®

Don Pendleton's

MAXIMUM CHAOS

The mob will stop at nothing to free a ruthless killer

Desperate to escape conviction, the head of a powerful mob orders the kidnapping of a federal prosecutor's daughter. If the mobster isn't freed, if anyone contacts the authorities, the girl will be killed. Backed into a corner, her father must rely on the one man who can help: Mack Bolan.

Finding the girl won't be easy. Plus, with an innocent life at stake, going in guns blazing is a risk Bolan can't take. His only choice is to pit the crime syndicate against their rivals. The mob is about to get a visit from the Executioner. And this time he's handing out death penalties.

Available October wherever books and ebooks are sold.

GOLD EAGLE®

Don Pendleton's Mack Bolan

CHAIN REACTION

An old adversary's illicit plot threatens global security...

When a Stony Man Farm nemesis is suspected in the death of two FBI agents, Mack Bolan gets called into action. The last time Bolan crossed paths with the shadowy criminal organization, he annihilated their operations in North Korea. Now the group has brokered a deal that would send weapons-grade uranium to Iran in exchange for a cache of stolen diamonds. Joining forces with a field operative, Bolan sets off on a shattering cross-continental firefight. Bolan has no choice: he must destroy the criminal conspiracy behind the threat. Once and for all.

Available October wherever books and ebooks are sold.

3 2953 01180639 7

GSB169